D0049402

I dangle my legs over the edge of the cliff, tapping my heels against the smooth dirt that crumbles down the side of the continent. I don't fear falling. The world below looks unreal and distant, like it's only been painted on. Falling is something I can't even imagine.

How many monsters run freely down there now? Thousands? Millions? Sometimes you can see something soaring below the clouds, larger than a bird but too far to distinguish its shape. From here the forests below look quiet, fake and imagined. The shadow of our continent blots out the sunlight for what must be miles across the infested landscape, but from here I can only see the edge of the darkness.

PRAISE FOR *INK*

"An enjoyable peek at a world very different from America, yet inhabited by people whose hearts are utterly familiar."

—Publishers Weekly

"Special."

—VOYA

"The work of a master storyteller."

—Julie Kagawa, *New York Times* bestselling
author of The Iron Fey series

"A modern day fairy tale."

—Amber Benson of TV's *Buffy the Vampire Slayer* and
author of *The Witches of Echo Park*

PRAISE FOR *RAIN*

"Takes readers on a brilliant and tense ride. Sun continues to impress with her witty dialogue, smooth plot and lovable characters.... A must read!"

—RT Book Reviews, Top Pick

**Books by Amanda Sun
available from Harlequin TEEN**

**The Paper Gods series
(in reading order):**

Shadow (ebook novella)
Ink
Rain
Storm
Rise (ebook novella)

HEIR
TO THE
SKY

AMANDA SUN

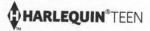

HARLEQUIN®TEEN

Recycling programs
for this product may
not exist in your area.

ISBN-13: 978-0-373-21191-3

Heir to the Sky

Copyright © 2016 by Amanda Sun

This edition published by arrangement with Harlequin Books S.A.

For questions and comments about the quality of this book, please contact us at CustomerService@Harlequin.com.

HARLEQUIN®TEEN
www.HarlequinTEEN.com

Printed in U.S.A.

For Alice, who traveled every step of this journey with me.

....

ONE

THE ROCK BRIDGE is the most dangerous part of the climb, and so I lower myself to my hands and knees to crawl along it. On either side of the sparse grass, the layers of slippery rock spread out like frail wings of stone. They look like they will support my weight, but I know a single step on them and they'll crumble, tumbling toward the earth far below Ashra, falling endlessly until they disappear from sight.

I used to throw flower petals over the edge of this floating continent to see how long I could track them, to see how far the fall really was, down to the mossy green and blue blurs of the world below. The blossoms would float on the wind, tumbling round and sometimes blowing back onto the outcrop, clinging to the silvery stone as if they, too, were afraid of falling.

I take another step, cursing these slippery red shoes on my feet. There's no fence out here like there is around the village of Ulan. There's no reason for one. No one ever comes out this far, past the borders of Ulan and the farmlands, past the citadel and the landing pitch and the great white statue of the Phoenix, May She Rise Anew. This part of Ashra is too rocky to develop or inhabit, too sheer and dangerous to trespass like much of the continent to the northwest and the east. And so it is its own lonely wall, one that keeps out the masses and invites solitude.

The soft sole of my right shoe scrapes against the bare grass that clings to the edge of the outcrop, and I stumble forward, my fingertips clinging to the jagged rocks. The wind tangles in my hair as I look up. A bird is soaring alongside the edge of rock; some kind of gull, I think. His white wings are outstretched as he easily rides the current, dipping and diving gently as his head tilts, and his beady eye stares at me.

"Don't worry." I laugh at him. "I can make it." I pull myself onto the outcrop one arm after another. My shoe finds traction again, and I heave myself up onto the soft, rich grass, the danger of the rock bridge finally past.

I take a breath and stand, brushing the gray dust from my scarlet robe, the golden tassels of my rope belt swaying in the wind.

A clearing of emerald green spreads out to the edge of the continent, a flowery field bursting with rich and vibrant color clinging so close to the edge. The fireweed blazes purple and red, the poppies burn with searing blue and fiery orange pistils. It's why I climb up here, why I risk everything to be here. It's a floating luminous realm for one.

The gull caws into the gust of wind as I step toward the edge. If I reach out, I could touch his outspread wing. Instead I look down past the tips of my shoes, past the sheer edge of Ashra. The view down to the earth is dizzying. It looks like a world of mottled green and blue, what little I can see of it. The clouds blot out most of the view as always, leaving the earth a mystery.

It's hard to believe we ever lived down there, trolling the dregs of that land like the bottom of a dark ocean. But the annals say we did, those dusty leather-bound tomes in the citadel library that almost no one reads but me. No one wants to remember; it's too painful to think of what we've lost.

Oceans are another piece of earth knowledge left over in the annals. We have a deep, cold lake on Ashra—Lake Agur—that during the season of rains spills over the edge of our floating island in a thin waterfall of azure and foam tumbling toward the earth. The current is dangerous, and the citizens of Ulan are forbidden from swimming in it, but we all do anyway, in the southern swell where the current is weak and the waterfall is far away. Streams flow into the river like veins into a heart from all across the continent.

Ashra is a small island, compared to the earth stretching below that doesn't seem to have an edge to it. Our home in the sky is maybe three days' walk from edge to edge, longer than it is wide, but no one bothers to go past the farmlands, and the farthest I've been allowed is to camp in the northern outlands with Elisha. My father would notice if I went farther, although one of these days I might just slip away and traverse it anyway.

Lake Agur is a closer option for a quick day of youthful rebellion, but you can always see the borders of the sparkling expanse, and the world around you never grows very dark when you swim to the bottom. You can always see the sun glittering above you, even if it takes several minutes for you to surface.

There's a rustling in the grass, and I turn. A pika stumbles through the blades. He is half rabbit, half mouse, a sprig of fireweed clenched between his teeth. He blinks, maybe surprised to see someone this far out of Ulan.

"I didn't mean to disturb you," I say, and his nose twitches, the fireweed sticking up at an angle as he tries to stuff another piece into his greedy mouth.

I smooth my red dress beneath me as I sit down, the pika scurrying off with his prize. I dangle my legs over the edge of the cliff, tapping my heels against the smooth dirt that crumbles down the side of the continent. The sun shines brightly above, the cool morning air gusting around me. I don't fear falling. The world below looks unreal and distant, like it's only been painted on. Falling is something I can't even imagine.

How many monsters run freely down there now? Thousands? Millions? Sometimes you can see something soaring below the clouds, larger than a bird but too far to distinguish its shape. From here the forests of earth below look quiet, fake and imagined. The shadow of our continent blots out the sunlight for what must be miles across the infested landscape. When Ashra lifted into the sky, it left behind a dark and jagged chasm in the earth the annals call the shadowlands. None of us know much about it, of course, whether it's completely in darkness or what might lurk in those caverns and crevices. From here I can only see the edge of the darkness.

"Kali!" A voice shouts, and it startles me. I lurch forward, digging the palms of my hands into the grass as my heart catches in my throat. My shoe falls from my foot as I tense, and it tumbles toward the suddenly real forest miles below as I gasp in the cool air, gripping the blades of grass with shaking fingers. Slowly, carefully, I slide back from the edge, pulling my legs underneath me. The slipper looks like the back of a sunbird now, small and crimson as it dives toward the mystery below. I stare at my bare foot. What am I going to tell my father?

"Kali!" the voice calls again. I take another breath and stand, walking back toward the outcrop. The pika is nowhere to be seen, and the blades of grass tickle against my sole.

I see her right away, her hands cupped around her mouth as she leans over the base of the rock bridge up to my realm of one. "Elisha!" I shout down. "You nearly sent me tumbling over the edge!"

"You're being dramatic," she says. Her black curly hair is pulled back with a looping purple ribbon, her cream tunic fluttering over her olive slacks. "You do realize the ceremony starts in half an hour, right?"

I sigh, looking down at my bare foot.

"So?" she says, resting her hands on the front of her legs. "Let's go!"

"One minute," I say, and I turn around to the burst of wildflowers for one last moment before I start down the steep outcrop. The jagged edges of rock slice against the sole of my foot as I climb, the dust gathering on the front of my dress.

"What happened to your shoe?" she asks.

"I lost it when you yelled at me," I say to the rock surface. You'd think Elisha would worry about distracting me on this narrow rock bridge, but she knows I've climbed it a hundred times. She thinks I'm as invincible as I do.

"So you're going to do the ceremony in one shoe?" She giggles. "I'm sure the Elders won't notice."

"If they do, you're the one who'll be in trouble."

"Sure," she says, rolling her eyes. We both know I'm the one who gets in trouble, even when it's her fault.

My feet finally touch the long grasses at the bottom of the outcrop, and I push myself upright.

"Ashes, your dress," she says, and then her hands are all over my robe, trying to wipe off the dusty grains of rock embedded in the fabric.

I laugh. "They *do* look like ashes. Maybe I'll get bonus points for authenticity."

Elisha rolls her eyes. "Let's hope *you* rise anew when Aban kills you."

"Blasphemy," I tease in Aban's deep voice, and we both snicker as the wind gusts at our clothes and hair.

Then the bell tolls in Ulan, and the smirks drop from our faces.

"Come on," Elisha says, grabbing my hand. We run toward the village and the citadel, standing proudly in the distance, its tower made entirely of blue crystal.

Elisha is the only one who knows the real me. We've been friends since I wandered into Ulan when I was three and deathly bored. Her family lives in the village, and I visit often. The population is smaller now after the Rending, so hierarchy doesn't mean as much as it did in ancient times. But my father is still heralded as the Monarch, and he insists on some amount of pomp and display. He says it settles people to know someone's in charge. They feel at ease knowing there's someone noble and dignified watching over them, whose life is dedicated to serving them and their best interests. So I carry on all removed and dignified in front of the villagers, and it's only Elisha who sees me for who I really am—another girl, like her, who wants to pull funny faces and drop buckets of water on the Elders and climb the outcrops of Ashra. A girl who wants to squelch handfuls of sand at the bottom of Lake Agur and come up just as her lungs are bursting. Someone who's free, who flies through the wind like a sunbird or a butterfly. Someone like Elisha.

But that isn't who I get to be. I'm Princess Kallima, daughter of the Monarch, heiress of the Red Plume and all of Ashra. The Eternal Flame of Hope for what's left of mankind.

I'm the wick and the wax, my father always tells me. I must burn for others, even if it means I will burn and crumble for those whose path I light. "We cannot return to those dark days," he says, and I know he's right, but it doesn't mean I always like it.

The dusty sand of the roadway feels hard and cool against my bare sole as we run toward the citadel. A hum grows louder in the distance, the vibration echoing through me as we hurry. It seems too far away as I gasp more air into my lungs.

A dark shadow casts over us, an oval of darkness on the ground that moves faster than we can keep up with. I glance around the blue sky and see it, the wooden belly of the airship as it creaks and hums its way past us. The gears on the sides spin and the plum-colored balloon wobbles back and forth in what little breeze there is, but it's the humming engine that keeps it moving through the air toward the landing pitch.

"What were you thinking?" Elisha huffs beside me as

we run. "The Elite Guard's already arriving. You could've gone to the edge of Ashra after the ceremony."

I open my mouth to answer, but no answer comes. She's right, but I'd thought I could escape for just a moment, just freeze time and not have to face all of this.

A momentary thought. A dream snapped in two like the pika's fireweed sprigs.

"At least you'll get to see *him* again," she teases, but the guilt comes over her face as I don't smile back. "I'm sorry," she says, regretting it right away.

I shake my head. "Jonash isn't awful." And he isn't. But he's not my choice, either.

We hurry on, the citadel feeling like it's never closer. We stop a few times to catch our breath, and I look down at my foot, smudged black from the dusty roadway.

A chime sounds through the clearing, and Elisha and I exchange worried looks. The bells are already ringing. Is it that late? She reaches for my hand and pulls me along the path, toward the bells chiming in the gleaming crystal tower of the citadel.

Maybe Aban will burn me alive, after all.

We finally reach the side of the stone building, and two of the Elder Initiates are there, straightening their robes and tying red rope belts around their waists. They look up in alarm as we stumble toward them.

"Kallima," one of them says, his brown hair slicked back and his sandals scraping against the dirt. "I thought you'd be inside already."

I pant. "Did Aban start already?"

He nods. "The Elite Guard arrived ten minutes ago. Elder Aban's already reading from the annals." Soot and ashes. I'm doomed.

"Your Highness," the other says, a dark woman whose golden earrings swing back and forth as she reaches out her hand. I take her hand and she pulls me up the stairs into the citadel.

"Good luck," Elisha shouts, and then the world around me is dark and silent, closed in by the shadows of the palace hallways.

TWO

I HAVE A momentary wish that the Initiate would pull me toward the northern hallways, toward the arched ceilings of the library and the rows of annals themselves. I'd rather bury myself in there, surrounded by piles of books, than face the crowds of the Rending Ceremony. But my absence wouldn't go unnoticed, so there's nothing to do but follow her toward the south of the building instead, into a great room lit by candles and chandeliers of glass, where my father stands with his arms outstretched like a scarecrow. Three attendants are crouched around him, straightening his robe, fastening his ceremonial gilded sword and buttoning the endless gleaming buttons of his official Rending Ceremony costume.

He peeks over his shoulder at me, his gray wiry beard pressed against the fine gold-and-red embroidery of the crisp robe he wears. "Kallima," he says, his voice filled with relief. "So Elisha found you." An attendant murmurs an apology as he turns my father's head forward so he can properly affix the plume of the Phoenix to his coat. "Where have you been?" my father asks the front of the room.

I don't like to lie to my father, but like any loving parent, he worries too much when I go near the edge of the continent. There hasn't been an accident on Ashra since I was two years old, and yet he still fears that I'll lose my footing and fall off the edge of the world. I don't think I could survive without my realm of one, so I bite my lip and gently betray him.

"At the lake," I say. "So many flowers are in bloom now." Two more attendants rush toward me, and I'm forced to raise my arms to the side like my father. They mumble to each other about the gray soot on my dress and the ragged ends of my golden rope belt. I wait in guilty anticipation of them noticing my missing shoe.

My father chuckles under his breath, and though I can't see his face, I know his eyelids are crinkling at the sides as he smiles. His blue eyes are always filled with warmth, even when he scolds me. "My Kallima," he says. "Always fluttering away."

The attendants tug at his sleeves and yank my hair back, brushing the brown matted waves into a more presentable tangle. Two of my father's attendants move to the side of the room and reach for the heavy golden headdress to bring it toward me. I groan quietly. It's beautiful, but it weighs a ton, pressing me into the ground. Whenever these ceremonies end and I get to take it off, I'm always surprised I don't float away.

The headdress is like a crown, but made of thousands and thousands of golden beads and cones and iridescent shells from the creatures that lurk in the mud of the lake. The strings of beads end in tiny plumes of red, usually the feathers of sunbirds but sometimes dyed gull or chicken quills if they need replacing. The headdress tinkles and chimes as they carry it toward me and lower it slowly onto my head. The beads drape across my forehead and dip along the sides of my head, where they fasten together in the back and drape through my hair. Every movement I make, no matter how slight, sends them clinking and jingling together in a melody that is said to evoke the Phoenix herself. May she rise anew, and all that.

The government on Ashra pieces together like a Phoenix, as we learn when we're little. The Elders are the feathers, surrounding the people—the Phoenix's beating heart—with truth and light. Some are just tufts, like the Initiates, and others are long wing and tail feathers, guiding us in the right direction with the sun and wind on our backs. When a child is born, the Elders visit the home to bless the child with welcoming rituals and gifts. The Elders study the annals to help us serve the Phoenix and each other, to take care of this floating world she entrusted to us. They're revered and welcomed as they journey the floating continents of our world—Ashra, Burumu, and Nartu and the Floating Isles. Nartu and the Floating Isles are so remote and small that they're usually grouped together. Only scholars live out there, retired Elders included.

After the Elders come the Elite Guard, who've arrived from their home in Burumu on the airship that passed over Elisha and me. The Elite Guard are the sharp talons of the Phoenix; they keep us safe from danger, although now they are much more ceremonial than in the past when monsters threatened us. In the time of the Rending, they formed to protect what was left of mankind. Now they serve as a reminder, and as a force against future dangers, should they arise. We stand upon them for support.

The Sargon lives in Burumu and is a lord below my father's ranking. He is the Eye of the Phoenix, ever watchful for unrest or trouble. And there has been some in the past, for Burumu is a small island of limited resources, and things have become tense from time to time. But none of us want to go back to dark days, and so it's never amounted to much at all.

And my father, the Monarch. He is the beak of the Phoenix, speaking truth and leading us all toward the future. His word is law. He lives here in Ulan, in the citadel, which is a smaller town than Burumu but it allows him the peace and quiet to thoughtfully govern us.

And me, his heir? I'm the Eternal Flame that ignites the Phoenix, the hope for the future of our floating world.

All of this symbolism is etched into my headdress. It's no wonder it weighs so much.

My father wears a circlet of feather-shaped hammered gold, the plumes of sunbirds hanging along it in a much more subtle pattern. His face crinkles up again as he smiles at me, and despite the hundred pounds pressing on my head, and the weight of who I am in my heart, I smile back.

"Ashes, child," he says suddenly. "Your foot!"

They've noticed. I can't look down easily with the headdress on, but I can feel the attendants lifting my foot up and wiping it with cloth, maybe the hem of their own tunics.

"I lost it on the way," I say sheepishly.

The doors at the end of the hallway burst open, and two of the Elder Initiates stride in. "Your Majesty," they say to my father, the Monarch. "If you please."

"Yes, well," he says, looking at me worriedly. After a

minute he laughs. "I suppose you'll have to lose the other shoe, as well," he says.

The attendants exchange looks.

"Sir, but Elder Aban will…"

"Oh, he can take it up with me later, if he survives the rise in his blood pressure."

I love my father, and he loves me.

I kick off the spare shoe and bite my lip to hold back the delighted grin at the expressions of the attendants and Initiates. My father quickly squeezes my fingers before they place a red and gilded annal in his hands and a short ceremonial staff in mine, a golden beam that ends in a rich crimson plume that tickles against my sleeve.

I follow my father through the hallway, and then we are upon the steps of the citadel. The sunlight is blinding after the darkness of the corridors. The minstrels are plucking at the goat-string harps and the trumpets are blaring as the crowds cheer for their Monarch. Father looks noble and kind as he descends the steps toward the crowd. I wait at the doorway and watch him. Banners of crimson stream in the wind, and the giant statue of the Phoenix towers over the courtyard. There are garlands of flowers strung around her neck and bouquets of red and orange laid at her feet.

It seems a little ridiculous to me at times, but the annals and my governesses have always been clear—without her, mankind would have perished, consumed by the monsters that overrun the earth below. She saved us all with her sacrifice, and so we celebrate the Rending every year since, commemorating our deliverance from certain death.

My father has reached Elder Aban in the courtyard below, and the trumpets blare loudly as the crowd looks up for me. I take a deep breath and grasp the plume staff tightly, walking slowly down the stone stairs in my bare feet, one clean, one scuffed and dirty. I long to glance at Aban's reaction, but I know I must look straight ahead into the crowd, smiling gently and looking wiser than I feel. The steps are grainy and rough and scrape the soles of my feet. Despite the bright sunny weather, the stone stairs are cold from the thin air up here in Ashra.

The crowd and minstrels are quiet, staring at me as I descend. I think only of how ridiculous it would look if I tripped headfirst, or if I burst into dance or suddenly turned and ran. I could end this whole ceremony, I think. It's not that I want to destroy it, but the potential, just knowing I could do so, swirls endlessly in my head.

At last I reach the bottom step, and the crowds bow their heads. It all seems too silly to me. I walk through the village all the time with Elisha and no one bows to me. But today there's such a separation I can feel it. They bend around me like heat bends around the wavering flame of a candle.

The Elite Guard stand in crisp rows to the side of the Phoenix statue. They're dressed in uniforms of the customary white, with a single red plume pinned to their lapels. Some have golden pins or medals of iridescent shell depending on rank.

I see him immediately, of course. Jonash. He's in the front row, at the right side of the lieutenant. It's hard to miss him. He's looking at me, too, his blue eyes shining and his dirty blond hair cropped neatly on his head. But there's no time to think about him now. Aban has come toward me to receive the plume staff, and I place it in his old, shaking hands while my father reads from the pages of the annal.

His voice resonates through the courtyard. "So it was," he reads, "that in those days, the land was covered with the thick darkness of a plague brewing. They came from every direction—creatures bent on destroying mankind and civility. On four legs, on six, on wings and in scales, above and beneath the surface of the earth. They knew only hunger, blood and malevolence."

Elder Aban steps toward the Phoenix statue with my plume staff. I clasp my hands together over my dirt-stained dress, standing as still as I can. I can feel Jonash's eyes on me, but I dare not look. I pretend that he's not there at all, that he doesn't even exist.

My father's voice rises as he reads from the gilded tome. "But there was one creature who lived in light, not in darkness. In flame, not in bitter ice. There was one who was merciful and generous and giving. She saw our plight and took pity us. She gathered us under her wings, to protect us from the foul monsters outside."

The people stare blankly ahead. We've heard this story. We hear it every year. But it's distant to us. It happened nearly three hundred years ago. Well, two hundred and ninety-nine. We've never seen the monsters written about in the annals. We don't even know if it's true.

"The people walked from the mountains, from the valleys, from the oceans and the islands. We gathered upon this place, Ashra, when it was then part of the earth."

Aban has placed the plume staff at the Phoenix's stone talons and is backing away with his head bowed toward her. There is a small string in his hands, almost invisible unless you know it's there. This is the big finale, the culmination of the Rending Ceremony.

"And then," my father's voice booms, "with a blast of her fiery wings, she tore the roots from the ground and rent the earth in two." Aban pulls the string, and the plume staff erupts in a burst of flames that travels up the garlands around the statue. "She lifted us high above the darkness and the fangs and the endless hunger that infested the earth. She burned to ashes like the sun, raising us to freedom and deliverance."

"May she rise anew!" the crowd shouts as the rings of fire blaze around the statue. The people cheer and wave their red banners as my father hands the annal to Aban, who closes the book and lifts it into the sky. I step toward the statue now, the flames dangerously close. My face is hot from the waves emanating from the fire. But this is proof of the Phoenix's favor, and I must do this task to instill courage in the village. I quickly reach my hand toward the plume staff, now only a gold handle with a burned quill end attached to it. The longer I hesitate, the hotter the gold will get, so before I can rethink it I wrap my fingers around the handle and pull it away from the statue's talons. I lift it high above my head like a baton, my headdress tinkling in my ears as the crowd cheers.

"From fiery sacrifice to ash, from ash to rebirth," my father shouts, "we, too, will rise anew! Let us never return to those dark days. Let us never throw away the gift of a new rebirth on Ashra and in the skies!"

The people cheer, and Aban nods, and the official ceremony is over. Now is when my father usually ascends the steps and I follow, but today he's got more news to share. I see him look at me for a moment, his eyes kind and a little remorseful. And there's nothing I can do but nod, because our lives are for the people, and I know this. We are the wick and wax, and we still burn for Ashra's freedom.

"There is one more announcement you've been waiting for," my father says, raising his hands. The elaborate red-and-gold sleeves coil around his elbows and the crowd quiets down. He looks toward the Elite Guard, and the lieutenant salutes. He marches smartly into the courtyard, then turns sharply to face the crowd. When he glances at his troop, Jonash steps forward. He doesn't march the way the lieutenant did, but walks gracefully and solemnly toward us.

"Next year is the Three Hundredth Anniversary of the Rending," Father says. "And it is time to secure the continuation of Ashra and her lands—Burumu, Nartu and the Floating Isles." Ashra had been the original continent—the others broke off during the Rending and sailed through the sky, shattered shards of a broken past.

But it's the future that concerns me now.

Jonash's eyes burn as intensely as the last of the flames that devour the garlands around the Phoenix. He falls to a knee before my father, who nods at him.

"I am pleased to officially announce," my father says, each word an iron link in my chain, "the betrothal of my daughter, Princess Kallima of Ashra, to Second Lieutenant Jonash, son of the Sargon of Burumu."

Jonash's eyes meet mine, and his hand rises palm up like an offering. I know what is expected of me. I rest my hand in his, and he presses his forehead against the backs of my fingers. His skin is cool from the breeze, but my fingers are warm from the golden staff fetched from the fire.

The people cheer and applaud as Jonash rises to his feet and stands just behind me. The Sargon is lower ranking than my father the Monarch, but Burumu has the densest population and the greatest output of resources that complement Ashra's agriculture. The union is perfect to continue the peaceful ruling of the floating kingdom on which our lives play out.

Jonash's hand rests in mine as we ascend the steps behind my father, the cold stone scraping against my bare feet. I feel as though I have changed into someone else just now, as if I have ceased to exist.

The candle of my life burns, tears of wax trickling down its melting sides.

THREE

JONASH DOESN'T SPEAK to me until we are inside the great room, where my father and I stretch out our arms, and the attendants begin to unravel the cumbersome costumes that adorn us.

"Kallima," he says. "It's a pleasure to see you again."

"And you," I answer, always diplomatic and polite as I am supposed to be. Two attendants come to lift the headdress off my head, untangling the strings of beads that have twisted and knotted into my hair. But with Jonash here, I don't feel any lighter. The world still feels stiff and heavy. "How was the journey from Burumu?"

He smiles, his blue eyes full of warmth and his cheeks flushed with a bashful glow. Elisha is right when she says he's handsome, but his looks don't move me at all. "It was well enough. Airships are bumpy, troublesome things."

I haven't been on one since I was seven years old, when

I toured Burumu and Nartu with my father for the 290th Anniversary of the Rending. The airships are patched together like the hot air balloons I've read about in the annals, and they float from side to side in a pudgy, indecisive path. I'd wanted to see the ocean below Burumu on that journey, but the clouds were thick that day, only the peaks of the mountain range poking through. I remember how wonderful it was to look out at the lesser floating isles, though, the small pieces of continent that are too rocky or inhospitable for people to live on or gather resources from. They looked so strange, their roots and crumbling soil holding on to nothingness as they floated in the air.

"How are things in Burumu, Jonash?" my father says as I duck my head down so the attendants can untangle the last strings of the headdress from my hair.

"Well, thank you," Jonash answers. "My father sends his regards, and his apologies that he could not attend the ceremony."

My father laughs gently, his warm eyes twinkling as his skin crinkles. "We understand the burden of the Sargon. Burumu is a bustling place."

"Yes," Jonash answers. "He does his best to deal with the unrest."

"Unrest?" I say. My father frowns, his gray beard drooping with the expression. This is the first I've heard of this unrest. And my father has never been one to coddle or patronize me. In fact, he's always kept me well involved in political affairs. I'm the next in line, after all. Ignorance wouldn't suit either of us.

"Nothing to trouble Your Highness, of course," Jonash says quickly. "It's nothing more than a trifling thought.

Burumu is a larger city than Ulan, and sometimes the past weighs heavily upon our shoulders."

Burumu is a larger city, this much is true. On Ashra we have Lake Agur, the rolling hills full of wildflowers and the comfort of the Phoenix statue and citadel. Ours is a farming community protected from the harsh winds by a sheer mountain range on the northeast side. There is too much to do in a day to sit around and talk about unrest. But Burumu is a city of resources, where they mine gold and smelt iron and copper. It's where the airships are assembled, and the land is scarcer. Many of the families in Burumu try to immigrate to Ashra, but we need to preserve the continent so that future generations won't run out of food. Is this the source of the unrest? We strive hard not to allow inequality in the kingdom, but there will always be some jobs more desirable than others to sustain the community.

I shake my head in disbelief, putting on my best regal voice. "We know what it is to have a common enemy, the monsters that drove us into the skies. We know that to squabble among ourselves would be to ignore the gift of freedom the Phoenix has given us."

"My daughter is right, as always." My father smiles. "The situation in Burumu is nothing more than that—a tiny squabble before the past is remembered. Otherwise the Sargon would be quite bored, with nothing to manage."

I feel uneasy. My father is lying, I'm sure of it, and whether it's to me or to Jonash is the question. But the conversation has ended, and to continue it would be to embarrass him in front of company. I'll ask him later, when it's just the two of us.

"Indeed Burumu keeps one busy," Jonash ends politely,

but his eyes never leave me. "It's always a pleasure to get away for a while and to seek other joys."

He means well, I know. He's charming, polite and well mannered. He's handsome and intelligent. But I don't feel anything for him, no matter how hard I try. He's like the floating continents—beauty and pageantry above, and no substance below. It makes me sad to think this, and I'm flooded with guilt. I haven't even given him a chance.

I attempt a smile, feeling like a complete fake.

"Your Highness," he says, but I shake my head.

"Kali is fine. There's no need for formalities now the ceremony is done."

"I suppose not," he says. "Then, Kali, might I request the pleasure of your company tonight?" His cheeks blaze, and every word from his mouth is slow and thoughtful. "I'd hoped to visit Ulan and see more of Ashra. The Elite Guard will be staying a few days to partake in the celebrations, but I'm afraid I won't feel festive when I don't know anyone in the crowds."

He smiles, but my stomach twists. I'll have to spend more and more time with him, until we're married next year. And then we'll live together in the citadel, and we'll be looked on to provide a happy example to the people. We'll share every meal, every moment, every night. We'll have heirs to keep the bloodline going. My face warms. Perhaps I can learn to love him, I think. I desperately will myself to love him, to make this easier.

I don't. But maybe I could. Someday.

Or maybe not.

"I'm afraid I'd had plans with my friend Elisha..." I

begin, and I can't believe the words are flowing out of my mouth. My father won't approve of my discourtesy.

Jonash's face turns pale; his warm eyes falter. "I... I see," he says, his fingers fumbling across the golden plume pinned to his lapel. "Of course I understand. I..."

"Oh, ashes and soot," my father chimes in from the corner. "Elisha can go with you, can't she? It wouldn't be proper without a chaperone anyway."

Jonash hesitates, uncertain how to respond.

But I know what to do. I know what my father has gently asked of me.

"Well, then," I say with regret. "I'd be delighted to accept."

"I... Oh. Wonderful," Jonash says. He's lost in the silent conversation between my father and me, the words unspoken that duty comes first. He nods his head. "Shall we meet at the fountain, then, after dinner?"

"Won't you dine with us tonight, Jonash?" my father says. "I couldn't forgive myself if I treated my son-in-law-to-be with such discourtesy as to leave him to scavenge for his own supper."

"My gratitude to you, Monarch," Jonash answered. "But it's the lieutenant's birthday, and he's asked us to join him for the occasion. Er... I'm certain I could explain to him."

I roll my eyes. It seems eloquence isn't one of Jonash's better skills. "That isn't necessary," I pipe up pleasantly. "You can always join us tomorrow."

Both men look at me gratefully, and I wonder what we're all actually thinking. Does Jonash feel as I do about the arranged engagement? Does he have someone he cares for on Burumu? If he does, or if he longs for freedom like me, then he hides it well. If he, too, burns for the people, I can't even see the wax tears dripping from the light of the wick.

"At the fountain, then," he says. "When the skies are darkening. I'll wait."

I force another smile, and an attendant escorts him out.

FOUR

ONCE JONASH IS GONE, and my father has been pulled away by the Elders and their pressing Rending Ceremony matters, I'm finally alone and free. I step barefoot through the dim hallways, twisting toward the library in the north. Except for the outcrop on the edge of the continent, the library is my most favorite refuge. Hardly anyone bothers these days with the dusty tomes and endless red annals stacked along the back shelves. There's no need to look into the past anymore. Life is busy enough to just survive the present.

But I love to read the rich stories of the earth and the world before the Rending. I want to dive into the oceans teeming with rainbow fish and turtles and dolphins. I want to feel the soft manes of horses, which seem to be a type of giant goat, and the striped tails of the raccoons. I want to know about the cities that used to be, ones where thousands of people lived all in one place. I want to know about the strange customs and technologies that have been lost to us for nearly three hundred years. And just once, perhaps, I'd like to see a dragon, or how small the two moons must look, gleaming down onto a world so far below the floating continents.

The oldest annals are difficult to read because the language is archaic and the print faded. I've asked the Elders for help, but even Aban doesn't have the knowledge to read them. It's surprising, really, because the original Elders were the first to write things down at the beginning of the Rending, to keep track of old memories and wisdom from earth to save our heritage. You'd think the Elders would have taught each other as they went along, keeping the knowledge alive.

I run my fingers along the tops of the tomes, aching to know what's written in the gold-edged pages. I grab the fiftieth one in the row, the one where the language is almost readable. I open it up about one hundred pages in, where one of my favorite illustrations is splashed on the page. The manuscripts hold so few images, but this is one where the Elder scribe couldn't help himself. He has imagined what the ocean would look like, a lake without end. He's drawn what he imagines sea snakes and dolphins and fish to look like, and he's painted them all with the reddish-brown iron ink they manufacture in Burumu. He's tried his best to be accurate, but he's never seen the ocean, either, except for glimpses from the edge of the continent. We have fish in our lakes, but I imagine the ones in the ocean are larger and vividly colored, splashing about with fangs and fins and glittering scales. I wonder if his sketch is even close to what sea creatures really look like, frothing about against the shore.

I fit the book neatly in its space on the shelf and take out the very first of the annals. I've looked at it many times before, but its faded ancient letters just stare back at me, their looping script holding secrets I can't unlock. I run my fingers along the red text, flipping the crinkled pages slowly. There's a single illustration in this tome, on the ninetieth page. It shows the bottom of the continent Ashra, the roots of the trees bound in a tangle around the dirt that lifts into the sky. There is a fissure sketched in, where Burumu and Nartu are breaking off from Ashra under the pressure of the Rending. Below the continent the Phoenix rises into the air. Her dark red-brown wings gleam with a cloud of sketched glory, and she clasps monsters of every type in her talons. They are miniscule in the drawing, but I can make out twisting horns, slithering limbs and feathers. A great hole has been ripped in the earth below her, and along the rim of the hole tiny sketches of people wail upon their knees, reaching out for Ashra as it rises up. These were the unbelievers, who didn't heed her call and were devoured by the monsters. I press my thumbnail against them, thinking how small they are. I pity them, but I envy them, too. They knew about the oceans and the mountains. They knew all the things I wish to know. Even if their lives ended in despair, they were free until that last bitter moment.

No, I think. There's no freedom in being hunted down. Their lives were forfeit before they were even born.

A shuffling in the library startles me. It's always quiet here, especially when everyone must be out celebrating the Rending. I quietly slide the first of the annals back into its place on the shelves so I can peek at who's approaching.

I call out softly. "Elisha?" Maybe she's searching for me to talk about Jonash and the engagement. But then I hear two men's voices arguing just beyond hearing. Something doesn't feel right, and I shrink behind the shelf as they approach.

"One of the Initiates must have said something," the first voice says.

The second one snaps, "We don't share it with the Initiates. It's reserved only for the senior Elders."

That's Aban's voice. I'd know it anywhere. A moment later, Aban steps into view, his cream robe swishing against the floor and the tassels of his red belt pounding against him with every step.

"Then how did it reach them?" the first man says. He stands in a crisp white uniform, two dark red plumes laid on either shoulder and a gold chain draped over his chest. The lieutenant of the Elite Guard. Why would he be here? Jonash had said they would be out to celebrate his birthday, but the lieutenant's brow is creased and his face anxious. The Elders use the library all the time, but I've never seen anyone from the Elite Guard set foot in these dusty stacks of tomes.

"It can only be the work of an Elder," the lieutenant insists. "The others cannot read the early texts."

"The Elders are loyal to the Monarch," Aban spits back. "They would never join the rebels."

Rebels? Rebelling against what? I wonder. Life on Ashra and her lands is peaceful, with no need to rebel.

"An exile, then," the first voice says.

Aban shakes his head. "And how do you suppose they got off Nartu?"

It's the first I've heard of exiled Elders. It's true that the life isn't for everyone, but Elders who retire or Initiates who give up their instruction often *choose* a life of solitude on Nartu. Don't they?

"It is your fault for not keeping Burumu under control," Aban says. "The rebellions should have been quashed by now, not spreading. And if they've learned of this!"

Learned of what? And who has read the early texts? Too many questions flood into my mind at once. I think of the unrest Jonash mentioned, the one my father hesitated to mention in front of me. Is it so serious as to pit the tempers of Aban and the lieutenant against each other? The Elite Guard and the Elders have always worked together to serve the lands of Ashra. All our roles build the Phoenix together to protect its beating heart, our people. And what the lieutenant suggests is ridiculous. Even the Elders can't read the earliest texts.

None of it makes sense. But if the unrest is bad enough to worry either group and make them accuse each other, then there is more happening than my father has let on.

My thoughts muddle with confusion as I peek over the tops of the annals. Aban and the lieutenant have stopped at a small desk on the other side, where the Elders occasionally place the annals to study them. Aban reaches around his neck and produces a small key on a string. I've never noticed a key around Aban's neck before. He turns toward a cupboard near the desk and fits in the key, turning it with a creak. He rustles through the darkness and produces a bloodred tome with gilded pages. It looks just like the rows of annals on the shelf, and every volume is accounted for. Why would there be one locked in the cupboard?

Aban lifts it onto the desk with an echoing thud and begins to flip the pages.

"I'm telling you," the lieutenant tries again. Aban whispers to himself in what sounds like a foreign tongue, his eyes scanning the words as his finger runs down the page.

My hand goes to my open mouth. He's reading the ancient script. He's reading the early annals.

There's an illustration on the page, but I can't make it out from here. I can only see where the block of text ends and the fanciful sketching begins.

The lieutenant leans over, impatient. "Well?"

Aban falls silent, his finger stopping at one paragraph. "It's just as they're saying," he says, his voice nearly a whisper. "The barrier, the generator…word for word, it's what's on the flyer. Show me again."

The lieutenant reaches into his pocket and flattens the crinkled piece of paper. Aban compares the information on the paper to the lines he's pressed his trembling finger against in the annal. He nods, his face ghostly white.

The lieutenant snatches the paper back and balls his hand into a fist. He quickly turns back to Aban. "And no one has seen this annal but the Elders?"

"And the Monarch, and you," Aban says. My father knows of this secret tome, as well?

The lieutenant holds the edge of the paper to the candle that flickers on the desk. The flame licks up the side as the paper curls in on itself and burns. "Are there other copies of the book?" he asks.

Aban closes the massive tome with effort, and I stare over the tops of the shelved books to glance at the volume number. It glints, a single line golden in the dim light. The first of the annals. But that's impossible. Another copy of the first volume hidden under lock and key? It makes no sense.

"Only this one," Aban says. "And the one on the shelf,

but it was dealt with nearly two hundred years ago. I believe the others were burned."

Burned? Dealt with? Quietly as I can, I slide the first volume of the annals off the shelf and crouch down, placing the heavy book on top of my red skirts. I flip soundlessly to the image of the Rending, staring at it. What could be different about this volume than Aban's special copy? What was "dealt with" two hundred years ago?

Then I see it, though I've looked at this drawing so many times before. Now that I know something's wrong, it jumps off the page at me. The Phoenix is a much darker red-brown sketch than the rest of the fading drawing. I look carefully in its filled-in wings. There are rings of red encircling the space below the floating continent. There is some sort of mechanism buried in the Phoenix's tail, some sort of...of machine.

The Phoenix has been drawn later, to cover something previously drawn. But what exactly, and why?

I slide the heavy book to the floor and peek through the shelves again to watch the men. Aban appears to think for a moment.

"Ashes," he says. "There was an Initiate many years ago. He had a talent for deciphering the older annals. In the end he wasn't suitable, and we sent him away. Perhaps he made a copy, or found another, and has deciphered its meaning. But he went to Nartu so long ago. And the retired Elders wouldn't risk their safety by revealing the truth."

"Then he's made his way to Burumu, his message with him," the lieutenant said. "It must be stopped."

"I agree, but carefully. If you did your job, Lieutenant, we wouldn't be in this mess in the first place."

"I could say the same," he grumbles.

"The Sargon better control the rebellion. It must not advance here."

"The rebels are disorganized and marginalized anyway," the lieutenant says. "We can easily stop the people. But ideas spread like wildfire. We need to discredit this information as lies."

Then a lighter voice rings out, friendly and unburdened. "Kali?"

It's Elisha, looking for me.

My heart seems as loud as the citadel bells. Aban rushes the tome to the cupboard, locking it as the lieutenant looks around nervously. I'm not sure what I've stumbled on to, but I know it isn't wise to let on that I've been here the whole time. Even with my rank as the Eternal Flame and heir, I feel the fear flicker inside me. They could erase me, too, if they wanted. It would be easy. I'm just one person, noble or not.

"Kali, are you in here?" Elisha shouts. Her voice echoes in the domed ceiling of the library. I glance down the row of annals, press my hands against the thick concrete wall at the end. There's no way to leave this corridor without walking past the two men.

Aban slips the string with the key back under the neckline of his robe and clasps his hands. He and the lieutenant step toward the entrance of the library just as Elisha appears in front of them. She knows how much I love books. She knows where to find me.

"Oh," she gasps, surprised. "Elder Aban. And the lieutenant, isn't it? From the Elite Guard?"

"Elisha," Aban says, his voice cool and collected. I can't see any of them now because I've shrunk back against the wall. It's as if I'm watching a play, like this couldn't really be happening.

"I'm just looking for Kali," she says cheerfully.

I hear the swish of his robes as he steps forward. "She isn't here," he says, his voice strange and urgent. "She's in the courtyard, I'm certain."

"Oh, I doubt it," Elisha says. Her voice is unburdened and innocent. She has no idea what's transpiring. "She hates crowds. Don't you know she's always in the annals?"

"Elisha, if you'll just check the courtyar—"

"I'll only be a moment, Elder."

No, I think. *Elisha, listen to Aban for once.* The world beats to my heightened pulse. Nothing seems real, as if life has become a theatrical performace. If only the stage would open up and swallow me into the darkness. What will happen if they find out I'm here?

And then she's there, staring at me as I look back like a pika caught stealing fireweed. "I told you!" She laughs in a peal of bells. "But what are you doing all scrunched up like that?"

Aban steps around the side of the shelf, his face a mask of horror. He quickly recovers, bowing his head. "Your Highness," he says.

I rise to my feet. I can't show them how I'm shaking. I clear my throat and nod my head. "Aban," I say as calmly as I can manage. "Elisha. Ashes and soot, I must have fallen asleep." I rub my eyes, blotting out the horrible scene around me. When I look again, the lieutenant is staring back, his mouth slightly open. I can't read Aban's expression at all.

Elisha laughs in disbelief. "Well, that's not like you," she says. "Falling asleep in the library? With the annals? You love reading the annals!"

Adrenaline pumps through my veins as I stare at her. She's not helping, not at all.

"The Rending Ceremony," I try. "It must have taken it right out of me." I stretch my arms out wide and try to force a yawn. None comes. Do they believe me? Or can they see the worry on my face?

A single bead of sweat drips down the side of the lieutenant's forehead. "Your Highness," he says.

I nod and put on my official voice, lifting my chin up. "Lieutenant." My voice wavers, just a little. He doesn't know me well enough to notice, but Aban will.

I wonder for a moment if I should just confront them, ask what it was all about. I'm the Monarch's daughter, after all. Their job is to protect me.

But something in me warns it isn't a wise move to tell them I know. Something whispers inside me to run, and to run as far as I can. Someone changed the first annal two hundred years ago, if I understood Aban correctly. And the Elders and Elite Guard don't want us to know what, or why.

"Well, now that I'm awake, Elisha, let's get to the celebrations in Ulan."

She smiles and takes my hand, pulling me through the stacks of the library and away from the frowning faces of Aban and the lieutenant.

I'm not sure what I've stumbled upon, but I know it's something big. I know my father will explain it to me if he knows, and if he doesn't, he'll protect me. Once he knows what I've seen, they won't be able to do anything to me. And anyway, as the next in line to govern Ashra and her lands, there's no reason I shouldn't know what Aban and the lieutenant were talking about. I don't know why the incident made my heart race; it's either for the good of the kingdom, or it's treason, and either way I would be in the right to question it.

But a feeling of doubt casts a shadow darker than the hallways of the citadel, and for the first time in many years, I feel truly frightened.

FIVE

"HERE," ELISHA SAYS, pulling a pair of beige sandals out of her bag. "I grabbed these for you." She giggles, holding the shoes out to me as she keeps pulling me forward.

"Elisha." I tug gently against her hand, and we stop in the corridor near the stairway. "Wait. I have to talk to my father."

She frowns, the shoes resting in her hand against her slacks. "What's wrong?"

I shake my head. "I'm not sure, but I need to talk to him first. It's Aban and the lieutenant."

She nods and helps me slip on the sandals before she follows me to the meeting room. Two guards flank either side of the doorway, tall spears in hand. It's just a formality, of course. The number of humans left in the world is too small to fear each other.

At least, that's what I'd thought. The sketch of the

Phoenix and the talk of rebellion has shaken everything I thought I knew. I wish the lieutenant hadn't burned the paper. I need to see what was on it.

I rest my fingers on the cold door handle, and one of the guards turns his head. "Are you looking for the Monarch, Princess?"

"I don't mind if he's occupied with the Elders," I say. "It's an urgent matter."

"I'm afraid he's not in there," the guard answers as I push in the door to the meeting room, empty and still. "He left fifteen minutes ago, I believe for the village square with the Elders. Some meet-and-greet celebrations."

My chest feels empty, as though I'm out of breath. Everything feels so wrong, and I can't explain why. What does it mean that there are two first volumes of the annals? What was dealt with two hundred years ago? And what in ashes is the unrest now in Burumu?

"Thank you," I tell him, my throat dry, and I turn toward the citadel steps.

Elisha wraps her arms around my arm, leading me into the sunlight outside the great doors. We pass the Phoenix statue, a few stragglers from the celebration still wandering the courtyard. They wave at me, no longer enthralled as I've become one of them again. I do my best to smile and wave weakly at them.

"Kali? You're acting so weird," Elisha says. "What happened back there?"

"I wish I knew," I say. "Your uncle lives in Burumu, doesn't he? Have you heard anything about a rebellion?"

Elisha's eyes widen with surprise and she shouts, "A

rebe—" Then she notices my urgent face and drops her voice down to a whisper. "A rebellion?"

I nod. "The lieutenant and Aban were talking about it. They had some kind of paper being passed around with some big secret on it. Aban had a key around his neck, Elisha, and he brought out this duplicate of the first annal that he could read. The first volume!"

"They have been studying it a long time," she says. "Maybe they're finally getting somewhere?"

"No, I mean, he could *really* read it. The ancient language and everything. I heard him."

She frowns. "Why would the Elders pretend they can't read it when they can?"

"I don't know. And earlier, Jonash told my father there was unrest in Burumu."

"That's nothing new," she says. "You know life is harder there. Work is grueling and there's little space to live. They all want to move to Ashra. Maybe they're just exaggerating when they say it's a rebellion."

But I'm unconvinced. "Aban was really worried," I say. "He said something was 'dealt with' two hundred years ago. The ink in the first volume was different somehow. The Phoenix looked newer than the rest of the drawing. And there were these rings and some kind of a machine buried in the drawing, under the Phoenix." I know how crazy I must sound. I can see it on Elisha's face. But she's my best friend, and I know she'll take me seriously, even if she thinks it's nothing.

We reach the end of the courtyard and start along the dirt path to Ulan. It's not a long way, and we can already see the tops of thatched roofs and wooden shingles. Folk songs played on goat-string harps and carved flutes float up like a cloud from the town.

"Aban is the most loyal person I know," Elisha says after a moment. "He'd die for the Monarch and for you. He would."

"You're right," I say, and she is. I can't help but wonder if my imagination is running away with me, if the pull for escape and adventure isn't making a bigger deal out of this than it really is.

"They probably just don't want to worry you, and it will all smooth over. I'm sure there's a reasonable explanation. Besides, the Elite Guard is based in Burumu. They can deal with problems there. Isn't that the Sargon's job? And so what if the drawing in the annals isn't as old as you thought, or the Elders can read them? What does that have to do with us now?"

I sigh, trying to let go of everything.

Elisha nods as we approach the fountain. It gurgles with cool water filtered down from the lake, and one of the women from the village gathers it up into a mauve clay urn which she rests on her shoulder. She smiles at us, and we smile at her.

"We're safe now, Kali," Elisha says. "Monsters can't reach us this high. Any rebellion will quickly fizzle out when they remember how fortunate we are. We've been safe for hundreds of years, and things will continue this way when you're Monarch, too." She sidles closer, her voice dropping. "Or is it Jonash that's on your mind?"

I nudge her away as she giggles. She thinks I'm lucky, and that the whole thing is romantic. She's bought into the royal distraction like everyone else. "I don't love him, Elisha."

She stops giggling and sits on the edge of the fountain, her fingers wrapping around the cool stone. "I'm sorry," she says. "But you have a whole year to get to know him. Maybe you'll fall for him."

I sit beside her, the stone lip of the fountain scratching the pads of my fingers. The trickling water sounds like the gurgle of the waterfall on the edge of Lake Agur, and it fills me with the urge to run there, or to my outcrop on the edge of the continent. "What if I still don't love him in a year?"

She shrugs. "Then break the engagement."

I let out a laugh. "My father would kill me." I dip my fingers into the water and splash her. She winces dramatically as the drops spatter on her cream tunic.

She splashes me back, the water spraying my dress a dark crimson. "He'd come around," she says. "You're everything to him."

She's right, I know. He would understand if I broke off the engagement. But it would disappoint him so much. I don't know if I have it in my heart to do that to him. He wants Ashra's future to be secure. Jonash is a good match, politically, and in almost every other way. And then I remember that the night isn't our own. "By the way, he's joining us tonight."

Elisha's eyes just about pop out of her skull. "Jonash is?"

I roll my eyes, leaning back against the edge of the fountain and swinging my sandaled feet in the air. "After dinner he wants to meet us here. There's some sort of party for the lieutenant's birthday first. Unless, you know, rebellion calls them both away." One can hope.

"Unlikely. Well, we better get in all the fun we can before our night turns political." Elisha jumps to her feet. "Come on."

Elisha is like the sun to me. She's always shining, always optimistic. She has moments of sadness and hardship when she dims, like everyone else, but it doesn't bother her that she's fixed in one spot. She has no desire to leave Ashra, no curiosity about the monster-ridden earth below or the strange past before the Rending. I try to shed my worries now, to enjoy the fun of the Rending celebration.

Ulan is vibrant and bustling with out-of-town guests. Groups of Initiates walk through the crowd in their white robes, carrying sticks of chicken glazed with honey and tiny cakes of puffed flour and dusted sugar. Villagers dance in the square, wearing dresses of red and orange and yellow, the colors of the Phoenix and of our redemption. Elisha runs to the open window of one hut, where a man passes her the sticky-sweet skewers of honeyed chicken. We lick the hot, sweet meat as the honey dribbles onto our fingers. After, we buy two glasses of foamed pygmy goat milk blended with crushed red field berries, and then stuff our mouths with miniature puffed cakes and gluey spirals of bright orange melon paste. We eat and drink until the sugar overwhelms us and our foreheads pulse with headaches, and then Elisha grabs my sticky hands in hers and we dance in the square, spinning around and around as the sun begins to set, as the candles are lit in every window and along the edges of the wall.

Ulan is the only part of the floating continent to have a wall. It begins at the citadel and curves past the fountain and around the edge of the farmlands. It ends abruptly in the tangled forests, where the trees make their own wall of roots and thorns and brambles. At first, our ancestors never bothered to build a wall, since the edge of a floating continent isn't something to be defended, nor is the village built directly on the brink. The schoolhouse is between the town and the farmlands, and children learn from an early age not to go wandering in the grassy fields that stretch toward the southern edge.

But when I was two, a terrible accident happened. One of the teachers in town was running late that morning. She'd raced to the henhouse to gather the eggs, and one of the chickens had gotten out into the farmlands. She'd just chased it down when she smelled her morning loaf burning in the oven. And so she rushed in to deal with that as well, and the whole time she'd left the door to her cottage open and her toddler son had wandered out into the long grasses to look for her. The villagers are still haunted by his screams, the helpless cries that pierced the morning quiet as he toppled suddenly off the edge of the continent.

His mother never got over the horrible tragedy. No one blamed her, of course, but she drowned in the guilt that my father said only a parent can suffer. Her heart heavy with grief, she jumped off the edge six months later, and so we built the wall to protect others from the same tragic fate.

The wall is mainly stones mortared together with a thick clay paste. I don't know how well it would stand up to someone who wanted to topple it over, but it's strong enough to hold against the strength of any child. I was only two at the time myself, so I can't imagine the symbol of grief the wall is for the older citizens of Ulan. It is hauntingly beautiful with the Rending candles placed along the length of the edge, villagers bending to light them as the sky grows darker. The flames flicker against the stones, casting dancing shadows and light echoed by the fireflies gleaming in the forests to the north. They look like tufts of Phoenix down floating on the wind, carried any way they please, lighting the continent with their orange-and-yellow glow.

I feel claustrophobic suddenly, longing to go back to my outcrop and think about the hidden tome Aban concealed in the cupboard. I can't face Jonash, or my father, or any of the politics ahead of me. It's risky to climb the outcrop at night, although I've done it before to watch the rainbow of fireflies alighting on the wildflowers. Maybe I can go to the edge of Lake Agur and listen to the waters, close my eyes and pretend I'm sitting on the shore of the ocean.

I close my eyes now, imagining away the crowds of celebration. "Elisha," I say, "let's ditch the festival. Let's go where that Burumu boor can't find us."

A deep voice answers, and it isn't Elisha's. "And where's that?"

I open my eyes, and Jonash's blue eyes study mine, the pale purple dusk shadowing the crinkle of his forced smile.

I'm horrified. The guilt sinks deep in the pit of my stomach, resting uneasily. Elisha stands to the side, her eyes wide and full of shared embarrassment.

"I'm so sorry," I blurt out. "I didn't mean anything against you."

Jonash laughs a little. "I'm certain you didn't," he says, but I know he's only being polite. I can see the confusion in his eyes, the expectation of an explanation. "Do I really come off as boorish?"

My cheeks blaze. "Of course not. I'm only feeling a little claustrophobic," I try, waving my hand around at the crowds. By now the barley and malt have made their ways through the crowds, and the dancing has become much louder and far less coordinated. "It's…it's just been a long day."

One of the dancers approaches, singing the verse of a ballad too loudly as he merrily shakes his glass at us. Jonash gently rests his hands on the man's shoulders and turns him so he dances away, back toward the crowd. "I think I understand," he says. "Shall we all three escape, then?"

Elisha's eyes twinkle, and I know she thinks it's Jonash being perfect again. And she's right, of course. He's being a gentleman about the whole mortifying situation. He offers his arm, and in front of the crowds, with my embarrassing words in mind, there's nothing I can do but take it graciously. I link my arm around his and we walk toward the fountain, the blue light of the citadel's crystal shining like a beacon in the growing dark. "I thought we could go to Lake Agur."

"Too many mosquitos and flies at dusk," Elisha says. "Why not the outcrop?"

Jonash raises an eyebrow. "The outcrop? Sounds intriguing."

I want to shake Elisha. I will, later. The outcrop is my place, one I refuse to share with Jonash. "It's nowhere important. But the outlands near the lake would be lovely."

"Anywhere," he says. "I've had enough politics for one night, as well."

"The lieutenant's birthday," I answer, and the scene in the library floods back along with all my doubts.

The lights and songs of Ulan fade behind us as we start

down the dirt path toward the citadel. Halfway along we turn down the northeastern path, past the landing pitch where the airship bobs like a puffy cloud in the dim light.

I slip my arm away from Jonash, pretending to smooth my hair back in the cold nighttime wind.

"The lieutenant seemed a bit off today," I hazard. "Has anything happened?"

"Off?"

"The unrest in Burumu is perhaps on his mind?"

Jonash slows, his head tilted to the side as he thinks. "Not that I'm aware."

"What is the unrest, exactly?"

He pauses for a moment as we walk in silence. "Just a little grumbling over ration allotment," he says finally. "Nothing to trouble Your Highness."

"Kali is fine," I remind him. "And I'm glad to hear it. Because the strangest thing happened today, and I'm not sure what to make of it."

"Oh?"

I'm hesitant to share with Jonash what's happened, but maybe he'll know more about it than me. "The lieutenant and Elder Aban were in the library. They were discussing a rebellion, and the annals."

"The annals are rather dusty and educational for the lieutenant's tastes." Jonash laughs, and Elisha politely laughs with him.

But I don't like that he's avoided the word *rebellion*. My instinct says it isn't the first he's heard of it. "The lieutenant had a paper from the rebels," I tell him, and the laughing stops.

I tell them the rest of the story, about the drawing of

the Phoenix covering up part of the original illustration, about the red rings and the machine scribbled out by her tail. I tell them about the secret first volume Aban had under lock and key, and the discussion of an Initiate who may be causing trouble from Nartu. I tell them how the lieutenant wants to discredit the information as lies, which means there's a dangerous truth embedded in it. Jonash's face darkens, and then I know I was right to worry, that it hasn't all been in my head.

"Have you spoken to the Monarch?" he says. His voice sounds off.

I shake my head. "He's been so busy with the celebrations. I'm going to tell him as soon as I return tonight."

"I would advise against it," he tells me. "The Monarch has so much on his plate. I can assure you whatever the issue is, my father and the Elite Guard in Burumu can handle it."

His advice annoys me. It's like a patronizing pat on the head. "That's the thing," I say, before I can stop myself. "If this was a serious matter, you'd think the Sargon would've spoken up by now. Surely he doesn't allow rebellion to take over Burumu?"

Jonash presses his lips together, likely to stop whatever words are dying to flow out. "Are you saying you have no confidence in my father, nor in me?" he says.

The question snaps me back into diplomacy. This is my fiancé, and I'm speaking without any tact at all. I don't really care what he thinks of me, as I quietly seethe at him not taking me seriously. But I love my father, and I'm risking too much fanning flames between our families.

"Not at all," I say, and I'm sure my face is flashing my irritation. "But something isn't right about all this, and I won't stop until I understand what it is. And that begins with informing my own father, who should know all rumors floating about the length of the sky."

Jonash nods, but his eyes seem dim and distracted. "I see," he says, but his tone disagrees. I assume he's embarrassed, that whatever this rebellion is, it's gone beyond the reach of his father, the Sargon, to deal with it. It's a losing situation for him—if he doesn't know of the rebellion, then he's incompetent, and if he knows but can't handle it, then he's equally ill-equipped. Neither bodes well for an heir like him.

But the thought is mean-spirited. I didn't know about the rebellion, either. Perhaps it's new information that the lieutenant will share on their return. "I… I'm sure you will be able to address it when you return," I offer.

"Indeed," he says, and his eyes still look sunken in his face, but at least the anger has faded from his voice.

The path is dark now, the shining crystal of the citadel far behind us. Elisha reaches into her bag and pulls out a cast-iron lantern, carved all over with the shapes of stars and feathers for the light of the candle to dance through. We stop so she can strike the flint and light it, and she passes the lantern to me as well as the flint, which I slip into my pocket.

"Are we really going to go all the way to the outlands?" she says, and the candlelight flickers across her worried face. "I was only joking about the outcrop, you know. The sun's set too quickly." She looks around, and I know she fears the animals in the forests around us. We don't have many predators on the continent, and they're no bigger than deer—dwarf bears and wild boars mostly—but they're protected by law in case we're ever in desperate need to hunt for meat in years of drought or famine. There have been sightings of small dragons before, lighting up Lake Agur with fiery breaths, but they turned out to be a combination of lizards, fireflies and children's wild imaginations. Monsters have never flown this high, but Elisha still fears the darkness. I'm sure our discussion of rebellion isn't helping.

"We can turn back if you want," I say. "And go tomorrow, in the light."

"I was hoping to see the fireflies," Jonash says, crestfallen. "I've heard they flash in every color in Ashra."

"You two go ahead, then," Elisha says, and I shoot her a warning look in the lantern light. *You're going to send me alone with him?*

She arches her eyebrows in protest. *He's the son of the Sargon*, she's thinking. *He's a gentleman.* But neither of us knows him, not really. I doubt he'd hurt me or force anything on me, for that would certainly break off the engagement and cause a terrible feud between our families and our continents. No, I'm much more afraid he'll try to win me over, or that he'll lean in for a kiss and I'll lean away and everything will become terribly awkward.

"Let's all go on, then," Elisha says after a moment. "But only for a quick look, and we'll head straight back."

"Agreed," I say. "It's only about ten minutes to the clearing anyway."

We walk the rest of the forest path in silence, listening to the wind rustling the leaves. I wish I'd brought my cloak. The nighttime air is always freezing in the sky.

The trees pull away then, and the outlands are before us. The tall grasses bend in the wind, rustling with the sound of the cold breeze. Fireflies thread through them like garlands of candlelight, flashing green and yellow and orange. I hold the lantern behind us to let our eyes adjust, and then the pink and purple and blue fireflies lift up, hovering above the grasses in wreaths of color.

Jonash steps forward, watching their colors flash. They go dim in front of him, blacking out along his entire path in their fear. But a moment later they light behind him, surrounding him in distant light.

"Go on," Elisha whispers, nudging me forward. I wish she'd stop pushing me. But seeing Jonash in the field surrounded by those lights, seeing him appreciate the beauty of Ashra, makes me realize there's so much about him I don't know yet. Maybe this is an opportunity. He listened to my concerns about the strange extra tome that Aban and the lieutenant whispered over, even if he was a little patronizing. He didn't take offense to what I said in the village. Elisha's right that I do owe him more of a chance.

The grass scrapes against the sides of my ankles and the gaps between my sandal straps. The edges of the blades are sticky with sap and dry from too much sun. Dimmed fireflies accidentally bump into my arms and legs as I walk, and the lantern swings patterns of stars and feathers around the grasses. The fireflies darken in swarms around me, like snuffed-out candles.

"It's wonderful," Jonash says as I reach his side. "We only have yellow and orange fireflies in Burumu."

"Most villagers in Ulan don't come out as far as the outlands," I say. "The edge of the continent is uneven here and difficult to see in the fields." He looks alarmed, so I raise my hands to reassure him, the lantern swinging back and forth. "It's out that way," I say. "You can see it easily if you look for the moons hitting the rock."

He peers over, so I take him closer to the edge to look. To me it's like a lighting strip, silver and shiny as it loops along the side of the clearing. The two moons in the sky, one a crescent and one waxing full, beam down on the sparkling crystal fragments embedded in the stone of the continent's edge. It's like a glittering warning sign curving along the outlands. "See? Easy to spot once you know what to look for," I tell him.

He crouches down to look at the sparkling stone. "I see it. It's like a thread of glistening silver."

I turn away, swinging the lantern at my side. The fireflies scatter from its light. "We should go back soon. Elisha will get spooked if we wait too long."

"Of course," he says, straightening up. "Only a little longer, and then I'll escort you both, I promise."

I roll my eyes, glad he can't see my face. I don't need his escort. I know every stone of Ashra, every curve of rock and packed earth. Nothing can harm me here. Only the wild animals need be avoided.

He follows a flashing blue firefly then, dangerously close to the edge. I wonder why he continues to veer so close now that he knows how to look for the silvery lip of the continent. Perhaps he's fearless like me. Or perhaps he's just foolish.

Now it's as if he's walking along a thin rope. My heart is fluttering. It wouldn't do for my fiancé to drop off the side of the world. The Sargon wouldn't be pleased, and neither would my father. "You're too close, Jonash."

He doesn't answer, but stretches his arms out to the side

to help balance. The fireflies shy away in clouds of twinkling light.

I take a step forward. "Jonash," I try again. "Come away from the edge. The sheer crystal is slippery." I take another step. "I'm sure it's different on Burumu, but here…"

I don't have a chance to finish my sentence. He begins toppling from side to side, and the horror claws at my insides. Before I realize it I'm leaping forward, throwing my arms around his waist to pull him into the tall grasses. He whirls around from the impact, the weight of him unbalancing my own footing.

I feel the scrape of the sharp crystals as they dig into my ankle, as my foot slips over the edge of the continent.

There's no time to scream or think. My balance is off, and I'm falling backward, away from Jonash's grim face. The lantern jangles against the cliff as it drops from my hand and tumbles sideways over the edge. Jonash's hands on are my wrists, pulling them from his sides before we both go over. He falls stomach-down onto the grasses as my other foot slips over the side, shards of rock and dirt scraping the insides of my arms as I cling to the continent.

The cold wind gusts against me as I hang on. My feet swing and flail, but there's nothing but air around them. The world is dark except for the glowing fireflies and the silver strip of crystal rock.

My wrists are slipping from Jonash's fingers. I can barely breathe. "I can't…"

"Kali, hang on," he says. "Elisha! Help!" His shouts send the fireflies whirling in clouds.

I can hear Elisha yelling something, but my pulse is racing in my ears and I can't make out a thing.

Jonash's hands slide up my wrists, and he curls my fingers into the grasses and the thin layer of earth that clings to the bedrock. I grasp at them, but the grasses come up in handfuls. Is he that much of an idiot to think they'll help keep me from falling? "Pull me up!" I scream at him.

The coolness of his fingers is gone, and the grass slips away. The edge of crystal rock scrapes the skin from the palms of my hands as I fall off the edge of the world.

I can hear screams, but I can't tell if they're mine. My body tumbles through the air, spinning over and over until I don't know anything but cold gusts of black wind. The moons blink their stark white faces in a blur of light that tumbles over itself until I'm completely dizzy. The rainbow lights of the fireflies stretch away like stars until I see nothing but blackness.

I'm going to die. I'm going to hit the earth and the impact will kill me.

I can't see in the darkness as I tumble round and round. I don't know when I'll hit, but it's coming. I can't tell if I've been falling for minutes or hours. The skirts of my dress are tangled around my legs. The wind whistles in my ears until I can't hear or feel anything else.

I start to slow then, and the world stops tumbling. Have I died? They say when you die, the Phoenix burns a hole in the world and clasps you gently in her talons to take you away. But there's no fire here, only cold air and a strange humming noise. And then a pale light spreads around me.

I look at my hand, drenched in a faint kaleidoscope of colors. It's almost invisible, like when I catch a glimpse of rainbow light dancing on my hand from the ripples of Lake Agur. I've slowed so much it's like floating in honey, the air thick and sluggish around me. I'm still falling, but drifting like a feather, buoyed gently down like I'm sinking into the lake.

And then there's a strange sucking sound, and the rainbow lights waft from my fingers. I'm falling at full speed again, my back to the earth and my eyes cast upward. I look up at the two moons as they beam, unyieldingly bright in the sea of darkness.

I hear a great crash as if I'm in another world, and I feel a sharp pain everywhere at once. Then there is nothing but blackness and void.

SIX

THE FIRST THING I hear is the mournful sound of strange birds calling in the sky. They drone sour notes, followed by a long pause, and then more wails. I hear the stuttering of what might be a squirrel or some sort of pika. The air is thick and the breeze warm, like a flame tickling across my skin. I've never felt any wind like this before.

My eyes open slowly, the daylight overwhelming. My head throbs as I try to figure out where I am and what's happened.

The fall. I've fallen off Ashra, down to the earth below. It seems impossible. I should be dead.

I rake my fingers against the ground and come up with sharp brown sapling needles. My eyes have trouble focusing on them even though my hand isn't far away. My body feels like stone, every muscle crying out as I roll slowly onto my side.

Elisha, I think. *Jonash.* I remember the feel of the grass as it slipped from beneath my fingers. All those times I spent on the edge of my outcrop, never imagining I could fall.

I almost can't believe it.

The branches of trees make a patchwork of sunlight that streams in from my left. Against my legs is a carpet of cold and damp. I squeeze my fingers and splay them. Moss, I realize. It's thick moss I've landed on. I bend my knees and slide my legs against the fuzzy moist earth.

It isn't anything like the rough drawings in the annals. It's wild and beautiful, and so alive.

I take a deep breath, and wiggle my fingers. There's a sharp pain when I turn my left wrist, and a pain in my chest when I breathe too deeply. But I'm alive, even if I'm injured.

I sit up slowly, my headache nearly knocking me down again. The spots in my eyes are clearing and the world is growing sharper.

I've landed in some sort of forest, though the trees are sparse and crooked. The whole floor of the woodland is covered in thick green-and-purple moss. Yellow-and-blue ferns unfurl in large floppy fans, and tiny sprigs of red flowers cluster like berries in the undergrowth.

The sour-sounding bird takes off with a rush of wings, his deep black feathers catching my eye as he soars past me. I look past him, up into the sky, to the looming dark island above. Ashra. It's massive, even from so far away. Giant roots tangle through an upside-down pyramid of rich brown dirt that clings to the bottom of its rock bed. The edge of the continent is jagged and fractured from where Burumu and Nartu broke off. A mist of water pours like a thin cloud from the side of the continent, like a tiny tail of white that vanishes halfway down to the earth. The waterfall of Lake Agur.

The earth. I'm on the earth. My world, my friends, my father…they're all high above on that floating continent, completely out of reach.

The thought jolts into me. The unrest in Burumu. The rebellion, the strange extra book and Aban's key and his discussion with the lieutenant. My father has to know. How can I tell him now? Is he in danger?

I rub the side of my head with my right hand, the moss and tree needles matted in my hair. How long have I been out? A single night? A day or two? Do they know what's happened to me? Elisha and Jonash would've gone for help right away. They'll have the airships out looking by now.

But the airships have never flown this low. They're bulky and unstable, difficult to maneuver. And finding me in this forest would be like finding a pika nest in the outlands, requiring more skill than the pilots have. They're not even sure the ships would hold up to the difference in air pressure down here.

On top of that, it's always been too risky to let the monsters know we're still alive on the floating continents. Some of the beasts have wings and could be willing to fly up to devour what's left of us.

My blood runs cold. The monsters. I'm like the unbelievers left behind in the illustration from the annals. It won't take them long to find me. The annals said they can sniff out a human from miles away.

They're probably already coming for me.

I rise to my feet in panic, but a deep, painful breath sends me tumbling down again. I cry out in agony and press my fingers against my ribs. My head twists to the side as I squeeze my eyes shut, tears stinging the corners. I've bruised my ribs, maybe broken them. I can't outrun monsters like this.

I look around the sparse forest. I need some kind of shelter, some sort of safe place.

But there isn't one. That's why the Rending happened in the first place.

My heart thrums in my ears, the panic rising in my throat. Will the airships search for me? Will the people think a fall like that killed me? I shake my head. No—my father will look for me, I'm certain. He'll hold out hope until the end. But he won't find me in time. The earth is too vast. I wonder if I can even spot the airships from here. It doesn't matter, because even if they could see me, they can't retrieve me.

My every breath sounds earsplitting in the silence. No, I can't give up. I've scaled rock bridges and swum closer to the waterfall of Ashra than any of the villagers in Ulan would dare. I've walked the edge of the outlands in the rainbow of fireflies hundreds of times before falling. One time, when Elisha and I were kids, we ran into a wild boar, and I chased it away with a stick while Elisha cried. I can do this. I won't be defeated.

Safe places, I wonder. I could climb a tree. Can monsters climb? I'm sure some can, but anything's better than sitting here on the ground like a pika on a platter.

I limp toward the nearest tree, resting my good wrist on the lowest branch. Hundreds of ants scurry up and down the splintered bark, but it's no time to be squeamish. I press my sandaled foot against the trunk and wrap my other hand lightly around the branch. With a strong push I lift myself up. The pressure on my ribs and my left wrist make me cry out before I can stop myself, and I fall to the ground.

Tears of frustration burn in the corners of my eyes as I shake the ants off my fingers. I've climbed hundreds of trees on Ashra. Now, when my life depends on it, I'm helpless.

They'll never find me in time, never find a way to reach me. But I can't give up hope. I'm still alive, after all. I survived the fall.

I rise to my feet again, shaking the ants off the hem of my skirt. If I can't climb the tree, then I need to find another way to hide myself. It's been almost three hundred years. Maybe the monsters have all died away. Maybe they've forgotten about humans. Maybe there are still some sort of village ruins I can hide in until help comes.

If help comes.

I shake the thought away. There's nothing to do right now but move forward. I walk along the edge of the trees, listening to the mournful songs of the birds, the rustling of the leaves. Surely if the monsters were near, the birds would stop singing, wouldn't they? So as long as they sing, I'm safe.

I step past the wide leaves of the blue-and-yellow ferns and follow the line of trees toward the shadow cast by Ashra. The ground slopes down toward the gaping hole of missing land, where the floating island fit centuries ago. The land is jagged like the edges of a deep wound, sharp caverns and deep chasms. Nothing grows in the shadowlands, but on the edges, where the sunlight filters in, sprigs of hopeful trees and vines and weeds sprout in a desperate tangle.

It would be a good hiding place, but the road is steep down to the shadowed crater—climbing back up would be difficult. And the airships won't see me underneath the continent. I imagine they'll search the perimeter where I fell. Jonash will be able to show them the spot, so I shouldn't stray too far.

I know they can't reach me, but I cling to the hope anyway. It's all I have.

I walk along the perimeter of the steep hillside for a while, listening carefully, watching my step, watching the skies. *The Phoenix is with me*, I think. She wouldn't let her heir be extinguished. It's a test and also maybe a blessing. I've always wanted to see the earth, and it's every bit as wild and breathtaking as I've imagined.

The forest is full of insects I've never seen before, long iridescent bugs that beat two or three pairs of wings as they float from one strange plant to another. A tiny yellow lizard with a bright and glittering blue tail spreads out on the wide leaves of the ferns. And the breeze, that strange wind, carries warmth and heat in it. Surely it must be still warm from the flames of the Phoenix tossing Ashra and her lands sky bound. There's no other explanation I can think of. The winds on Ashra are cold, but we're closer to the sun, so the reason must be residual heat left from the Phoenix's ashen sacrifice.

I walk along the perimeter of the forest for what seems like hours. There's no end to the wild lands, no place I can find shelter or a clearing to wave at the airships if they come.

My stomach growls, and I tense at the sound. How long has it been since I've eaten? I think of the honeyed chicken and the puffed cakes at the festival. I reach into my pockets but only find the small piece of flint Elisha passed me with the lantern in the outlands.

I look around the sparse forest, wondering if there's anything I can eat. The clusters of tiny red berries cling to the moss underfoot, and I wonder if they're safe or poisonous. A bird calls out in the sky. Maybe I could take a fallen branch and whittle it with the flint to make a spear. But I've never had to hunt before. I'm not sure if I'd know how to lance a bird.

I bend down and wrap my fingers around a bunch of the berries, pulling it toward me until it plucks free from the brown stem. Each berry is barely the size of a tiny bead. I lift the bunch toward my nose and smell them. They're pungent, a sickly smell like rotting. I squish one of the berries and the dark red juice runs down my hand like a trickle of blood.

I'm not sure what I'm looking for. I don't know how to tell if they're poisonous or not. But I'll starve if I don't eat anything. Surely one cluster wouldn't kill me. And if I'm sick, then I'll know for later.

I reach the berries toward my mouth and bite down on one. The tough skin punctures and sprays my tongue with bitter juice. I cough and sputter, spitting out the taste. The cluster drops and bounces gently against the moss while I wipe my mouth with the back of my hand. Not edible, then. Not even close.

My stomach claws against my insides, and my throat is parched. There has to be water somewhere nearby. The trees and moss and birds couldn't survive without it, could they?

I trudge forward for what feels like another hour, the remnants of the bitter juice sticking to the insides of my cheeks. My tongue feels like a slab of stone, thick and dry in my mouth.

At last the trees thin, and there's a small clearing of bright

green tall grasses. The tops of them splay out like the grains
we grow in Ulan. I peel the chaff away and pop the seeds
I find into my mouth, crunching them desperately before
swallowing them. They catch in my dry throat and I cough
while my fingers unravel another seed from the grass. If
only I'd grown up in the village like Elisha. Then I'd know
if this was a crop of wheat or oats or barley, or anything at
all that I could eat. My education was all about the Phoenix
and how to govern with authority and grace. It was history and language and etiquette, which fork to use when.
It seems ridiculous now, standing in this wild landscape.
Which fork to use? Why not teach me which wild plants
to eat, how to find water, how to identify crops? How far
from reality have I been living?

I scrape at the tops of the prickly grass until my fingers
bleed, swallowing down every seed I unwrap. They scratch
my throat as they go down, and still my stomach growls as
if I've eaten nothing at all.

The wind dips the grass, and I notice a small mound in
the distance that doesn't move with them. It's just a little
curve, a tuft of grass that doesn't match the others. It's pale
yellow, sticking up just above view. I narrow my eyes and
try to see more clearly.

Two dark black eyes stare back at me.

Every nerve in my body pulses. A beast. And it's watching me.

My mind races. Is it a monster? An animal? It's immov-
able, like a stone. I raise myself onto the balls of my feet
to see its head better. Its yellow tufted hair fades to purple
stripes on either side of its eyes. Its nostrils drip with con-
densed breath as it stares back at me. But that's all I can see.

I pull my hands slowly back from the grass tops. What now? If I run, it will chase. If I yell, maybe I'll scare it. If I fall over dead, perhaps it will go away, but it may also devour me.

I reach into my pocket for the sharp piece of flint. It will have to do until I can get my hands on anything else. If I survive this, I'll whittle a spear from a branch. Ashes and filthy soot, why did I spend all that time aimlessly walking in a world of monsters?

My foot lands on the leathery leaf of a yellow-and-blue fern, and it snaps in two with a loud crack. The beast lurches forward, a horrible growl echoing through the clearing. It looks like a giant barn cat from Ulan, but massive, the size of the giant Phoenix statue in the citadel courtyard. Its matted fur is striped bright yellow and vibrant purple, and its fangs look like horns curving out of its mouth. Its paws pound against the ground as it comes for me.

A monster. Not an animal, not harmless or friendly. It's a monster, out for blood.

I dart into the trees, clutching the flint in my bleeding fingers. I hope the maze of trunks will slow him down, but I don't dare to look. I run as fast as I can, my legs tangling in my long red skirts. I can hear his panting and the fall of his huge paws as they tear up the carpet of moss beneath us. I know I can't outrun him, but instinct takes over. My chest burns as I try to take deeper breaths.

Then a force like a stone wall shoves me to the ground. The monster's foul breath floods my nose and his sharp claws dig into my shoulder. I wrench myself to the left, reaching with my flint as his weight holds down my right side. I slice wildly at the air above me, hoping to hit him.

The jagged rock scrapes across his moist nostrils and he cries out, shaking his head as dark plum-colored blood trickles down his nose and on to his curved fangs.

I twist onto my back as the hold of his paw loosens and I strike again, going for his eyes. He rears back and I scramble to my feet, taking off across the field. He's behind me, and we're running again.

A shadow falls over me like a dark cloud. The entire clearing becomes night in an instant. A screeching sound vibrates through my head and I cry out, falling to my knees in pain from the high-pitched noise. The giant cat screeches a horrific version of the wails I've heard from barn cats in Ulan, and then a blast of wind nearly knocks me over.

The shadow lifts from the clearing, the sunlight streaming back in, the tall grasses flattened to the ground from the gale.

I look up and swear under my breath. A dragon has snatched up the massive cat in its talons. A dragon. A real one. Its black-and-red wings stretch out across the clearing as it lifts into the air. Its snout is long and sharp like a beak, and tufts of spiky fur sprout from its head and its breast like a shield of bone needles. Another gust of its wings flings me against the ground. The giant cat squirms in the dragon's sharp talons as it lifts him away. It shrieks once more, and I clasp my hands over my ears from the pain.

Then the dragon and the cat are gone. My ears ring as I sit there in shock, panting, my hands bleeding over the flint at my side. After what seems like an eternity, the birds in the forest start chirping again.

And then the tears come, fast and hot in my eyes. I sit

there as the sun begins to set, as the sky tints purple and orange and red, all blurred through my blubbering.

I'm going to die here on this forsaken wasteland.

No one is coming for me.

SEVEN

LIGHT HAS NEARLY left the sky by the time I get a hold of myself. There's only a pale purple glow that lights the clearing as I wipe away the last of my tears with the sleeve of my dress.

Reason starts to flood back into me. *For shame*, I think. Would I sit and sob about rebellion with Burumu? Would I merely weep if a dragon attacked Ashra? What kind of leader would abandon hope and logic in a time like this?

I still don't have a weapon or a safe place for the night, and now I've wasted what was left of the daylight. I'm an idiot, a complete and utter dull cinder. I don't have a chance to survive, but I refuse to die. And so there's nothing to do but keep burning, like always.

I clasp the flint in my hand and search the underbrush of the trees for a fallen branch. It's hard to see in the plum-colored light, but eventually my hand falls on a stick that's about as long as my arm. I sit down with my back to the trunk and pull the tiny sprigs off along the length of the branch, then take my flint. I squint in the fading light to see what I'm doing. Should I use the flint to make a fire? But I'm frightened it will attract more monsters.

My whole body aches for water. I put the branch aside and grab a wide leaf from the yellow-and-blue fern. I snap its wide center vein apart and suck on the sticky sap inside. It doesn't help much, but I'm clueless and desperate. At least I can pretend it feels better.

I scrape the flint against the wood again, and this time the rock splits in two. I feel around the ground for the second piece. Its sharp edge nearly cuts into my fingers. It's a better weapon than sharpened wood, I realize, if I could tie it to the spear somehow.

I reach for the rope belt around my dress and grasp a length of it in my hand. I hold the tasseled end across the flint, sawing back and forth with the sharp edge. The fibers slide apart and I tie the smaller flint piece to the top of the branch, wrapping the string round and round and tying knots. There's a small but natural groove in the branch that seems to hold the flint in place. I can only hope it doesn't completely fall apart when I thrust the spear at something. I take the original piece of flint and slip it into my pocket as a second weapon. It's completely dark now, and I can't see my handiwork, but there's a small comfort in holding the homemade spear in my hands.

The two moons shine high above in the pitch-black sky. The breeze isn't as warm as it was in the daytime, and I find myself shivering as the night goes on. Sprays of stars glisten through the dark clouds that float above, but a large and vacant blot in the starry map lets me know Ashra is hovering there, silent and safe in the sky.

I stare up at my home. The fireflies will be out in the outlands. The pikas will gather fireweed and thistles on my outcrop realm of one. The Rending celebrations will continue, the candles flickering along the stone wall in Ulan. Burumu will bustle with its own festivities, and the scribes on Nartu will have tea and cakes and discuss politics with each other until dawn.

Or maybe they'll think their princess is dead, and the festivities will stop. Maybe they'll trade the bright red-and-orange garlands for black veils, the goat-string harps for the mournful carved flutes.

I have to get back to Ashra. I have to let my father know I'm alive, that I need him to come and get me. I doubt they'd see a fire from up there, even if they were looking. They'd never know it was me who'd created that pinprick dot of flame on this vast earth below.

In the distance something shrieks, and another thing howls. The sounds are inhuman, monstrous and strange. Throughout the night I find myself starting to doze off, my head slipping against the tree trunk, and then one of those shrieks will pierce the sky, and I'll jolt awake, my blood running cold. What's even out there? It looks as though, now that humans are gone, the monsters eat and fight each other. Or perhaps they've always done that from what I've read. Except for the Phoenix, they've never shown sentient thought about anything.

I close my eyes, and the nighttime blurs into strange thoughts that dance around my head. I wake to thunder that rolls above me in the clouds and air that tastes sour on my tongue. The sky flashes lavender, and then everything is black again while the thunder rumbles. Why hasn't the daylight come yet? My back aches from the thick bark digging into it, but it's the only reassurance I have that nothing is creeping up behind me.

The air buzzes with electricity as another bolt of lightning streaks through the sky. I try to lick my parched lips. Please, I think. By the ashes of the Phoenix, please, let it rain.

And then the drops fall thick and hard, drenching the tall grasses as they sway from the weight.

I try to catch the water in my hands, but the sticky blood on them taints it. I rub my fingers together, washing as best I can and trying again. Then I gather up my skirt to catch water, but it soaks into the fabric, weighing down the cloth. I take the corner and squeeze it into my mouth, but only a few drops come out.

I feel around beside me in the dark and rip off one of the wide fern leaves, shaping it between my cupped hands. It's almost impossible to wait until it fills, and I tip the raindrops I've caught over and over into my mouth. They taste sweet and warm, and though most nights with dinner I have honeyed berry juice in a golden goblet, right now I've never had anything more delicious than tepid rainwater in a fern leaf.

But once the edge of my thirst has faded away, all I can feel is the cold of being pelted by the rainstorm, my dress waterlogged and pulling me firmly to the ground. If a monster came now, I probably couldn't run fast enough.

I shiver in the rain, reaching for the flint in my pocket. But I can't make a fire now. Everything is soaked, the tall grasses bent over from the heavy deluge.

I close my eyes and think of the warm fireplace in my bedroom of the citadel. I think of the crackle of the logs at night as they sputter and pop with bright flames. I shudder in the cold even as the rain slows and the clouds move on, as the shrieks and piercing wails of monsters echo in the dark around me. I think of my father smiling, of him dancing me around the room when I was only seven on our trip to Nartu.

The rebellion. I have to warn him, have to find out what's going on. I think about the strange light I passed through as I fell from Ashra. The pale rainbow glow was as slow as honey around me. Is that why I survived? Was that part of the drawing that had been scratched out?

Thoughts drift to strange images. I jolt awake, and the sky is flooding with light. The sun is starting to warm the breeze that drifts over the muddy field the clearing has become. The battered tall grasses are hunched over but starting to reach again for the sunlight. Birds are chirping in the trees, and squirrels and pikas are chattering.

I reach for the spear beside me and stand. Every muscle aches. My muddy skirts pull with weight, so I lean the spear against the tree and wring them out. I consider cutting them shorter with the flint, but I worry I'll freeze if the nights get any colder. My feet and sandals are covered in cold muck, and they squelch as I shift my weight to stretch. I take a careful breath, but the horrible pain in my ribs is still there, like a rope tied too tightly around my chest. At least my left wrist feels a little better, so it must be only twisted and not broken.

I've survived a whole day in a land overrun by monsters. I will survive another.

I take my spear and start walking along the edge of the clearing. My stomach throbs with hunger. I search the skies but keep going. I don't want to go too far from the edge of Ashra's shadow, in case the airships are looking for me, but

I also need to find food, more than just those sharp grains from the tall grasses.

Ashra floats in the sky like a beacon. I lift my hand upward, as if I could touch it.

"I'm right here," I say quietly. "I'm alive. Come find me." I think of Father and Elisha, of trying to hold on to Jonash as I slipped off the edge. How could this happen? I've walked that edge a hundred times. I bitterly wish for a minute that I'd left him to fall off the edge himself, instead of me. But then hot guilt curls in my stomach. I wouldn't wish this monster-ridden landscape on anyone.

I feel tears gathering in the corners of my eyes, so I blink them back and try to think rationally. Food first, water and shelter, and then self-pity. The forest stretches around the perimeter of the shadowy land as far as I can see. In the distance is a line of mountains looming far away, some of the peaks dusted in snow. Winged beasts in the sky far away, some like giant birds and others more like the dragon I saw yesterday. Ashes. This world really is flooded with the beasts. The rest of my view is blocked by a thick jumble of trees on a wide hill. I look to my right, along the tree line. There's a cluster of greener bushes and ferns in the distance, where the terrain turns rocky. Could it be a river?

I walk back along the right tract of forest. It's not lost on me that I'm almost retracing my steps from yesterday, returning to the patch where I originally fell. If I'm right, that there's water there, I was probably no more than an hour's walk from it yesterday.

My ankles sting in the sandals Elisha lent me. They're slightly too small, and they rub red blisters into the backs of my heels. I think about taking them off and walking barefoot, but I'm afraid of this landscape and what I might step on.

"Elisha," I say, and the loudness of my own voice startles me. "I made it to the earth I couldn't stop talking about. If only you could see me now." I laugh a little, because there's nothing else to do.

A shadow swirls over me and I look up to see the long spiked tail of a feathered monster that swoops up and over the forest. I quietly thank the Phoenix that it didn't choose me for lunch.

The sun is at the top of the sky by the time I reach the rocky ground. I listen to the faint whisper I can hear over the chorus of birds in the forest beside me. I think it's the sound of trickling water, and I hurry forward, stumbling over the clusters of sharp rocks that scrape against my ankles.

It appears like a dream, a long creek babbling over a stony bank, the water clear and sparkling in the afternoon sun. I stagger forward, bending my tired knees and dipping my hand into the water. It's ice-cold, and I put my spear beside me so I can fill my cupped hands and drink. I splash my face and shake the beads of water from my hair. I scrub the dried blood from my fingers and unlace my sandals. The water stings against my blistered skin and I can only stand to put my feet in the water for a few moments at a time. I peer into the darkness of the bottom and look for signs of fish, but I can't see anything darting around. It doesn't look deep enough to warrant fears of underwater monsters or the sharks the annals warn of that live in the oceans.

After a moment I lie on my back, my legs still dangling in the water up to my calves. Burumu, Nartu and the Floating Isles are so far that I can't even see their borders from here. Only Ashra hovers in the sky, the tangle of roots and dirt hanging down from its shape, the mist of the tiny waterfall foaming off the crystal edge.

There's a speck in the sky near the rim of the floating continent. Could it be an airship? I flood with a panic to signal it, but the thought just as quickly flies from my head. It's impossible. If I couldn't see the monsters flying around the lands from Ashra's heights, there's no way the airship will see me on the ground.

The water laps under the breeze and the world feels peaceful and calm. But the lapping gets louder, even when the breeze stops. Something isn't right. I sit up on my elbows slowly, and look.

A monster is across the bank from me. It's as big as a caravan, its shoulders at a height nearly halfway up the tree trunks. Its body is covered in soft cream fur, but its long tail is slippery and striped, the end of it dipped into the water. And it has three heads, *three*, each drinking and gulping from the stream. One is dark purple with horns and a long bearded snout like a goat. Another is like the giant cat from before, but with a mane of shimmering gold. And the third is scaled and sharp with lizard-slit eyes. I stare as my heart pounds in my chest. The water trickles down the goat head's beard and beads in the cat's mane. It shimmers off the lizard scales like oil. And then the tail of the monster flicks out of the water, and it's a snake, with a black tongue that slithers in and out of its mouth.

By some miracle the monster hasn't seen me yet. So I soundlessly slip my legs out of the water and grab my sandals. I place the leather on my raw, blistered skin, but the pain makes me wince. I can't run in these. I slip my foot back out, resting a hand on my spear and the other on my flint shard.

I'm terrified to stand up. It will see me, I know. So I sit, thoughts rushing, trying to think of my next move.

That's when the goat head sees me and bleats. The cat head blinks, its lip curling back in a hungry snarl. The lizard licks its eyelid with its sticky pink tongue.

The monster steps into the creek, where its massive cream paws sink into the water. And then it darts forward, water spraying in an upward cascade that momentarily hides it from view.

I turn and run, the rocks sharp against the soles of my feet.

I doubt I'll be lucky enough for a hungry dragon to come by this time. It's over—it's going to eat me.

EIGHT

I SPRINT AS fast as I can, barefoot across the slippery jagged rocks and onto the grassy plain in front of me. Maybe I should run to those ancient tangled trees on the hill to my left, but the monster would catch me before I made it up the steep muddy slope that leads to them.

I race forward, not knowing where I'm going, waiting any moment for the sharp claws to dig into my back. When the claws don't come, I risk a quick look back.

It's still there, chasing me, the cat's head with open jaws and the lizard's scales grating against each other as it runs. The goat head bleats angrily, water still dripping from its gray beard. The ground rumbles as the monstrosity stumbles along behind me, but its legs are stubby and uncoordinated. It can't run as quickly as the yellow-and-purple cat from yesterday, which is why it hasn't caught up with me yet.

I keep running, every breath burning against my ribs, the

searing pain slowing me down. The grassy ground is bumpy and uneven, and I keep stumbling over the tiny pockets of soil and moss strewn over the landscape. A massive bird with a lizard tail swoops over us and snaps its beak, but it doesn't snatch the monster or me. It's a reminder that if this monster doesn't eat me, something else will.

I huff and pant as I slow. My body is exhausted and starved, my ribs cracked and throbbing. I'll have to face it. There's nowhere to hide.

Against every scream in my head I force myself to turn as I heave in fiery, stinging breaths. I hold my spear tightly in my right hand, its sharp point wavering at the three-headed monster galloping toward me. The beast digs its claws into the ground, and a huge ripple waves through its matted fur as it forces itself to a stop. The cat head is growling, the lizard flicking its tongue. At the back of the monster, the serpent tail weaves back and forth, its fangs dripping with venom as it watches me. The goat head stares intently at my spear.

My own voice startles me. "Come on, you ashen ugly!" He's so much bigger than the wild boar from my childhood. But he stands between me and survival. And I will survive.

It lunges forward, claws in the air. I slice at the goat head with my spear and hit nothing but air. I grunt with the effort as I swipe again. The goat grabs the branch of the spear in his mouth and holds fast. Icy panic washes down my spine as I yank at the spear, trying to get it free. The cat growls and snaps with his sharp teeth, and I step around the left side of the giant beast so it can't reach me. The paws make an uncoordinated turn, and we circle one another, the spear lodged in the goat's mouth.

And then the goat grates his teeth, and the spear snaps in

two between his jaws. I cry out, swinging at its head with what's left of the branch. It clubs him near the ear and he shakes his head, bleating his foul breath at me.

I swing the club again, turning slowly with the monster. There's no time to grab the flint in my pocket. The snake is hovering close by, and I'm sure he'll strike the minute my eyes are downcast.

And then there's a blur of movement, and the snake lets out a gag as he's yanked backward. A creature draped in mottled beige fur, with curved incisors like a wolf's, forces the snake's fangs into the monster's side, and all three heads bellow at once, the sound ripping through the air. It sways and tilts and snaps at the wolf creature as it climbs on its back and throws its arms around the lizard head. The action throws the monster off balance, and it collapses on its side with a rumble that shakes the ground. The fanged wolf head falls backward against the softness of the fur.

It takes me a moment to realize what I'm seeing.

The creature isn't a monster. He's wearing a fur cloak, the wolf head and fangs part of a hood. His face underneath is painted with vibrant colors, but he's human.

A human. On the earth. My mind races as I try to process what's happening. He pulls out a dagger and cuts at the beast while I stand completely stunned.

They weren't wiped out. The unbelievers who were left behind, the ones illustrated in the first volume of the annals, have survived. They've survived for these long three hundred years.

The tongue lolls in the lizard's head, and the cat's eyes roll back. The goat head collapses against the ground, its eyes turning vacant and glassy. The snake tail wavers in the air like a tipsy festival-goer in Ulan, before flopping onto the ground like a coil of rope.

The boy doesn't look at me. He steps over the goat head and squats down by the snake tail, lifting it by the neck and shaking it around a bit before letting it slump back down to the ground. A minute later he reaches for a quiver over his shoulder and slides it off, two dozen wooden arrows scattering over the ground. He takes the snake in his right hand, the arrows in his left, and squeezes the serpent's head until its eyes bulge. Venom drips down its fangs and onto the arrowheads as he changes them out for new ones.

I open my mouth to speak, but I'm so overwhelmed that nothing comes out.

A minute later he glides the arrows back into the quiver and shoulders it again, neatly pulling the matted fur cloak over top. He's still looking at the ground when he asks, "You need venom?"

"Sorry?" I say.

He stands up slowly and turns to face me. I'm surprised to see we're nearly the same age, at least as far as I can tell. His brown hair is cut jaggedly, two yellow and purple stripes painted under his eyes; the colors remind me of the giant cat from yesterday. His arms are tanned and muscled, though hidden by the strap of his bow and the beaded leather lacing that crisscrosses his right forearm. His ripped leather tunic is covered with straps that hold the quiver on his back, a row of daggers on his hip and a pouch at his other side, half hidden by the creamy fur of the cape. Around his neck is a string of iridescent shell circles that remind me of home; they're like the shells that decorate my headdress for the Rending Ceremony in Ashra.

"Venom," he says again. "Do you need any?"

"I…" It takes me a minute to understand what he's asking. The snake's venom, he means. "No," I stammer. "Thank you."

He nods. "Where are your weapons?"

I look down at my broken branch, the rope and the flint scattered on the ground by the goat's head.

He frowns. "That's it? You're either brave or crazy." He bends down to retrieve the flint, and that's when I see the lantern fastened by his pouch. A large dent caves in the side of the lantern, the black iron riddled with carved stars and plumes. Elisha's lantern that I dropped over the edge of the outlands.

"That's…that's my lantern," I say, pointing at it.

He reaches a hand for the lamp, lifting it slightly to glance at it. "Yours?"

"Well, my friend's."

He stands and tilts his head up to Ashra, hovering silently in the sky. Then he turns to me. "Did you fall? From the floating island?"

"Yes," I say, tears stinging in my eyes. I can't believe I'm talking to a human on the earth. It's more breathtaking than anything I've read in the annals. "Yes. Two nights ago, I think. I don't know how long I was unconscious. I need to get back. Is there a way?"

He doesn't answer my questions but looks at me intently. I feel too on display in my ripped, muddy robe, my corded belt cut and unbraiding, my feet bare and blistered and my hands covered in scrapes. Hardly the best first impression for the Heir of the Eternal Flame.

He reaches for the leather that ties the lantern to his belt and loosens the knot with his slender fingers, holding out the iron handle to me. "Welcome," he says, with a shy hint of a smile.

It catches me off guard, to think a human has taken down a caravan-sized monster and now welcomes me to the monster-ridden earth. "Thank you," I manage.

The handle creaks as I take it gently, the sunlight streaming through the cutouts on its surface. *Oh, Elisha*, I think. Homesickness swirls in every fiber of my body. I don't know how to think or act here, or what the boy is thinking of me right now. The candle inside has shattered from the fall, only a small jagged piece of it left at the bottom. I undo my rope belt and tie it through the loop of the lantern handle, fastening it to my hip.

Then the boy turns to the monster again, and with his dagger he slices into the fur at the nape of the goat's neck. The squelching sound turns my stomach, and I look away as the blood trickles onto the ground. If I'd grown up in the village like Elisha, I probably wouldn't be such a baby about it, but we never slaughtered animals in the citadel. I take a deep breath and turn back to face it, to face him. I can't afford to be a coward down here, or I'll never make it back to Ashra.

"Could I... Could you tell me if there's a way to get back to the floating continent?" I ask. "Do you know a way?" He keeps cutting, not even looking at me. I feel stupid for asking the question then. Of course there isn't a way. He wouldn't live down here if he could escape.

He keeps cutting along the fur, pulling back the skin to expose the fat and muscle. "What are you doing?" I say. "It's already dead."

"If you don't mind," he says, "I have to work quickly, before the venom spreads. Perfectly good waste of meat."

"You're…you're going to eat that thing?"

"Why not?" he says, cutting strips and laying them on the ground. "He was going to eat you." I shudder, but he continues. "If I had time to do it properly, I could get a great deal more than just a hunk of meat. But the snake's venom is spreading, and the scavengers will be here soon. We need to be gone before that happens."

"The scavengers?"

His blade never stops moving. "Pack of nasty beasties," he says. "They can smell a rotting chimera carcass a mile away."

Chimera, I think. So this type of monster has a name. I shudder again, thinking of all the scavenger monsters that it will attract.

"Can I help you?" I say, eager to get away before they come. He looks at me for a minute, then nods, cutting across the large piece of fur dangling from the goat's neck. He tosses it on the ground, and the edges curl upward. I nod and kneel beside it. I only hesitate a moment before smoothing out the sticky inside and loading the chunks of meat onto it. I'm so hungry, so desperate, that for a moment I consider shoving the glistening raw meat into my mouth. But I know I'll get really sick, so I try to force the impulse down. The meat is warm and bloody, staining my hands pink. The iridescent flies try to land on it as I shoo them away.

It's amazing what you can do when you're faced with no other option.

"It was… It was clever to use the snake tail to kill the chimera."

"The best way to take down a monster is with the weaknesses it presents you," he says.

I say nothing, only take another chunk of the bright red meat and place it onto the skin.

"I was looking for you, you know," he says, wiping the sweat off his forehead with the back of his arm. He goes back to carving.

Looking for me? "How?" I say. It's not like I planned to fall from the continent.

"There's a barrier around the floating island," he says. "When you passed through it, it set off a light in the sky like a star. I saw it two nights ago, and I've been searching since. That's how I found your lantern."

"A barrier?"

He nods. "You must've wondered why you survived the fall?"

I remember then, slowing as I fell, the air sticky like honey. The rainbow lights dancing faintly on my fingertips. "But I've never read about a barrier in the annals."

"What are the annals?"

I choke back my surprise before I blurt anything I'll regret. Of course he hasn't heard of them. It's the Elders who have kept the records on Ashra, high above in the sky. And then I remember the second volume Aban kept hidden, the writing about a barrier and a generator on the flyer the lieutenant burned. "Did the survivors of the Rending keep records?"

"The Rending?" he says, which answers my question.

"Of the Phoenix," I say. "You know, the day Ashra was sent into the sky. The day the unbeliev— I mean, that some humans were left behind. Your ancestors."

There's a horrible cluster of wails in the distance. The sound of it chills me to the bone.

"Time to go," he says, and wipes his dagger on the grass

before sliding it into his belt. He reaches into his pouch and pulls out some string that he uses to tie the bundle of meat inside the strip of fur.

We stand, and he notices my bare feet. "You can't go far like that," he says.

"I had to leave my sandals at the creek after the chimera chased me."

He gives me a sympathetic look as he adjusts the fur cloak over his shoulders. "We'll have to go back later, okay?"

The wails come again, and I tremble. "It's fine. Anything." *Just don't leave me here alone*, I think, but I don't say it. I don't want him to think I'm afraid. As heir, I'd never be allowed to admit that to anyone.

He nods, and takes off running toward the steep hill crowned with a tangle of trees. I follow him, running as fast as I can with my aching ribs. It's easier to run without those sandals after all, the grass soft and pliable under my feet. He's faster, though, probably used to running for his life down here.

That's when I think about the others like him. Because he can't be the only one to survive, can he? There must be others as swift and equipped as he is.

When we reach the edge of the hill I hear a frenzy of howling behind us. I turn to the distant mound of the chimera. A dozen wild doglike monsters are crawling over it like maggots, tearing flesh and chomping with their large fangs. One of the giant birds I've seen circling the valley is hovering over the carcass, the wild dogs snapping at its legs while it scrapes at them with its talons. I can't look away from the horror of it.

That could've been me they were feasting on. It nearly was.

I feel the strong grip of the boy's hands on my wrist, and

I turn to look at him. His shining eyes are looking into mine, the paint on his face smeared by sweat. "Only look forward," he says, pressing my hand into the thick grass. My fingers are still stained pink from the raw chimera meat.

It's enough to snap me out of it. "Thanks," I say, grabbing at the thick tufts to pull myself up the hill. We scramble up the steep hillside to the sickening slurps and growls of the scavengers behind us. My ribs burn, and my left wrist throbs. When I'm almost at the summit he's already at the top, reaching a hand out to help me. But I want to show him I can do it, so I make my way, slowly, and he waits.

When I get there I collapse, panting as I rest a hand on my stinging side.

He looks alarmed. "Are you injured?"

"My ribs," I say. "I think I broke one or two when I fell."

"You can't climb, then?" he says, looking up at the tall tangle of ancient trees.

I tilt my head back, looking up. I have to admit the truth. "I'm…not sure."

He nods. "Rest now," he says. "I'll make a fire." He walks toward the trunks, gathering branches that have fallen, and discarding those soaked by last night's rain. He expertly sorts them as I sit there, useless, and I start to realize how lucky I am that he's found me.

I'm going to survive, I think. *Only look forward.*

NINE

I RUB MY ribs with my hands, trying to stop the aching pain. I wish I could go back to the creek and wash my fingers properly. They're sticky and rank with the smell of raw meat. I wipe them against the ground for a bit, my elbow clanking against the iron lantern at my waist.

Suddenly the boy's standing above me with an armful of branches. He puts them down and arranges them in a cluster, the sides of his fur cloak spreading out against the ground like wings. "What's your name?"

The question startles me. In Ashra and her lands, everyone knows who I am. "Kallima," I manage. "Kali, for short."

"Kali," he says. "And are you all right now, Kali?" He smiles again. He smiles a lot for a monster hunter, I think. His face should be battle-worn and hopeless, like the unbelievers in the annals. But it isn't, not at all. He's cheerful and healthy, capable and pleasant. Elisha would laugh at me for using words like that. *Healthy and capable?* She'd sidle up to me and whisper in my ear. *What are you really trying to say?* And she'd be right. I blush at the thought.

"I'm sorry that was your introduction to earth," he says, pulling up tufts of dried grass that grow in little huddles near the campfire.

I clear my throat. "I... I would like to extend my gratitude for your fortuitous assistance."

He squints a little, twisting his head to the side. I realize at once my mistake. I've turned on my regal voice, rending us apart by status and education. I look like a patronizing show-off, and the formal acknowledgment makes us both uncomfortable. "Thank you," I add, with an awkward cough.

"No problem." He shrugs. Aban's blood pressure would skyrocket if someone answered me in such a casual tone on Ashra. The freedom of being a normal girl, floating on the winds of possibility, is thrilling.

But then my cheeks burn as I realize I haven't even asked him his name. He saved my life, but it's all been a blur, a shocking revelation that there are survivors on earth. He's handsome and charming, and I haven't even thought to ask. "What's your name?"

"Griffin," he says, and he reaches into his pouch and produces two pieces of flint like mine. He strikes them together, the sparks flying on to the tuft of dried grass he's placed on his knee. He blows gently, patiently, and I'm afraid to speak in case I distract him. It takes a few tries, but eventually the smoke spirals up from the patch of grass, and he places it carefully under the branches, blowing the spark until it licks the undersides of the wood.

Then he places the fur bundle of meat in front of him, untying the string and placing it back into his pouch.

"Griffin," I finally repeat. I've never heard a name like it in Ashra. Most parents think it's fortuitous to name your children after the Phoenix or her attributes. Jonash, for example, has the word "ash" in it, while Elisha's name uses an older variant. My own name is more unusual, but my mother had wanted to name me after the butterflies that gather near Lake Agur. Even though she died in childbirth, my father upheld her wish and named me Kallima.

But I've never heard a name like Griffin. It doesn't sound like any of the older words for Phoenix or "to rise," "ashes," or "plumes" or "embers."

"What does it mean?" I ask.

He's silent for a moment, adjusting the branches as they kindle in the growing flames. Then he passes me a longer stick, which he's skewered a strip of the meat onto. "It was the first monster I killed," he says, gazing into the fire.

I think of how quickly he attacked the chimera, how he didn't hesitate even when his life was at risk. I'd been grateful to survive a day. He's been surviving his whole life. "How many have you killed?"

He turns the meat on his on stick. "Like the stars," he says. I glance upward, but the sun is only low in the sky, not yet setting, and all I see up there is Ashra, looming silently. "I'm a monster hunter."

"A monster hunter?" The thought turns my stomach. "You track them willingly?"

He smiles, the yellow and purple paint under his eyes creasing with the expression. "I fight back," he says, and now I can hear the pride in his voice.

Everything I've ever wanted to know is in my reach,

but I'm almost afraid to ask. "Are there others down here? Other monster hunters like you?"

The smile falls from his face, and he reaches over to adjust my stick of meat closer to the flame. It's obvious I've never cooked over a campfire in my life. "Some," he says. "Not many."

"But there are humans," I say.

He looks into the fire, turning his meat as the fat drips into the flames. "There are a few of us who've survived."

I'm not sure what to ask next. I've wondered my whole life about the earth below, scouring the annals for clues. Now I'm here, and there's an actual monster hunter I can ask. I wonder if he's seen the ocean. Maybe that's where he got his shell necklace? But there's one question still burning in my mind, brighter than the others. I take a deep breath. "You said you were looking for me. You saw the flash in the sky."

He nods. "We always rescue the fallen."

I frown. It doesn't make sense. "No one's fallen from Ashra in fourteen years," I say.

"From the other floating mountains, I mean."

No, I think. That's impossible. No one's fallen off Burumu or Nartu in my lifetime, and no one lives on the smaller continent fragments of the Floating Isles. "How often?" I ask.

He crosses his legs, resting his elbows on his knees. "Four in the last year," he says. "Maybe five in the few years before that."

"No, you're wrong." I blurt it out, before I can stop myself. "I would've heard about it. It would've been huge news."

He shrugs, turning his stick of chimera meat over the

fire. He doesn't care if I believe him or not. Why would he lie to me? What does he have to hide?

There's a loud screech in the distance, and I cover my ears with my hands, the stick pressed against my temple. It's farther away now, but I know that bloodcurdling sound. It's the dragon again, crying out. Suddenly none of my questions matter.

"I need to get home," I say. "Back up there, to Ashra."

Griffin smiles gently, but doesn't answer. He's striking, I think, with his kind eyes and his array of furs and weapons and tools. He doesn't look like someone on the run for his life. He looks self-assured and confident, unlike anyone I've ever met before. He looks the way I used to think of myself—invincible—before my fall and pathetic attempt at survival. I can't help but feel like a fraud now, a dulling, fading cinder in front of a brilliant spark.

He takes hold of my branch and looks carefully at the chimera meat on the end, before nodding. "It's good now. You can eat."

My stomach growls on cue, and I pull the meat closer to sniff it. Monster meat. But I'm starving. It's too chewy and burning hot, and it scorches my lips and tongue as I bite into it. It tastes faintly like the pygmy goat meat we have in Ulan, but gamey and a little sour.

"I don't know of a way to get back," Griffin says, his voice so quiet I barely hear him. "I'm sorry."

I pause and stare at him. Staying here isn't an option to me. I have to get home to my father. I have to quell whatever unrest there is and protect my people. I'm the wick and the wax, the only descendant of the Monarch who can burn for the good of Ashra.

And more than that, I'm a lost child who needs her father's warm and loving arms.

Griffin sees the look on my face, his eyes shining with pity. "Hey, try this," he says, his voice upbeat. He reaches into the pouch at his hip and pulls out a tiny blue vial, sealed with a cork stopper. He pries the cork from the end with a pop and presses his finger against the opening, tipping the vial upside down before righting it again. He reaches over and shows me the tiny dark crystals glittering on his finger. Then he dusts them with his thumb over my chimera meat. "Much better," he says, his cheeks turning the slightest pink as he returns the cork to the vial and stows it in his pouch. "From the lava lands."

I take another bite of the meat, my tongue pressing against the crystals. They flood the meat with charcoal-like sharpness and rich flavor. It must be some kind of black salt. My eyes must show everything, because he laughs at my expression.

"Good, right?" he says, and I nod. I can't imagine how difficult it must be to get salt here, but from the way he handled the vial, and how he didn't even put any on his own dinner, I know what he's done for me is precious and generous. I eat every bite, my stomach reeling as it finally gets food.

"It's not so terrible down here if you can survive," he says. "You'll make a new life. It will be all right."

I shake my head. "You don't understand. I need to get back to my father and my old life. If I could only reach the airships…"

He stops midbite. "Airships?"

"You can't really see them from down here, but they

ferry passengers from one floating island to the next. You know?"

His eyes are wide, and although he must have seen hundreds of monsters, the novelty of airships clearly sparks his interest. "Ships," he repeats. "In the sky?"

"Yes," I say. "Only they don't come down this far. I thought I saw one last night, but it only looked like a speck from down here. If we could...I don't know, rope a dragon or something. Just get a little higher."

He laughs, reaching again into his pouch and pulling out some sort of leather bag with a stopper. He opens it and passes it to me. I sniff at it.

"Water," he offers.

It tastes warm and leathery, but it's refreshing after the salty meat. I know without Griffin I would be dead by now, mauled by the chimera and the scavengers after it. "You can't 'rope a dragon,'" he continues, chuckling. "Unless you want to be its lunch. But we could get higher up." He points at the mountain range in the distance, the spiky backbone that runs along the horizon of the pockmarked valley to the south. "Could these airships see you from the mountain top?"

My heart jumps at the thought of it. They look like they'd be tall enough, if we could manage to climb them. And the airships fly over those mountains on their way to Burumu. I know, because I remember looking out at them on that trip for the 290th Rending Anniversary when I was seven. It had only looked like a spiky, snow-peaked line then, but I'm certain it's the same mountains.

I pass back the flask and Griffin gulps what's left of the water. "Could...could you take me there?"

"If that's what you want," he says. It's big, what I'm asking, and yet he's willing to do it. "But it's a long way. And you won't make it without shoes."

"I can go back for my sandals," I say, but he shakes his head, pointing at my blisters.

"They weren't the most practical pair, were they? Anyway, those scavengers won't leave until the chimera is a tiny stack of bones. I have family who can help us, not far from here."

Other survivors. Other humans. And a way home, too. "We can take them with us," I blurt out. "You can come up to Ashra—that's what the floating island is called. You'll be safe from the monsters, I promise."

Griffin smiles kindly, but there's something in his eyes that I can't place. Doesn't he believe me?

"We'll set out in the morning," he says. "It's too far to make it before nightfall."

"I understand," I say. "You don't want to be caught out there with the monsters in the dark."

His lip curls up in amusement. "No," he says, his hand on the string of his bow. "I don't want *you* to be out there with the monsters in the dark."

My cheeks burn. I'm useless down here, nothing but a liability to him. In the dark I'd probably trip over a chimera and right into its mouths.

"It's all right." He grins. "Not everyone is called to hunting, you know."

"You think I'm not cut out for it?" I say, looking myself over with dramatic flair. "What was your first clue?" Might as well be good-natured about it—I'm no hunter.

He laughs. "Only the lack of weapons and armor." I'm pleased he doesn't say anything that would alter my opinion of him—that I'm a sheltered girl pretending at being brave; that my hands are thin and pale from an easy life; that I wouldn't last a week out here on my own. It might be true, but I don't want him to think it.

He leaves the side of the dying fire and grabs the nearest trunk in the ancient tangle of trees. Before I can blink he's halfway up, the soles of his leather shoes gripping the sides as he scrambles up like a pika. He walks soundlessly along one of the thicker branches, pushing on the boughs with his foot as he tests their strength. Then he unfastens the strings of his fur cloak and spreads it across a jumble of the branches, tucking it under and around to keep it in place.

He returns to the trunk and sidles down, and then he's beside me again, reaching out his hand.

"Your ribs," he says. "Can I have a look?"

My cheeks flush. I know he's asked innocently, that he wants to know how bad the injury is. But even knowing this, the thought of hiking up my dress to show him my bare skin is a thought I can't help but choke on.

He looks unfazed, expectant. Of course, I think. What kind of society has he grown up in? Probably one where privacy has no meaning. This is survival.

I nod and slowly gather my dress up the side of my leg, pausing at my thigh. He waits quietly, and I try to think of him as a medic as I pull the fabric the rest of the way up, past my underclothing and to the bright red skin over my ribs.

He stares for a minute, then reaches a hand forward. "May I?"

I nod. His fingertips are cool against the hot skin, but as he presses, it feels like fire bursting in my chest. I gasp and cough, and he pulls his hand away.

"They'll heal," he says. "The break isn't all the way

through, so the bone won't puncture your lung. But you should try not to run if you can, so it can mend."

I lower my dress to cover myself again. "I'll keep that in mind the next time a monster comes at me."

"Better a broken rib than to be bitten in two." He shrugs. "Come over here."

I follow him to the gray trunk and stare up to the cloak in the high branches above. "I can't climb," I tell him. "I already tried."

"Of course you can't. Not with those broken ribs." Griffin turns, his broad shoulders protruding from his sleeveless leather tunic. He looks over his shoulder at me. "Put your arms around my neck."

The closest I've ever been to a boy my age was two nights ago, when I held Jonash's arm in the fields of the outlands. I hesitate, then gently put my arms around his neck. He reaches up and pulls at my wrists, clamping my arms tighter around him. And then my feet lift off the ground as he starts climbing the tree with me on his back. It pulls on my chest, and my ribs blaze like fire. I squeeze my eyes closed, hot tears stinging in the corners. I sway back and forth as he ascends, so much slower than before. I want to cry out, to tell him to put me down, but I can't. We're halfway up, and there's nothing to do but hang on and wait.

His arms bulge as he pulls me upward, his feet pressed tightly against the flaking trunk. I can feel his every breath heaving under the weight of me. We're almost at the tangle of branches when he says to me, "Doing okay? Can you reach?"

I force my eyes open and see the thick branch near me. "I don't think I can," I pant. "I think my wrist is twisted."

"No need to climb," he says. "Just hang on for a minute." So I grab hold of the branch with my right wrist, and then loosely with my left, and I hang there in the air like a Rending pennant, knowing that if I let go my leg would probably snap in two when I hit the ground.

Without the weight of me, he scrambles quickly the rest of the way, and then he bends to take hold of my arms and pull me upward. I help as much as I can, folding over the branch like a tent and then lifting one foot onto the bough, followed by the other. Somehow we manage together to get me up to the softness of the cloak tucked over the branches.

"It's sturdy," he says, pressing on the fur with the leather of his shoe. "Have a seat."

I sit slowly, and I find the nest of branches holds more weight than I'd thought. It's steady and curved.

"Rest now," he says. "We'll stay here for the night."

The sun is only just starting to set in the sky, but the day has completely drained me. Searching for water and food, running from the chimera, learning that the earth has human survivors—all of these, coupled with the fresh meat and water in my ravenous stomach, press on me with the weight of severe exhaustion. I barely hear Griffin as he climbs back down the tree, as he buries what's left of the fur-packaged meat in the dying ashes of the fire. The ashes make me think of the Phoenix, of her promise to save us from the earth and its scourge of monsters. She has sent Griffin to save me, I know. She will wrap me in her soft warm wings. She will keep her promise to rise anew, so that we will be saved from this plagued world once more.

The thoughts comfort me as the hazy pull of sleep overtakes me.

TEN

I HEAR THE chimes of the bells in the citadel's crystal tower, see the smiling face of my father. I run to him, Elisha beaming at his side. The Phoenix statue is draped in red garlands and Aban stands near us in his white robe, the first tome of the annals in his hands. Everything is ready for the Rending Ceremony, and I've returned from the outcrop just in time.

Millions of red petals fall through the air like snow, cascading over the courtyard and hiding my father from view. There are too many now, the entire courtyard bloodred with the blossoms, and they're falling in my eyes and tangling in my hair. All I can see is crimson and scarlet drowning the world.

I jolt awake to see Griffin hovering above me, our stomachs almost touching. His chin nearly rests on mine, and his eyes focus on something behind me. His arm lances out and I hear a squealing hiss that makes me jump right against his warm chest. I scramble to get upright, but Griffin's body is stretched out above mine and I can't get around him to look.

He leans back a moment later, a long gray snake impaled on a broken tree branch in his hand. The snake has tufts of fur along its back and curling antennae that spiral into a yellowish color in the dusky light. I've never seen a snake that big, except for the chimera's tail.

Griffin tosses it over the side of the tree to the ground, where it squeals and writhes on the stick.

"Are you all right?" he says, sitting down at the far corner of the branch nest.

My eyes are wide, my thoughts disoriented from the panicked waking. "What *was* that?"

"Dream Catcher," he says. "They use their antennae to send waves into your dreams and keep you relaxed while they make the kill. They usually hunt birds in the trees, so they make the mistake of suggesting red flowers in the dream, which wakes up human prey."

I look down at the snake. He was the reason for my dream? "I thought it was safe up here in the trees."

Griffin shakes his head, running a hand through his jagged brown hair. "Safe-*er*," he says. "There's no place on the earth where the monsters don't hunt us."

I wrap my arms around myself, looking down at the snake on the ground. It would've killed me. If I'd climbed a tree that first night, one probably would've gotten me there, too.

"Don't look," Griffin says gently. "It's better not to think about it too much."

He's right, but it's hard to think about anything else.

"There's still time to sleep," he says. "Rest. I'll keep watch."

The sky is a deep orchid purple, the stars stretched out overhead like glittering crystal. The two moons hang low in the sky, near the horizon. Below us, the campfire gleams with the sparks of embers from the night before. "It isn't time to go?" I ask.

He hesitates, and I know if it was him alone, he'd be ready. "There's still time," he says, generous and patient.

My head and ribs throb, my back aching from sleeping against the bony branches. But sleeping in the fur cloak was still much nicer than the night before, propped against a scratchy tree trunk in a pouring thunderstorm. Neither is what I'm used to—a rich, fluffy bed full of goat fur blankets and feather-filled pillows.

I want to be stronger. I want to be like Griffin, able to survive down here without complaint. I don't want the softer, easier life I've always had, marking me inept and useless.

"I'm ready," I say. Griffin opens his mouth to protest, but I look at him with hard eyes, and he gets the message.

"Okay," he says, and I help him untuck the fur cloak from the branches. He fastens it around his neck and motions for me to put my arms around him again. With the cloak on, it's like hugging the stuffed animal pika I've had since I was a child. The fur cape looks matted, but it's soft and warm as I hang on. Griffin slides down the tree slowly, his feet hitting the ground with a jolt that throbs in my ribs. Beside us the Dream Catcher has stopped writhing, but Griffin walks past it toward the gleaming embers of the fire. "Aren't you going to eat it?" I ask, pointing with my bare toe at the gray coil.

Griffin shakes his head as he digs through the ashes of the fire. It amazes me he doesn't burn his fingers. "Dream Catchers are way too poisonous," he says. "I can't even use their venom to hunt monsters. Even a drop on an arrow to bring down a hazu would come back to bite me when I ate the kill."

He pulls the package of chimera meat from the ground, the skin crinkly as he peels it back.

"What's a hazu?" I ask, kneeling beside him. He passes the meat to me; it has been charred overnight by the slow heat of the embers.

He takes a piece after I do, chewing on it as we sit on the grassy hill. "The hazu is a sky beast," he says. "You'll probably see some today. They tend to circle on the plains."

I wolf down the smoky meat, but there's no water in the flask today, and we can still see the scavengers in the distance near the creek. More have come, by the looks of it. I shudder.

"There's a waterfall we can drink from, but we won't reach it for a long time," Griffin warns me. But there's nothing I can do about it, so I just nod. He's wasted all his water on me, I'm sure. Then he slips off his soft leather shoes and places them in front of me. "Here."

"Oh, I... I can't."

He shakes his head. "The plains are home to scorpions and sole worms, and lots of thistle patches. I know what to look for, but you don't."

I look at the soft shoes, the edges trimmed with smears of paint. I slide one foot in, then the other. The shoes are too big and still warm from Griffin's feet, but they don't pinch like Elisha's sandals did. "Thank you."

He nods and rises to his feet, dusting off his leggings. "Ready?"

We descend the steep slope of the hill and turn to the left, toward the mountains in the distance. I'm glad to know every step is taking us closer to them, to the place where the airships will be able to see and rescue us. We walk slowly as I trip in his too large shoes. When I step right out of one, Griffin stops and pulls handfuls of grass, stuffing them into the toes of the slippers. The grass is feathery and ticklish, but the shoes stay on a little better, and we can cover ground faster.

The tangle of ancient trees on the hilltop fades behind us, and the valley stretches out in front. The landscape is a lot hillier than it looks, full of dips and dives. A forest spreads beside us, hiding whatever terrain might lie on the eastern side. As the sun rises, its orange light spills onto the thick underbrush that crunches under my feet. Griffin wasn't joking when he said the plains are full of coarse, spiky plants. I flood with the guilt of leaving him barefoot.

As the sun rises, the breeze turns warm once again. I'm still not used to the heat of the wind on this land below Ashra, the richness of the thick air I breathe in.

A shadow swoops over us, and I duck instinctively. It's a massive bird creature, the ones I've seen before with the long lizard-like tails. This one has curling horns on either side of its head.

"A hazu," Griffin points as it swoops away. He unties his cloak and places it around my shoulders. "Here. Wear this." He unfurls the hood of the cloak and drapes it over my head. The wolflike fangs hang down on either side of my forehead. "Hazus don't go after karus. Too much trouble."

Karus? "How many types of monsters are there?"

Griffin laughs, adjusting the cloak around me with his nimble fingers. The shell necklace around his neck glistens and clinks as he ties the karu fur tightly. "Lots," he says. "There are the sky beasts, beasts of the land, the fiery lava-land types, the ones in the ice lands and lots of water beasts. To name a few groups." His eyes gleam. "There. You look more like a monster hunter already."

The shells clink together again as he leans back. The bow and quiver on his back are exposed now, his feet bare. He's all weapons and pouches and leather strings everywhere, stretched over his toughened, tanned frame. I look nothing like him, and we both know it. But the semi-compliment makes us both smile, my cheeks blazing with undeserved praise.

We walk on, hazus swooping over us now and then. In the distance I can see giant monsters running in packs.

"You said you were named Griffin after the first monster you hunted," I say, breaking the silence.

"Killed," he says. "Not hunted. He hunted us."

"Oh," I say. "Is a griffin a beast of the land?"

He shakes his head. "Sky beast," he says. "Head and wings of an eagle, body of a lion." At my expression, he adds, "Half bird, half cat."

I don't remember lions from the pages of the annals. But I clearly remember the giant cat and the furry chimera head. "And it attacked you?"

Griffin's expression is dark, and we walk for a minute in silence. I know I've crossed a line, but I'm not sure exactly where. "I'm sorry," I say.

He shakes his head. "Sorry," he says. "It's not you. It…it was a long time ago. It attacked in the night. Killed both of my parents and had my sister in its beak to kill next. So I killed it first."

I lift my hand to my mouth. I can't imagine carrying a memory like this. It's exactly why the Phoenix saved us all, why we're so lucky to live on the floating continents. If only we'd known there were humans still on earth. We could've found a way to rescue them, to spare them horrible histories like this. "I'm so sorry."

He says nothing, only keeps walking along the uneven plain. I'm scared to ask if his sister made it, or where she is now. Instead I say, "There are no monsters on the floating continents, you know. You'll be safe there."

He laughs, which confuses me. What's there to laugh about? Can he not conceive of a world that isn't flooded with monsters? "Really," I promise.

"Just another kind of oppression," he says.

"What?" This is the most ridiculous thing I've ever heard. My father rules with benevolence. The lands are happy and monster-free. Yes, there's my concern about the rebellion brewing, but he couldn't know that. And my father always reminds me how important it is not to return to those dark days before the Rending. I know the rebels will remember that, too, in time. "You've never been to the floating lands," I manage. "How could you know what it's like there?"

"I know what the fallen have told us," he says. "And I know that they all decide in the end to stay here and not look for a way to return."

My body seizes with confusion and irritation. No one has fallen from the continents in fourteen years. It's a fact. Why does he continue to act like this is the truth? And I suppose if you're used to being free, wandering the earth without contributing to a community, you might feel the life on Ashra was oppressive. Everyone has to do their part there to survive, after all. But why make up stories to support your reluctance to come to Ashra?

"I'm sorry," I say finally, "but no one has fallen from the continents in fourteen years. There must be a mistake. Ashra and her lands are a place of refuge, not oppression. The Phoenix tore them from the earth and placed them in the sky as a safe haven from the monsters down here. No one was meant to be left behind."

"The Phoenix?" Griffin repeats. My eyes are wide, my pulse rushing. Has he never heard of her?

"She's the only monster who ever felt compassion for humans," I say.

Griffin laughs with scorn as another hazu blots out the light around us. "No monster has ever felt compassion for its dinner. That's why they're monsters."

My cheeks flush. "The Phoenix did. She saved us. Why do you think she sent the floating continents into the sky three hundred years ago?"

"Did she, now?" he mutters, but he says no more and keeps walking in silence.

It would be better if he kept arguing with me, I think. I don't like the uneasy feeling that I'm wrong. But I'm not wrong. I couldn't be. The annals clearly state what happened. There's no other explanation for the floating continents.

But the memory of Aban and the lieutenant, and the strange secret volume of the annals in the cupboard, leaves me unsettled. The rings sketched underneath the Phoenix's wings, the strange mechanism covered by the inky tail feathers and the lieutenant's paper. What do they mean?

When I return to Ashra, I'll show my father, and if Aban is really against us and refuses to help, we'll contact the scribes in Nartu to decipher them.

The plain slopes suddenly toward a greener valley, the plants growing less crunchy underfoot and softer, water-logged. The sun is at the top of the sky now. We must have walked for hours.

"Let's rest for a minute," Griffin says, and at that moment I realize how much my ribs are burning. We sit in the grasses, looking down the slope at the forest stretching out on the left, the mountain range far ahead. "I didn't mean to offend you," he adds.

A flood of hot embarrassment spreads across my face. He's saved my life twice now, given me shoes and a cloak to wear, food to eat and a place to sleep. And I fumed at him for not appreciating a life on Ashra that he can't even imagine. It's not his fault he doesn't know.

"You didn't," I say. "It's all just overwhelming, that's all." I pull my legs up and wrap my arms around them, resting my chin on my knees. "We have an order on the continents called the Elders. They're sort of the servants of the Phoenix and the people. Anyway, they've kept these record books for three hundred years, since the Rending. They're called the annals."

"You mentioned them before," he says.

I nod, staring at the edge of forest near us, the stretch of mountains so far away. "I used to read them all the time, wondering what the earth was like. I never thought I'd be here."

Griffin smiles, leaning back on the palms of his hands. "Is it how you imagined?"

"Not at all," I say. I could never have imagined this world

with its ravenous monsters and vibrant landscapes. The sun glints on Griffin's necklace, and I can't keep the question at bay any longer. I point at the string of iridescent shells. "Did you get them from the ocean?"

"Hmm?" He looks down to see what I'm pointing at. Then he loops his finger into the chain, lifting it as the circles clink together. "This? It was my father's. He used to be a fisherman on the ocean's shore."

"Then...you've seen the ocean." I know my eyes are gleaming. "What's it like?"

"I've only seen glimpses, never up close," he says. "Only rivers and lakes. My father moved away from the ocean before my sister was born." He grins then, at my excitement. "I guess you don't have oceans on your floating island."

His face is kind and genuine, warmth and honesty exuding from his every glance. He's not hardened or cold the way I'd imagine a monster hunter would be. He's human, I think. Just as human, maybe more, than those on Ashra. In a way, we're penned up there like cattle. Life is harder down here, but he's free, and it shows on his face. He's paid a heavy price for it, but he's free, and he knows it. I smile back at him, and there's a giddiness to it all, like for one moment in my life I'm not the Phoenix's heir. I'm not the wick and the wax to burn for others. I'm just myself, Kali, just a girl on a walk with a boy she's just met. A boy she wants to know better.

Then the world flashes black, a rush of feathers beating against my face, and suddenly I'm alone. Griffin is gone.

I look up into the sky and see the hazu as it flies away, Griffin struggling in its claws.

ELEVEN

"GRIFFIN!" I SCREAM. I stand there helpless, desperate. The hazu is so high in the air that I can't even throw my flint piece at it. I wish Griffin had given me his bow and quiver, but it's not like I know how to shoot anyway. I scream out for him, not knowing what else to do. I chase after them away from the forest, across the coarse orange plain.

It's all my fault, I think as I pant and trail the hazu. Griffin gave me his karu fur cloak. If he'd worn it, the bird would never have snatched him. It would've grabbed me.

The hazu screeches in the air, its long spiked tail snaking behind it. I'll never catch it, but I follow anyway, unwilling to let go of my only companion on the earth.

The giant bird screeches again and shakes its foot back and forth. I see Griffin climbing out of its talons and up its leg. He suddenly leaps through the air and grabs the hazu's right wing, hanging off it like a rag doll in the sky. The wing folds under his weight and the hazu veers sideways, plummeting in a downward spiral. It tries to snap its beak at Griffin, but he rolls along the side of the wing and the hazu comes away with nothing but a mouthful of its own plucked feathers.

They're going to slam into the plain, and I realize in horror that Griffin won't survive it. But just as they're almost to the ground, he climbs along the wing to the monster's back. The hazu flaps desperately and lets out a horrible screech. Dust clouds swirl under its wings as it fights its way back into the sky.

I'm nearly beside them now, and the bird's talons are hovering just above my height. I throw myself at its scaly leg and yank as hard as I can. My weight is nothing to the hazu, but he twists his neck back, startled. He shakes his leg to fling me off so he can lift higher into the air. Griffin looks alarmed and reaches forward to cover the bird's giant eyes with his hands so he won't see me.

The hazu squawks and kicks, its beak open as it snaps at the air. The motion gusts wind around my face, the click of its beak echoing in my ears. He's lifting into the sky now. The ground is whooshing away.

"Kali, let go!" Griffin shouts, and I drop from the bird's leg. My legs buckle under me as I land.

The hazu is struggling against Griffin, its talons flailing too close to my head. I scramble to my feet and run, tripping over the too-big shoes I'm wearing. I fall flat on my face with a mouthful of dirt.

"Kali!" Griffin cries, looking over at me. The distraction is enough that the hazu shakes the hands off his eyes. His neck curves around and his beak slashes into Griffin's back with the horrible sound of flesh tearing.

"Look out!" I shout, but he's already crying out in pain. There's a tangle of limbs and feathers that follows, the hazu flying in low circles as the two struggle. Griffin lifts an arrow out of his quiver and digs it into the nape of the bird's neck like a spear. It's a tiny arrowhead for such a big monster, but then I remember the venom he dipped it in from the chimera's snake fangs.

The hazu slams against the plain in a cloud of dust and grass, its wings unfurled on the ground, its long tail twitching. The movement throws Griffin off its back and he rolls across the ground, writhing.

I run as fast as I can, my breath heaving against my aching ribs. "Griffin!"

He looks over, his shoulders rising and falling with every breath. His blood stains the rust-colored dirt around him. "Kali," he pants. "Are you all right?"

"Me? What about you? You're bleeding."

"Am I?" he says, his eyes squeezed shut with pain. "How about that? It's been a while since a sky beast drew blood. I'll have to adjust my stats."

Is he serious? I blink, and then he lets out a small, forced laugh.

"Don't worry," he says. "I've hunted worse things than this overgrown chicken. Give me a minute, will you?" He heaves himself up to a sitting position as I kneel and offer my hands. The sweat drips down his forehead and smears what's left of the yellow and purple stripes under his eyes.

He takes my hands, his palms sweating and his fingers rough. I help him up as he winces and looks over his shoulder. There's a gash right through the leather of his tunic, near the back of his neck. It's bloody and torn, but it doesn't look too deep or life-threatening, as far as I know. Which isn't that far.

"It's kind of embarrassing." He laughs. And I wonder if it would've been better if I hadn't interfered with the hazu.

"I'm sorry. I just… I wanted to help you."

"I appreciate it," he says, his eyes crinkling as he smiles. "It's nice to have someone looking out for me." The comment leaves me feeling warm and forgiven. I've just met him, but he's so comfortable to be with, like an old friend. Elisha would like him, too, I think. She'd also probably waggle her eyebrows at me when his back was turned.

Griffin stumbles to the hazu, still and massive on the plain. He plucks the feathers on its stomach, one by one. It takes both hands and effort, because each plume is at least half our height. I've watched Elisha pluck a chicken before, in Ulan. So I step forward and pull out as many feathers as I can, until the sweat is dripping down my neck and chest. Griffin pulls three for every one I manage, even with his injury. But I won't let it slow me down. I rest my foot on the bird to brace myself as I yank the feathers out. I want to show what I can do. And Griffin doesn't tell me to stop or laugh at my feeble attempts. He says quiet, sincere thank-yous as I add my plumes to the pile. I'm an awful hunter, but he makes me feel like I'm good at it, like I'm useful.

When we've plucked a clean area, Griffin carves in with his dagger. "It'll make a nice visiting gift," he says, resting the meat inside one of the large feathers on the ground.

"You're going to eat another monster?"

He hums cheerfully as he cuts into its belly. "He was going to eat me," he says. It's his answer for everything.

There's more meat on the hazu than a village could use in a month, but he's taking what he can manage so he doesn't waste all of it. "I suppose the scavengers will come again."

"Everything needs to eat," he says. "Otherwise I'll have nothing left to hunt."

There's a tone of sadness in his voice, even if he's joking. He wants it to end. He wants the monsters to vanish.

"What do you mean, a visiting gift?" I ask. I sit beside the feather and rub the soft downy fluff between my fingers. "For your family?"

He nods. "We're nearly there. As long as they're still in the haven. We have to switch hideouts frequently or the monsters figure out how to get in. If they've moved on, then at least you and I will have a feast. And the waterfall's nearby, too, so I can clean this chicken scratch on my back." I roll my eyes. It's hardly just a scratch.

When Griffin's carved as much as we can carry, he folds up the feather and binds it with string, resting the package over his shoulder. We walk back to the slope down to the greener valley and follow the edge of the forest, the sun starting to descend in the western sky. I hope we'll make it before the sun sets, but I know I've slowed him down all day with my injuries and my tripping over his leather shoes. And now the encounter with the hazu, and the laborious plucking and gathering, have slowed us down even more.

But just as the sky is turning shades of orange and purple, and the swarms of biting insects come out of hiding from the warm daylight, I can hear the rush of water nearby. I look at Griffin, and he nods, a smile curling on his lips. "Nearly there," he says.

It's amazing how much greener the grass is down here from the rusty plain. It reminds me of my outcrop on Ashra or the fields around Lake Agur. There's an emerald sheen to everything, rich and alive and flourishing. The forest stretches out farther than I can see, but Griffin says there's marshland on the other side of it. He wades deeper among the trees, the swarms of insects landing on our necks and arms and faces. I swat them away as the sunlight dies, turning the forest a deeper olive green.

I'm about to ask how much farther when a voice calls out from above. It's a woman's voice, confident and assured. "Griffin!" she shouts. "Have you finally trekked your sorry behind all the way home?"

Griffin laughs. I look in the canopy above, but I can't see the owner of the voice. And then a rope drops from a tree branch and the woman slides down it. Her laced leather boots land softly against the grass. She looks maybe two or three years older than me, and she wears a mix of furs and leather and weapon straps just like Griffin. In her hand is a long spear, tipped with a jagged crescent of white bone. She wears a necklace of teeth or curved bones around her neck—I'm not sure which, but they're definitely from some kind of monster. Her skin is the most elegant black, like the darkest night sky, and she wears a gold armlet and earrings that sparkle in what's left of the fading sunlight.

"Aliyah." Griffin laughs as the two embrace. Her arm wraps around his back and lands straight on his wound from the hazu. She jumps back, grabbing his shoulder to spin him around like a naughty child.

"Two shining moons, you idiot, what did you do to your back?"

"Love bite from a little bird," he grins as she runs her hand across the torn leather.

She shakes her head. "You're nothing but trouble." And

then she looks at me, nodding her head in greeting. "I'm Aliyah," she says, holding out her hand. "This fool's sister."

His sister? The comment takes me off guard, and I falter for a moment. "I'm Kali," I answer finally, taking her hand.

"Welcome," she says, swatting a mosquito off her bare shoulder as she stares at me. I must make quite the impression in my ragged, muddy dress and my lack of tools and weapons. And I'm draped in her brother's karu fur and too-big shoes. "Have you traveled far?"

I think of my long fall to earth. Her question strikes me as funny, and horribly unfunny, at the same time. "You could say that."

"Kali is a fallen," Griffin mutters. Aliyah's eyebrows rise up.

"A fallen? Well, then, a double welcome," she says. "We haven't had a fallen this side of the mountain range in a very long time. You must be hungry and full of questions. Come, come. Sayra is just about to start on the meal."

"We're in good time, then," Griffin says, handing her the bound hazu feather full of meat.

"Look at that, he's some use, after all." Aliyah laughs. "I'll take this down to her. Will you come with me, Kali?"

"Thank you," I say, feeling shy. Their hospitality and happiness is overwhelming. I'd always assumed the earth was barren, but if there were humans, that they'd be miserable and barely surviving. Unbelievers lifting up their hands in lament and mourning like the illustration in the annals.

She leads us through the trees until I'm thoroughly lost in the darkness. And then she stops suddenly, crouching over a mossy patch of dirt. Griffin helps her smooth the moss and grass away, and there's a trapdoor underneath. She pulls on the iron handle and it lifts without a creak. There are stairs leading down into the darkness, a small flickering light glowing at the end of them.

"Welcome to one of our havens." Griffin smiles at me, and we descend into the darkness, Aliyah lowering the trapdoor behind us and sealing us in.

The stairway is steep and dark, but just as I'm worried about stumbling, Griffin's hand reaches out to me. "Here," he says. "Take them slowly."

Aliyah is already down the stairs, her silhouette outlined by the gleaming of the light in the distance. "Ignore him," she says. "A woman can do it on her own, Griff. You've come out of the day more damaged than she has."

"Sisters," he mutters near my ear, and withdraws his hand. There are only four steps to go, then three, and when we're at the bottom the short tunnel opens into a room dug out of the earth. The light is an oil lamp on a small wooden table, flanked on either side by beams of wood on stumps that make two benches. There's a long countertop on the far wall with a clay basin of water and an iron stove, with a pipe that runs up the dirt wall and out of the forest floor above. A skylight has been cut above the countertop, but it's fitted with another trapdoor that's closed and barred for the night. There's another girl our age at the basin, and she turns with a bright smile. Her skin is olive, her hair dark and frizzy like Elisha's.

"This is Sayra," Aliyah says, and we take hands.

"Kali," I say.

"She's a fallen," Aliyah adds.

"Welcome." Sayra smiles, and then she embraces Griffin. She throws her arms tightly around his neck, and the impact almost pushes him off balance as he laughs.

"Careful," Aliyah warns her. "He's got another bragging-rights scar back there."

Sayra's expression turns to concern as she sees the wound, but Griffin waves off their worry as he sits on one of the benches. He passes the hazu meat package to Sayra, who looks pleased. "Can I help you prepare it?" he asks.

She shakes her head. "Rest now, both of you."

The kindness of these three overwhelms me. We'd always been taught to look down on the unbelievers, in a way. They'd chosen to die by the monster's claw rather than work together to build a new life on Ashra and her lands. If I'd pictured humans living on the earth, I could never have imagined these three in their underground haven, sharing what little they have with nothing but smiles, looking so alive in the face of certain death.

Aliyah shows me the adjoining room, a floor of dirt swept clean and covered with beautiful quilts. They're stitched from furs and odds and ends of cloth, lining the room from one end to the other. It's the complete opposite of my room in the citadel, with its opulent fabrics and gilded edges and giant windows open to the mountains and Lake Agur. Sometimes, on dark, still nights, I could see the rainbow glow of the firefly clouds in the outlands, the cool breeze wafting around my balcony. There's no fresh breeze down here. It's small and stuffy, but cozy. I think that maybe I was wrong about the monster-ridden earth, that there were no safe places down here. This certainly feels like one.

Sayra appears in the doorway with a clay goblet of water, and I drink it down so quickly that I sputter when my dry throat sticks. She smiles and gets me another full glass from the pitcher, and then Aliyah invites me to lie down and rest while they make dinner.

"You're sure I can't help?" I ask, but I'm so exhausted I sway on my feet.

"You've done well to survive until Griffin found you," Aliyah says. "And he told me about your ribs. Best thing for broken bones is rest."

"Thank you," I say. The blankets are as soft as they look, and I can almost forget the hard dirt ground beneath them. In the other room I can see the edge of Griffin sitting at the bench while Aliyah removes his leather tunic and sighs, dipping a washcloth into a basin and dabbing at his shoulder.

Then I see the two huge gashes on his bare back, not from the hazu, but from something much older. They curve inward like crescents from the edge of his shoulders to the top of his hips. The two grooves are thick and scarred, split open like deep lash wounds from a whip. I can't imagine what kind of monster carved those marks into him. I can't believe he survived it.

"Another badge of honor, hmm, monster hunter?" Aliyah sighs. Sayra says something past hearing, and the three of them chuckle between Griffin's small gasps of pain. They mumble in a low and comforting harmony that reminds me of my father speaking outside my bedroom door to the guards in the citadel. The hazu meat sizzles and smokes, and the mouthwatering aroma fills the tiny underground haven.

Exhaustion overcomes me and I close my eyes, finally feeling safe for a moment in this vast and frightening world.

I am with Griffin, Aliyah and Sayra, and we are alive

and safe. I could never have imagined any of this even three days ago.

I sleep for maybe an hour before I awaken to the terrible clawing of monsters scratching through the roof above.

TWELVE

I SIT UP with a shout before Griffin and Aliyah come running into the room. I point at the ceiling, where a monster of some kind is clawing and sniffing high above the surface. They exchange glances before looking at me with sad eyes.

"It's all right," Griffin says. "They usually give up before they dig too far in. There's easier prey on the surface at night."

"Get her some water, Griff. You're scaring her," Aliyah says, and while he's gone she smooths my hair behind my ear. "You're not used to the monsters yet," she reassures me. "Give it time."

But I shake my head. I will never get used to the eternal fear of being hunted, of being mere prey to be sniffed out wherever I go. "Griffin said he'll take me to the mountain range," I tell her. "From there the airships will be able to see me and rescue me. I've told him they'll take all of us, too. You can come live on the floating continents, where it's safe."

Surprise plays in Aliyah's wide eyes as Griffin returns with the water and a plate of the fragrant hazu meat. Sayra has drizzled it with scarlet honey and spices, and it reminds me of the chicken I had with Elisha at the festival. I breathe in its hot fragrance before I take a bite, while Aliyah raises her eyebrows at Griffin. "Did you tell her you'll take her to the mountains, brother?"

He hesitates while I drink the water. "Yes, I did."

"I see."

I don't understand why they're all so cautious about going to Ashra with me. They've never been up there. How are they so sure they'll hate it? Surely it's better than mere survival down here.

"When will you go?" Aliyah asks.

"Sunrise. Kali says the airships will be looking for her, so we need to get there as soon as possible."

Aliyah shakes her head and takes my empty plate and glass from me. "She's in no condition to travel, and neither are you. That wound will split right open unless you take a couple days to heal up first."

"But the airships," I say. I don't mean to be ungrateful. It's just that if I wait too long, they won't search for me anymore. They'll think I'm dead. Which they probably think anyway. Who could survive that fall? And they don't know about the barrier that saved me.

"You're easy pickings for the monsters ahead if you don't take the time to heal," Aliyah says. "Rest now." She leaves the room, and as much as I don't want to admit it, I know she's right.

"Don't worry," Griffin says. "I promised to get you to the airship, and I'll get you there."

"Why are you helping me?" I ask, the words surprising me as much as they surprise him. "I know you said you help the fallen, but you've done that. Why take me all the way to the mountains? Aliyah doesn't seem to think it's a good idea."

He chuckles under his breath. He's washed his face, and the paint is gone from his cheeks. He still wears his shell necklace, but his weapons and all their leather straps are gone, his chest bare. I can see the trails of old scars, bites and claw marks etched into his skin by different predators. "Aliyah's been protective ever since I can remember," he says. "She's all the family I have left. The two of us and Sayra are the only ones left from our village, so of course she always worries."

The only ones left? I don't know how large the village was, but three survivors means many lost. They have so little left, so much of a burden to carry. And now I'm putting him back out there, on what Aliyah thinks is a hazardous trek.

"I can't let you do it," I decide. "Show me the way to the mountains, and I'll go alone. Look what happened today. I can't put you in any more danger."

Griffin twists his shoulder so I can see the hazu's wound across his back, the one that sits atop the crescent moon gashes. "This?" he says. "I've had worse. It's brave of you to tell a monster hunter to mind his own business. And I don't mean to sound arrogant, but you're biting off more than you can chew. I'll take you to the mountains. I promised, and that's the end of it."

He leaves the room, and I lean against the wall. The

dented lantern tied at my hip presses against the blankets as I look down at the broken candle inside.

I don't know what lies ahead on the way to the mountains, but I know if I'm not safe alone, then it will be more terrible than I can imagine.

The next several days are a pleasant change from running for my life. In the daylight, the trapdoor in the main room is open, and the fresh, sweet air floods in. Aliyah, Sayra and Griffin take me to the waterfall to replenish our supplies. It's smaller than I'd pictured, not a raging angry current like the waterfall on Ashra, but steps of jagged rock, down which the water flows in frills of misty lace. The air is filled with the spray of cool water, and the birds call to each other through the forest. Griffin takes handfuls of the water and splashes them at us, and we run away like children, squealing, circling around to fill our basins and dump them over his head. I feel like I'm on the edge of Lake Agur with Elisha as we talk and laugh, as if the four of us have always been close friends.

But at night, the monsters claw at the top of the underground haven, snorting with their large nostrils and bellowing as they stomp around the forest. The three of them sleep through the horrible sounds, but I lie awake for hours, waiting for the ceiling to burst and the monster's fangs to rip through the dirt and into my flesh.

One morning, Aliyah stands with me near the waterfall and hands me a bow and a quiver full of arrows. "You need to be able to defend yourself," she says.

"You're a monster hunter, too, aren't you?" I ask.

She nods. "It's the path I chose when our village was destroyed."

"And Sayra?"

She shakes her head. "She's got a gentle soul. Monster hunting isn't easy. You have to grab hold of the fear that overtakes you when death itself charges. You have to take that fear and give it fangs. You have to lose everything so that you have nothing to lose. Sayra lost everything, but it made her turn inward instead. She helps in other ways."

I imagine Ulan, empty and destroyed. I can't even fathom what they've been through.

"I heard what happened to your parents," I say. "I'm sorry."

Aliyah smiles gently, then sits on a stone ledge beside the waterfall. The beads of water glisten on her dark skin. "I'm sure you've wondered about Griffin being my brother," she says. "Of course we're not related by blood. My parents were good people. They found Griffin wandering in the fields, crying. He was barely a baby then. I remember them bringing him home. 'Aliyah, water!' they said to me." Her eyes gleam with the memory. "I went to the well by our house, and for the first time I found the strength to turn the handle myself and bring up the bucket. I was just a babe myself, really. Four years old."

I imagine Griffin and Aliyah as children, Griffin with a tuft of curly brown hair as he ran in the field.

"He had a broken arm and kept crying for his mother. We knew she must've been taken down by a behemoth or griffin. There were so many surrounding the village. Poor dragonling that he was. He was such a happy little boy once he felt at home with us." She laughs as she remembers. "He used to take my father's harpoon and pretend he was hunting sea serpents in the field behind our house." The smile fades from her lips, the waterfall rushing through the silence. "He changed when the griffin attacked our parents. It ripped the thatched roof clean off. Without my brother, I would've died that day. Sent the harpoon right between that griffin's eyes."

The weight of the memory presses on both of us as I try to imagine the horror of that day. But I can't, not really. I lost my mother so young that I have no memories of her. Losing my father would break my heart, but it would never be so vicious an end as the jaws of a monster. I can't imagine what Aliyah and Griffin have seen, what they've been through. "My deepest sympathies," I say, resorting to my regal upbringing. It seems larger than anything I can say or offer in exchange.

Aliyah forces a smile and stands up, wiping the water droplets off her arms. "It was a long time ago," she says. "And the only way to survive down here is to become stronger. And now you have some learning to do, don't you? Let me see your arm for archery."

She wraps a leather strip round and round my left wrist so the bowstring won't rasp against my skin. And then she shows me how to hold the bow, how to pull back the taut string with all my strength. My wrist stopped hurting two days ago, but the effort still burns in my ribs.

"Ready?" she says. "See if you can hit that trunk."

I nock the arrow and aim at the tree she's pointed out. The bowstring snaps forward but the arrows drops, clattering to the ground beside my feet. My cheeks blaze.

"First try," she says. "It takes getting used to."

The next fifteen arrows follow suit, leaving a mortifying trail that zigzags slowly closer to the tree trunk. At last, the sixteenth arcs through the air and far past the trunk into the tangle of ferns and underbrush.

"Better." Aliyah smiles. "Want to take a break?"

My ribs are aching, but I shake my head. "I want to get it right."

"I told you," Griffin says suddenly, and I look up, startled. He's sitting beside the spray of the waterfall. How long has he been there? He was soundless, like a barn cat. I never heard him approach. I flush with embarrassment. I hope he hasn't seen my pathetic volley of arrows.

"Told her what?" I say.

He smiles, his eyes gleaming. "That you're a fighter. That you don't give up."

I flush like the Phoenix herself is blazing through me. He's seen my effort, not my failure, just like before. I can't stop the smile from spreading over my face, and it only brightens the smile on his.

I pull back the bowstring with renewed strength. The ache in my ribs only fuels me on.

"Looks good," Aliyah says. "Lightly, now."

My fingers are feather tufts on the string. I let the arrow fly, and it soars into the underbrush.

"I missed," I say.

Aliyah nods. "But the strength behind the arrow improved."

The quiver is empty, and I bend to gather the arrows on the ground.

"I'll get them," Griffin says, and before I can protest he's vanished into the thick forest where my arrows have gone astray. I can tell from Aliyah's raised eyebrows that he's not always so helpful.

"Let's try something else," Aliyah says, handing me her crescent-tipped spear. "In case Griff blanks and you have to fight something closer range."

I look at the jagged bone fastened to the wooden staff. "What monster is that from?"

"Behemoth fang," she says. "Huge snarly beast from the lava lands. They roam near the village where Griffin and I grew up."

I hold the spear and arc it slowly, the serrated tooth of the behemoth piercing the air. "It looks really sharp," I say.

"It can cut through the flesh and bones of smaller monsters," she says. "Nasty beasts, behemoths."

"And you killed one?"

"Three," she says. "Griff and I together. They're not easy to bring down alone."

I swipe the spear around a bit as Aliyah guides my hands. She shows me how to hook the fang through the air, where to place my hands for the best control of the weapon.

"You tease each other a lot, you and Griffin," I say. "I'm an only child, but I always wished for a sister." Elisha is like my sister, I think. I miss her dearly.

"Griffin has a big heart," she says. "He saved me, but he's never forgiven himself for not saving our mother and father. And now he wants to save you."

The guilt floods through me like fire. "I told him I'd go alone to the mountains," I say. "I don't want to put him in danger."

"Oh, I know that," she says, and she smiles warmly, raising an eyebrow. "But I can see in your eyes and his that my speech might be a little too late."

I don't follow, and I tilt my head at her, confused.

"He has a big heart," she says again. "But he lives a dangerous life hunting murderous beasts. And though he looks all right and means well, he's very scarred, Kali, very fragile underneath all that tough monster-hunter guise. And if you're completely set on returning to the continent and leaving him behind…well, then I suggest you start letting him down now."

It takes me another minute to understand what she's saying. Griffin has been so kind to me, laughing and smiling and… Oh. My eyes go wide.

"Oh, no," I stammer. "It's not like that. I'm engaged. To a man on the continent."

Aliyah's eyes widen. She wasn't expecting that. And I can see how it must look through her eyes, that he's fetching my arrows and putting his life at risk to take me where I want to go; that we sit side by side every night on the bench, joking warmly as we eat the hazu meat Sayra prepares; that we splash in the waterfall and feast on the berries we pick in the warm afternoon sun.

So I clarify, because I also don't want her to think I'm leading Griffin on. "It's an arranged match," I explain. "I've only met him a couple times. I… I'm obligated."

"Arranged? Obligated?" She purses her lips, her gold earrings swaying against her neck as she frowns. "Who are you, exactly, back on your floating mountain?"

"I…" It's no secret, but I've never explained to them who I am. And suddenly I don't want to tell her. They seem to hate the people on the continents, but I'm not sure why. And I have grown so attached to the three of them, so quickly. I don't want them to think less of me.

Aliyah nods after a minute, allowing me my privacy. Gratefulness floods the guilty flame that flickers in my chest. "If you're promised to another, then you should find a way to let Griffin know, before it grows into something else."

"I don't think he feels that way," I say. We've only known

each other for about a week and a half now. Aliyah merely smiles. But she's planted the thought in my head and it's sprouting, and when I think about how Griffin smiles warmly at me, I feel the heat creep up my neck.

Then I shake the thought away. He saved my life, and the experiences we've been through fighting the chimera and the hazu and the Dream Catcher would tie anyone together. That's the source of the closeness I feel. It's a bond of gratefulness and shared survival, nothing more.

Aliyah's voice is low, almost beyond hearing. "Can you climb?"

It's a strange response to my answer. "Are we done practice with the spear?" I ask. But Aliyah doesn't laugh; in fact, she doesn't move her eyes from the underbrush.

Something's wrong. I start to turn, to look over my shoulder into the grass.

"Stop," she says sharply. The wood around us buzzes with insects and birds. I can't hear anything, but I stop, adrenaline rushing through me. "Listen carefully, all right? There's a pack of karus, and we won't make it back to the trapdoor in time." Karus, like the fur cloak Griffin wears. "Do your ribs hurt too much to climb?" I take a deep breath, the pain shooting through my chest. She sees the look on my face. "Then stay close to me." She slowly reaches for the curved bone dagger at her waist. "Practice is over."

THIRTEEN

I GRIP THE spear tightly, my hands trembling. I don't yet know how to wield it. Aliyah bends her legs, her wide stance low to the ground. "Come stand behind me," she says. "Slowly." I move around her as gradually as I can. It reminds me of the dancing we do in Ulan, and I can hardly believe this is real.

Then I realize where she's staring into the woods.

"Griffin," I whisper urgently. He's in there, gathering my arrows.

"He can handle himself," she says.

And suddenly, like the flap of the Phoenix's wings, chaos blazes everywhere. The karu breaks free of the trees with a large crash and a howl. His mottled cream fur looks just like Griffin's cloak, the long fangs part of his terrifying snarl. I swipe the spear down in front of me as a defense, but the karu charges at Aliyah beside me. In a blur she moves with the karu. He leaps into the air for her windpipe, and she ducks under him, thrusting hard with the crescent of bone. The squelch of weapon meeting flesh fills my ears as he arcs over her bent frame. She rolls to the side as he hits the ground hard and comes up again, all fangs and blood and fur.

I hold Aliyah's spear tightly, the behemoth fang pointed right at the monster. But Aliyah doesn't need help. She moves like Griffin, all speed and precision and skill. Her earrings and armlet catch the sun as she tangles with the karu. She doesn't need my help.

"Get to the trapdoor," she shouts above the monster's snarling.

I hesitate for just a moment, wanting to help. But then I remember how my help ended in Griffin getting slashed by the hazu, and I turn to race toward the haven's entrance.

My skirts scrape against the underbrush and ferns as I hurry through the forest. The staff feels reassuringly heavy in my hands. It won't snap like the flint one I made for myself. It's sturdy and skillfully made. But I don't know how to wield it.

And then a figure leaps out in front of me, and I stop running.

It's like the karu, but a little smaller. It's certainly a dog, its fangs curved like the karu but not as pronounced. The fur is soft brown, striped with vibrant black bands that run up and down its body. Its mouth is all teeth, its back legs tensed as it growls.

"Easy," I say, lowering my staff to put the massive fang between us. "Easy now."

It barks, snapping its teeth at the bone crescent which I pull back in time. Should I run to Aliyah? But I can't turn my back on this thing.

Then I spot something beige moving in the trees above. Griffin's here, but the monster hasn't noticed. He's moving silently, preparing to drop on the creature. I force myself to look ahead, to not look up and give him away.

The monster growls and steps forward.

"Just keep looking here," I say, backing up slowly. "That's right. A tasty, easy meal right here. Hungry? Here, boy."

The monster leaps, and Griffin drops from the trees onto its back. It howls and arches up, and the two tangle in a blur.

I thrust the spear forward, to drive it through the monster while his attention is divided.

"Kali, no!" Griffin shouts, but I'm already lunging forward, my weight shifted to my front leg.

I feel a sharp pain in my back leg as the spear clatters out of my hands. I hit the leafy ground a moment later, a headache ripping through my temple. The world is snarls and fur and the behemoth fang is gone.

There's a second striped wolf monster on me. He lunges to bite me, and suddenly Griffin is on his knees beside me, his arms wrapped tightly around the monster's neck. He holds the beast away as its jaws snap over and over, just in front of my face.

Griffin's row of daggers glints at his waist.

I reach for a dagger and pull it free, and thrust it as hard as I can into the monster's neck. There's a horrible gasping sound, and the monster's eyes go glassy. It collapses on top of me, and I cry out, the weight painful against my cracked ribs.

Griffin rolls the beast off me and onto the ground with a thud. Just then Aliyah runs out of the trees, and Sayra pops up from the trapdoor nearby, a bow in her hand.

"Is she all right?" Aliyah shouts, stooping down beside me. Griffin nods, panting as the sweat drips off his forehead.

"Karus?" Sayra asks.

"Three of them," Aliyah answers, looking at the teeth marks around my ankle. "Not too deep, Kali, but we'll have to clean it to stop infection." She looks at Sayra. "Any scarlet honey left?"

Sayra nods. "I'll get it."

"I'm sorry," Griffin says. "There was no time."

"It's okay," I say. "You warned me. And you saved me." I gaze at the two dead monsters; they look as if they'll suddenly come back to life, ready to bite. "What are those?"

"Karus," Aliyah says. "The adolescents are striped to better camouflage them. Their fur changes to cream when they're older to draw the eye."

"That way you don't see the rest of the pack sneaking up on you," Griffin adds. "Quick thinking to grab my dagger." He pulls it out of the beast, cleaning it against a fern leaf.

"You did that?" Aliyah says.

"I...I guess I did," I say.

She smiles and ruffles my hair. "Congratulations," she says. "You defeated your first monster." She tucks her curved dagger into the strap at her waist and disappears into the forest.

I don't feel proud, not at all. I feel horrible and vulnerable.

Griffin nods, even though I haven't said anything. "It gets easier," he says, his eyes kind as they look into mine. "We do what we have to so we can survive." He pulls me to my feet, and toward the trapdoor, where Sayra has appeared with a jar of honey to pour on the wound.

"We do what we have to," I repeat, looking at the dead monsters at our feet. Aliyah reappears, the massive cream-colored karu draped over her shoulders. It must weigh a hundred pounds; I can't believe she can carry it. *We do what we have to so we can survive.*

Griffin nods. "It's what makes us human," he says.

That afternoon, Aliyah teaches me how to skin a karu. She uses the same curved bone dagger, showing how to carefully remove the fur in one piece. It's a slow process, and I gag a few times, but she smiles patiently, never teasing me.

She shows me how to take sinew from the monster's tendons for string, and how to stretch the fur over a frame to dry it. She removes its bladder and throws it to Sayra, who turns it into a water flask with a strap of scrap leather. It's amazing to me, the amount of survival knowledge these three have. At night, by the light of the oil lamp, Aliyah carves one of the karu fangs into a tiny sculpture of a goat. It reminds me of the pygmy goats in the village. We have so much in common, I think, and also nothing at all.

A week passes, and my ribs start to ache less. Aliyah and Griffin help me practice archery, spear-wielding and dagger-throwing. Griffin is healing, too, the gash across his back fading into a pale scar. "We can go to the mountains soon," he promises.

One day, after dinner, we sit on the benches around the table joking and laughing. Sayra walks to a corner of the room and grabs a bundle of leather and fur. She places it in front of me while Griffin and Aliyah beam.

"What's this?" I ask. Griffin's eyes are gleaming as I take

the bundle apart. There are new leather boots, soft and laced like Aliyah's. There's the karu fur, fashioned into a cloak, and a leather sheath decorated with tiny pieces of karu bone; it holds a medium-sized dagger.

"For the journey to the mountains," Aliyah says.

My eyes fill with grateful tears that I blink back. "But you can't afford to share this with me. You have so little of your own."

"Says who?" Aliyah booms, reaching her long arms out to the sides. "I have a whole world to borrow from. You helped us slay the karus, Kali. You've earned these. And I'll visit the weapon smith in the lava lands when I want a new dagger."

I pull the dagger from the sheath. The blade is metal, not bone, and well-worn with scratches and pockmarks. It has a gleaming garnet set in the hilt that sparkles red and orange like a flame. It shimmers under the glow streaming in the skylight, but I know in the daylight it will blaze like the fire of the Phoenix herself.

"Thank you," I say, though it's not enough. "Thank you for this beautiful reminder that the Phoenix will rise anew." They look puzzled, and then I remember they know nothing of the Rending. "I'm so grateful for your gifts, and your friendship," I say, trying again. "I wish there was something I could give you."

Then I remember the one thing I have in this world, the one thing I brought with me when I fell.

I untie the lantern from my side and place it on the table. It's damaged and worn, not anything like their beautiful gifts, but it's all I have to give. "When you light this lantern, will you think of me?" I say. "The stars and the Phoenix plumes will remind you of Ashra, the floating continent I come from."

"We will treasure it." Aliyah smiles.

I've known them only a few weeks, but it feels like a lifetime. "Please," I try again. "Come with us to the mountain range. You'll be safe in Ashra."

Griffin frowns, lifting a hand. "Kali..."

"No, please, listen," I interrupt. "I'm not sure why you distrust us on the floating continents, but I can promise you we are good people. Food and land is shared. We are safe and protected. There are still forests to wander, and all kinds of trades to learn. Aliyah, you could craft your own weapons like your behemoth staff. And your carvings! I'm sure they would be so popular. Sayra would love to cook with Elisha in Ulan. There's opportunity for all of you."

"I'm sorry, Kali," Aliyah says quietly. "But we can't."

It's the most exasperating conversation I've ever had. I'm giving them an escape from the monsters, and they won't take it. "But why?"

"Because of the massacre," Sayra snaps.

Massacre? I sit there with my mouth open, confused. Griffin sighs and rests his head in his hands.

"Sayra," Aliyah warns.

"It isn't fair to her if she doesn't know," Sayra protests.

"Know what?" I ask.

Griffin shoots Sayra a warning glance. "Nothing."

But Aliyah says, "Kali, this will be difficult to hear, but remember that we are your friends, and that the other fallen have come to terms with this truth."

My blood is pulsing, my heart racing. I think back to the conversation I stumbled upon between the lieutenant and Aban. I know these things are linked. I know it.

Something wasn't right, but I'm frightened to hear it. "Tell me," I say. "Please."

Aliyah takes a deep breath and nods, her earrings tinkling like my headdress back on Ashra. "Kali," she tells me. "There was no Phoenix."

FOURTEEN

MY FACE FLOODS with heat as my heart pounds against my ribs. "I don't understand."

"The floating continents weren't sent into the sky three hundred years ago," Sayra says. "They were raised up three *thousand* years ago."

That can't be right. The annals only go back three hundred years. "But the monsters only overwhelmed the earth three hundred years ago," I say. "It's in the annals—our history books."

"Who wrote the books, Kali?" Griffin says gently. His eyes are gleaming with concern, deep hazel like the sand of Lake Agur.

"I know this is hard to accept," Aliyah says, and she folds her fingers in mine across the table. Her fingers are warm and calloused, like Griffin's. "I know there is a story the fallen have told, that a Phoenix used its last burning heat to raise up the continents. But the floating mountains are actually held aloft by a complex system of machines built by the Benu."

"The Benu?"

Sayra drinks from her goblet of water and sets it down with a thud on the table. "You have to wonder," she says. "If humans were meant to live in the sky, why wouldn't they have wings?"

It's a strange question, but a similar thought has occurred to me. It's dangerous for us to live on floating continents. I learned from my tutors how animals on Ashra adapted to the conditions. The annals say horses and cattle were brought up onto the islands with us, but that the early generations died because they couldn't breathe enough oxygen to sustain them at the severely high altitude. Only the smaller mammals have survived—chickens, pygmy goats, pikas. I've wondered if eventually humans will adapt, too—by getting shorter, maybe. Sprouting wings is a bit too far-fetched. Isn't it?

"The fact is that the floating continents were originally home to the Benu," Aliyah says. "Another race of humans who were adapted for flight."

I look from her solemn face to Griffin's. Are they playing a joke on me? "I believe in chimeras," I say slowly, "because I've seen them. And behemoths, and karus, and the Phoenix. But humans with wings? That's absurd."

"Why?" Sayra says. She fills my water goblet from a carved wooden pitcher. "In a world of monsters, can't you believe in one more?"

Aliyah shakes her head. "They weren't monsters, Sayra. They were human. The problems started when they were seen as monster hybrids instead of humans."

"Were they?" I ask. "Monsters, I mean." I can't picture

a race of humans with wings. Were they like birds, or bats, or butterflies? How could such a thing exist?

"They may have been some kind of hybrid," Griffin says. "But that's not the point. They lived in friendship with the humans on the ground. They were capable of thought and conscience, not like the monsters I hunt."

"Right." Aliyah nods. "And I don't know how or why the floating continents were raised in the first place, only that it was at least three thousand years ago. Maybe the Benu wanted to live apart from human ridicule, or maybe they were running from their own monsters and adapted to the floating continents by sprouting wings. I don't know. We don't have any of these annals like you have, Kali. We have only the traditions passed down from survivor to survivor, and stories from the fallen who've been pushed."

My jaw drops. "Pushed? We'd never push humans off the side of the continent. Surely they fell by accident. Anyway, there haven't been any reports of people falling in fourteen years."

"That you know about," Griffin says. "They were pushed, Kali. They said so."

"The fact is that the earth became overrun with monsters, and the Benu wanted to help us," Sayra continues. "They welcomed all humans to the floating continents. But there wasn't enough room for everyone. There weren't enough resources to go around. Nowhere to live, nothing to eat."

I don't like where this story is going. Not at all.

"The massacre you mentioned," I say, my throat dry, my thoughts shaken.

Griffin nods slowly, and whether or not it's true, they all believe it.

"Humans slaughtered the Benu," Aliyah says. "Hunted down every last one. Operation Phoenix was the code for the mission. They scourged the land, a new society rising from the ashes of the lost. The humans who disagreed with the massacre, our ancestors, were pushed from the sides of the continents. The barriers saved us from death, but without strength in numbers, without the fighters and the hunters and medics who stayed on Ashra, most of our ancestors were wiped out immediately by the monsters."

I'm shaking. I can't believe it. "How many survived?" I whisper. "How many humans are there now?"

Griffin's gentle voice answers me. "We don't know. Besides the three of us, we know of the weapon smith and his family in the lava lands. There are a few families who've done well on the other side of the plain, and there's rumor of an entire village by the Frost Sea."

I think of the drawing of the Phoenix in the annals, of how the wings covered the barrier and the strange machine deep in the crater made when Ashra lifted into the sky. I remember the unbelievers throwing their hands up in despair. Were they not unbelievers, but exiles? Thrown over the sides in a callous genocide?

"I... I'm sorry. I can't quite believe it."

"Of course you can't," Aliyah says, letting go of my hands to stroke the backs of them. "It's a horrible truth to face. But we want you to know it's not your fault. You're not responsible for the choices your people made hundreds of years ago. And you're not responsible for the fallen now."

But she doesn't know the worst of it, that I'm the princess and heir to Ashra and her lands. Whoever called for the genocide was a direct ancestor of mine. I am responsible.

"This isn't who we are now," I say. "You'd be safe on

Ashra. I'm certain they haven't been pushed, and I'm certain that help would be extended to you."

Sayra shakes her head. "We're afraid for them to know we've survived," she says. "They might think we're attracting monsters, that we pose a threat. They might try to destroy what's left of us."

I shake my head no. My father would be horrified to find out what our ancestors had done. Is this what Aban and the lieutenant were hiding? The bloody truth of our betrayal of the Benu? Is this what's sparked the rebellion, beyond the housing and hard work on Burumu? Are people being pushed off the edge for their involvement? Soot and filthy ashes, I think. Who else knows?

"And the Phoenix?" I say. "There's a great statue celebrating her by the citadel."

"The Benu worshipped the Phoenix," Sayra says. "They called her their ancestor, whether she was or not. Whether she even existed. That's all I know."

Then...did the Benu build the citadel with its gleaming crystal tower? Has everything I've ever known been formed of half-truths told in shadow, our history lessons steeped in bloody deeds and our annals tainted by deception? No. Someone would have remembered what really happened. Someone would have held on to the memory, family to family, of the truth behind the Rending.

The thought strikes me cold. The rebellion growing, the flyer the lieutenant burned. The fallen—they're the ones who've remembered or found out somehow. Were they really pushed from the edges of our world to be silenced? And what threat does history hold? It doesn't reflect who we are now. It doesn't mean we'd choose that bloody path again.

But Elder Aban had said the past was "dealt with" two hundred years ago, when the annals were changed. Was the conscience of the people burning with guilt? Did they need to erase this blot on our creed of peace and community that the Phoenix bestows? Genocide isn't something she'd condone. That this brutality is at the core of our history makes me shudder.

My father has led me to one day govern the people. I can understand the motivations for such a cover-up, as horrible as they are. Our beliefs—our society—would fall apart faced with such evil truths about the Rending.

Then I think of my own plummet down to earth. It was right after learning of Aban and the lieutenant. Is the cover-up continuing? I shake the thought from my mind. I fell off the continent by my own foolishness. I tried to save Jonash from the edge and fell myself. He and Elisha were trying to save me. It isn't the same at all.

"What will you do?" Aliyah says.

Griffin touches my shoulder gently. "You can stay here with us."

Aliyah smiles, sliding the dagger they've given me toward my closed fingers. "You have the great beginnings of a monster hunter," she says.

But I'm the wick and the wax. And if the rebellion grows, fueled by the deception about Operation Phoenix, there will be chaos. "I have to go back," I say. "I'm sorry."

There's an awkward silence where none of us are sure what to say next. But then Griffin nods. "Then it's settled," he says. "There's no point sitting around discussing ancient history. We'll get you to the mountain, and that's all we need to know right now."

A wave of gratefulness swells in me, and the awkwardness passes. Aliyah helps me try on and lace my boots while Sayra fastens the dagger around my hip. Griffin reaches around my neck and pulls my new karu fur cloak about my shoulders to see how it is for length. His fingers brush against my bare shoulders, and despite the weight of what we've talked about, I remember Aliyah's words to me at the waterfall.

There's a rebellion I have to think about, and dark truths I have to get to the bottom of. There's a spark in each of Griffin's fingertips, but I will not let them burn, because my life isn't truly mine. In a few days we'll both be back to our respective worlds, and this will all be a memory I'll carry with me to the sky.

It's just the way it has to be.

We set out at dawn, when the last of the monsters' scratching claws go silent on our roof of earth. The laced leather boots are snug and comfortable on my feet as I walk up the narrow stairs into the cool plum world before the sunrise. The karu cloak embraces my shoulders with its warm, soft fur as the mild morning breeze blows through the forest.

Aliyah stands with her behemoth spear at her side, because monsters could lurk at any time. This world isn't safe, no matter how different it has felt this past week.

Aliyah and Griffin embrace, holding each other tightly. Then Aliyah steps back and ruffles her brother's hair. "Don't get eaten, monster breath."

Griffin laughs and pushes her shoulder gently. "And give you the satisfaction of being right? Not a chance."

But Sayra has tears in her eyes that she's blinking back. They all know it could be the last time they see each other, just like every other parting. Sayra throws her arms around Griffin and holds him tightly, her body shaking as she tries to hide her tears. I can see how much she cares for him. Is that why Aliyah warned me not to let things grow between us?

"It's all right," Griffin says, warmth in every word. "It's only a week's journey to the mountains, and then I'll be back again in another week."

"Griff leaves for months sometimes, Sayra," Aliyah says. "He'll be all right. He has work to do, as do we." When Sayra keeps crying, Aliyah takes her gently by her elbows and turns her to look in her eyes. "Monster hunters hunt so we can stay alive. Griffin chooses to go. You know that."

I know Griffin has hunted monsters since his parents were killed. I know that my appearance here hasn't changed that, and that once I leave, he will continue hunting them. But I also know that asking him to take me to the mountains is more perilous than I'd realized. I know I'm the reason Sayra is crying right now.

"I'm sorry," I say to no one in particular, to all of them. "I can still go alone. I don't want to be the reason Griffin is in danger."

Griffin shakes his head. "Kali…"

"Kali," Aliyah interrupts him. She tilts her head back like a proud lioness, her jaw set. "Don't look back now. This is the path you've chosen, and Griffin's chosen his. We don't regret it."

I nod, but I'm unsure what to think. I don't know exactly what world I'm returning to. "And you're sure you don't want to come to Ashra with me? I can straighten this whole thing out. The past is the past, isn't it?"

"Operation Phoenix was three hundred years ago, but

as the story has been passed down, each generation has sworn to never reveal that the exiled survived. We put all humans at risk if we reveal this fact to those on your floating mountain."

It makes me sad that this is what she thinks of my world, that we would come after the survivors in fear instead of friendship. But she believes it completely, and to argue would only be awkward and offensive. So instead I tell her, "I promise I won't tell anyone you're down here." At least, I think, not until and unless I'm in a position to control Ashra's reaction. And that won't be hard, because the Monarch is my father, and he and the people will listen to their heir.

"Thank you," Aliyah says, her eyes gleaming. She steps forward to embrace me, her arms pressing the karu fur tight against my back, the tip of the behemoth spear cool against my cheek.

And then it's time for us to leave. Aliyah and Sayra walk to the waterfall with us, the sky turning a lighter purple as the sleepy birds twitter their morning chorus. Thunder rolls in the distance, and the air feels prickly. When we reach the waterfall, the mist of droplets is cold on my arms. The sun lifts, and the world floods with orange and pink.

"Let the two moons light your path," Aliyah says, while Sayra clings to her, looking from Griffin to the ground and back again.

Griffin waves a hand. "I'll bring back some basilisk scales for you, Sayra. Promise." And I remember what Aliyah said, that Griffin wants to save everyone.

We climb the stepped green slope beside the waterfall and follow the foaming stream through the woods, turning to wave until Aliyah and Sayra are out of sight. Griffin wears his karu fur cloak but no jerkin, his skin covered with leather straps and weapons and pouches. His shell necklace clinks against his neck as he walks, and on his right fore-arm he wears his crisscrossing beaded lacing from wrist to his elbow. He's painted fresh lines of yellow and purple under his eyes, too.

"Is it to help you see better?" I ask. "The paint."

He lifts a hand up to his cheek. "The purple helps," he says. "Mainly it puts me in the right frame of mind to hunt monsters. If I feel stronger than human, like I'm infused with power, then I know I can take them down."

"Like a good-luck charm, then," I say. The thunder still rolls in the distance, but here the air is clear and cloudless, the breeze warming on the rays of sun as they brighten our path. "I used to keep a red plume with me for luck. The Elders gave it to me when I was born." Every newborn on the floating continents is presented with one at birth, to symbolize the Phoenix's promise to us that one day she will rise anew.

"What happened to it?"

"It blew out of my hand and off the side of the conti-nent," I say. Griffin chuckles, and I laugh, too. "I guess it wasn't a good choice of charm for the sky."

"Tell me more about Ashra," he says, and the request surprises me. I thought he wanted nothing to do with it. The surprise must show in my expression, because he smiles. "All I know is that you fell off the edge," he says. "You know all about me, now. My parents, my sister, my career of choice."

"Career." I laugh. "I never thought of monster hunter as a career." Our boots land softly in the grass near the stream. "Did you ever say to yourself, 'When I grow up, I want to hunt monsters'?"

He grins, but the thought of it twists my heart. He hunts them because they killed his family. He shouldn't have to hunt them, but he does, to save whoever's left.

"I didn't have a choice of what to be," I say. "I've always been told what I need to be."

"Ah," he says. "A life of service, like me."

I want to tell him. I want to tell him everything—that I'm the heir to the floating continents, that I'm the descendant of the brutes who ordered the massacre. That I'm engaged to a man I don't love, that I'm the wick and the wax and that I can't burn for myself. My father once told me a light that burns only for itself is like a candle under a glass—quickly extinguished, useless to everyone. But to tell Griffin all this would be for this dream to vanish, and I only have a week left of it anyway. So I keep it to myself, as horribly selfish as it feels. Instead, I answer his first question.

"Ashra is very beautiful," I say. "There's a farming village called Ulan. The people raise chickens and pygmy goats, and they sow fields of wheat and oats and barley. In the summertime, you can see the long tufts of it swaying in the winds, like they're dancing."

"We used to grow wheat and corn in our village in the lava lands," Griffin says. "My mother—my real mother—baked the most delicious bread. I was so little when she was killed by a behemoth, but I still remember the bread." He closes his eyes as he walks, remembering. "It always smelled so good in the oven. I used to burn my fingers all the time because I couldn't wait for it to cool. She'd warn me, but I never listened." He laughs, and as we step forward we startle some iridescent insects that scatter around us. I think of what Aliyah said, how they found Griffin crying and wandering the fields. "Of course, now we can only gather wheat if we're lucky enough to find it wild. Sayra sometimes bakes acorn bread."

"Acorn bread?"

He makes a face, sticking out his tongue. "It's nutty and grainy and dense, but better than nothing. We can't harvest fields anymore. It's too dangerous to be in the fields for hours at a time plowing and reaping. And the cows and horses are long gone, so we can't break the tough soil open."

"I saw drawings of horses in the annals," I say. "I think they looked like deer, but larger."

"I've seen them on the plains," Griffin says, and the jealousy I feel is immediately surpassed by curiosity. "In small herds. I'd like to ride one someday."

The beauty in the forest around us dims under the sadness. "So much is lost," I say.

"But there's so much we still have," Griffin answers.

I shake my head. "How do you do it?"

"Do what?"

"Stay so positive."

He shrugs, his bow clinking against his quiver under the karu fur. "Sometimes all we have left is hope. If I give up, the monsters win. And I won't let them win."

The forest thins around us, leaving hilly fields of green that bump along the stream's path. I walk forward, the thunder rumbling in the distance and the sky so bright my eyes water. I glance at the mountains in the distance, rising up strongly, never failing, like Griffin's sense of hope.

FIFTEEN

WE'VE WALKED FOR a couple hours now, following the stream as it winds around the bending curves of the lush valley. We each have a flask of water in our pouch, but there's no point drinking from it when there's a gurgling stream rushing along beside us.

"Just a minute," I tell Griffin as I walk to the water's edge. He follows me, his eyes always scanning the perimeter of the clearing.

I pass a nearby apple tree on the way to the water, most of its petals gathered in crumpled piles on the ground. I dip my hands into the water, the cool bubbles foaming against my fingers as the current rushes toward the waterfall downstream. The water is sweet and fresh, and I splash some on my face when I'm done drinking.

Then I hear Griffin's voice, sharp and hushed. "Kali!"

I look up, and he's kneeling on the ground near the apple tree, waving his hand wildly at me to come over. Something isn't right. I hurry, half hunched in the grass. As soon as I'm kneeling beside Griffin, he reaches over and pulls the karu hood over my head.

"Stay down," he hisses, and we lie flat on the ground, trying our best to look like two karus napping under an apple tree. A cloud of butterflies and red bees lift into the air, disturbed from their pollen gathering on the dying apple blossoms.

A shadow drifts over us, and I can hear the flapping of wings. A deep purple dragon coils his limbs and tail, landing neatly beside the stream. The mustard-yellow insides of his leathery wings wrinkle and fold, while long, translucent crystals hang from his nose like a moustache, clinking as they sway back and forth. He leans down and snuffles the top of the water with his large nostrils.

"Storm dragon," Griffin whispers. "Maybe five years old. Just a dragonling."

It's only a fraction of the size of the dragon that grabbed the giant cat on my first day down here. It's the size of the chimera more so than a full-grown dragon. I can't believe Griffin spotted it from so far away.

The dragonling swirls its nostrils across the surface of the water, blowing little gasps of breath that send up sprays of white mist. And suddenly the long, buttery crystals on its muzzle gleam with bright electric light. Little bolts of shining lightning spark from the crystals as they hum with power. I want to ask Griffin what's happening, but I'm frightened to give us away.

The dragonling dips the crystals into the stream and the air fills with static energy. I can hear the zap of the current running from one crystal to the other, and then a large fish goes belly-up in the water.

"He's hunting," I whisper. The dragonling opens his slender jaw and crunches the fish, tilting his head backward to swallow it down.

"He's not the only one," Griffin whispers back. At first I think he means us, but then I hear the snap and creak of ancient limbs unfurling. I can't see another monster, but I can hear it. And then I see the tree branches, long and tangled and draped in moss, reaching across the stream toward the unsuspecting dragonling.

I put my hand to my mouth as the branches ensnare him in a wooden cage. The dragonling gurgles on his fish, scratching at the tree limbs as they unfurl around him.

It's not a tree at all, but another dragon, camouflaged as an old oak tree. He opens each ancient wing with a crack like a branch breaking in two. His mouth is carved from bark, his tongue mossy and green and forked, hanging out of his mouth around his polished, gray teeth.

The dragonling lights up his crystals and zaps the branches curling around him. He flings himself at their sides, snapping one after another in his jaws. But the long limbs of the oak dragon grow and lift him into the air, closing tighter around him.

I know they're both monsters, but my heart breaks for the tiny storm dragon. I stand up and then feel Griffin's fingers tighten around my arm.

"No!" he whispers, but it's too late. They've seen me. The storm dragon stops fighting the oak dragon, and throws his whole body against the wooden cage, snapping his teeth in my direction. I feel utter betrayal. I wanted to help him, but I see now that Griffin's right—if I save the storm dragonling, he'll only come after me.

The dragonling throws himself against the branches with

newfound strength, but the oak dragon is still more interested in his catch—either that or he's rooted to the ground. I wonder how long he's been lying in wait to catch his unsuspecting victim.

Griffin rises to his feet, his hand still around my arm. "Come on," he says sharply, and we run past the dragons as they screech behind us. The storm dragonling's call is like thunder, and as we race past them, I wonder if that was the rolling thunder I heard earlier. The oak dragon reaches a barb-tipped wing toward us, but his movements are slow and ancient, and we easily escape the trap.

We run until I feel the familiar sting of my bruised ribs, until I'm coughing so hard I collapse to the ground.

"Kali," Griffin says, and I notice he's barely panting. He must be used to running for his life all the time. "Are you all right?"

"Fine," I gasp. "Just...just one minute."

He nods, surveying the landscape carefully. The oak dragon won't come after us, and the dragonling can't. The bubbling stream carries on peacefully, as if we'd never witnessed the fight. After a moment I catch my breath. "I just wanted to help the baby dragon," I say.

Griffin smiles sadly. "You're thinking like a human. They're monsters. They only want to destroy."

I've seen kindness in animals many times, but Griffin's right—the monsters lack the compassion other living creatures have. "You know a lot about them."

"It's my life to know," he says. "The minute you let down your guard is the minute they win. There's nothing more dangerous than a cornered monster that has nothing to lose. So I have to be the same."

The sun is hot in the afternoon, the wafting breeze too

muggy against our faces. It brings with it swarms of mosquitos and flicker wasps, which fly so quickly they seem to vanish, until they flicker right beside our ears. They buzz and waggle their menacing stingers the size of my fist, but Griffin tells me to walk straight ahead calmly and I do, and neither of us is stung.

When it's safe, we talk quietly about Ashra and the earth below, about the generators the Benu built to keep the continents aloft in the sky, and whether they'll last forever. "It's not like we have any scholars left to study them," Griffin says. "But I've gone down to the shadowlands before to look at them. They glow with a pale blue light, the generators, and they seem to recharge by themselves, but I can't figure out how. There's definitely no sunlight getting in down there."

"Maybe the Phoenix's sacrifice provided enough residual heat to keep them going," I say, and he looks at me, pained, but unwilling to contradict me. "Look, I'm not saying I don't believe you about the massacre. It's hard to accept and believe, but…I have my doubts about some of the annals." Like that secret first volume, and what Elder Aban and the lieutenant are keeping from me. "But the Benu built the statue of the Phoenix at the citadel. She was clearly important to them. And maybe it's true that she sent the continents into the sky. It was just a lot earlier than we thought."

Griffin thinks for a minute, and then nods. "Anything could have happened three thousand years ago."

"Will Aliyah and Sayra be okay?" I ask. I can't stop thinking about them, left behind in the dugout haven.

"They're survivors," he says. "They'll keep going, until they can't. That's what survival is."

I know this. And Aliyah is strong. Not just her weapon skill and her survival knowledge, but her heart and her attitude. But Sayra…it seemed to crush her, Griffin leaving. "Sayra seems so heartbroken," I say finally.

"She's lost everything. Aliyah and I still have each other, but she lost her whole family when the griffins attacked. She had two older brothers and a younger sister, and her parents. All gone."

"It's horrible," I say. "It's not fair."

It's too warm, and Griffin slips the karu fur off his shoulders. It slides back on its strings, folding in against his spine like a curtain. When he steps forward, I can see the large crescent scars on his back. "Of course it isn't fair," he says. "Everyone has lost something. And everyone deals with that loss in their own way. Together, Aliyah and Sayra will survive."

We carry on in silence a little longer, and then Griffin looks at me, his hazel eyes gleaming in the sunlight. "You're looking at my scars."

My cheeks blaze red, and I swat at a mosquito that buzzes in my face.

"You're wondering how I got them." Griffin looks away. The mountains are out of view at the moment, the terrain jagged and blocked by trees. If I was on my own, I'd be afraid we'd gotten turned around.

"I… I was wondering."

His lip curves in a smile. "We have a long way to walk. If you ask me anything, I'll answer. And you do the same."

I wonder if he's figured out that I've held back about who I really am, if this is his bargain. But the more we go through together, the more I feel tied to him. When he looks at me with those hazel eyes that have seen so much,

I know I can trust him. I want to know him, and I want him to find me, too. The real me, the one hiding timidly in my own shadow. "Okay."

He grins. "Except this time, I can't answer. I'd tell you if I knew, but I don't. I've had these scars since my adoptive mother found me. She found me crying in a field near the village, after being separated from my blood parents."

"Aliyah told me."

"They figured the scars were from the behemoth pack that likely killed the rest of my family. I was only two or three. I don't remember. In fact, I don't even know my real age, my birthday...whether I was an only child or not." He laughs, but there's little humor in it. "Sometimes I remember my mother singing to me, and of course the bread she used to bake. But it's only vague glimpses in distant dreams. I couldn't sing a verse or bake a loaf to save my life."

"I'm sorry that happened, Griffin. I really am."

He slaps at a mosquito on his arm, the motion jangling the bow and arrows hanging from his shoulder. "The thing is, I had a wonderful childhood with my family. And until the griffins came to the village, they raised me with love. So there's nothing sad about it." He doesn't look at me, only keeps walking. But I'm moved by his courage and his heart, and I feel the ember Aliyah warned me about sparking, glowing from red to blue with its own life, ready to burn down everything I believe in and rise anew from the ashes.

"I had a happy childhood, too," I say, and I rest my hand on the inside of his elbow, my fingertips wrapping over beaded lacing and hot skin. "My mother died in childbirth, but my father worked so hard to be both parents to me. Even though he was always being called away for work, he never made me feel like I wasn't the first priority. I knew—I know—that he loves me. And that's one of the reasons I need to go back so badly. To tell him I'm all right. To show him he doesn't need to worry."

"We're lucky, then," Griffin says. "In a world of so much sorrow, we've both known so much happiness."

And I'm so glad that I've told him a little more about me. I'm glad that I'm letting him in.

We walk for five more days, dodging monsters and catching fish from the widening stream. When it's safe, we laugh and share stories by the campfire at night. When it isn't, we hide in trees from the pouring rains and shiver in our karu furs while the monsters lurk nearby. Sometimes I have to wait while he hunts a monster that's stalked us for miles. Other times I help alert him to their approach. He teaches me how to read the signs, footprints and scrapes on the trees, birds chirping to each other and strange shifts in the wind. I catch on quickly. I use my garnet-adorned dagger for the first time to help him carve up a catoblepas— like a wild, scaly, murderous cow, he jokes—and I help gather branches for campfires. He holds my hands gently in his and shows me how to strike a spark on the kindling. He brings out the precious vial of black salt from the lava lands and sprinkles it on my dinner when he thinks I'm not looking.

I do the same to his, when he looks away.

On the sixth day, the grass is getting spongy under our boots, as if the ground is saturated from rainwater. I look down, expecting lush emerald, but the grass is brown and sickly, and the trees are sparse.

The stream whisks to the west, where it branches off from a wide river, but the mountains lie to the south. So

we trample the squishy plants and walk into the marshlands, heading straight for the nearing backbone of the
mountain range.

A thick, ancient tree stands at the edge of the spreading marsh. Its branches have grown in a tangle around old
wooden beams laid halfway up the trunk—the remains of
a floor and one wall of a house. The window is broken, the
black metal frame bent and hanging out like a thin gnarled
arm. There's a rope ladder dangling in the middle of the
exposed room, and it's attached to a single plank of what
may have been the second floor. Griffin shakes his head,
and I know what it must have been—a survivor's hut, home
to one or two or a family, abandoned like so much of this
world. What happened to them?

The water underfoot spreads, and the marsh ahead is
a labyrinth of water and land. I can't be sure when I step
whether the ground will hold me, or whether it's only an
island of floating reeds. And at the end of the maze of water
and land paths I can see the base of the mountains rising up.

"One, maybe two days' walk," Griffin says. "Nearly
there. There's a pass up the mountain, so the climbing
shouldn't be too rough. But marshlands first."

I take a step and my boot sinks into ankle-deep marsh
water, murky and dark as it soaks into the leather. I'm about
to take another step, but Griffin's steady hand wraps around
my elbow and I hesitate.

"This way," he says, "unless you're wanting a bath."

We tread carefully through the maze of marshland. If a
monster swooped down from the sky, we'd be easy picking. We have our karu hoods up just in case, but Griffin
says there are lots of monsters here who think karu are just
fine to eat, so it's not much help.

By the time the sun is setting, the mountains still seem so far away, bathed in mist and fog that rises up from the marshlands. I'm not sure how we'll make camp in this soggy landscape, but I don't ask. Griffin's face is all concentration, looking carefully at each reed island, trying to figure out if it will hold our weight. He takes one step and the water goes up to his knee, gushing into his leather shoe and soaking his legging dark brown.

The light is slipping from the sky, and we're no closer to a possible rest point. "Griffin," I say.

"We'll have to keep going," he says. "You all right to keep walking for a bit?"

It's going to be miles, but there's nothing we can do. "Can't wait," I say, and he smiles.

"You don't have to be *that* nice. A little complaining's all right." But when I'm with Griffin, I want to say everything I can to make his heart lighter.

The marshland is thicker here, and our steps are slowed by squelching mud. We hang on to each other to avoid falling into the thick sludge. It's hard enough to see where to step next in the fading light. I wish for a moment I hadn't given the lantern away.

But as the last of the sunlight falls, as the sky turns that deep plum color dotted with gleaming stars, something amazing awakens in the marshlands.

I've seen the rainbow colors of the fireflies in the outlands of Ashra, but I've never seen anything as beautiful as this. The entire marshland begins to glow with incandescent light. Ferns gleam with ghostly, glow-in-the-dark leaves that unfurl in great coils. Fireflies light with luminous blue green that matches the ferns, and the edges of the water glisten with schools of tiny shining fish, thousands of them. It's as if the air and the earth have reversed, as if we're walking through the glitter of luminescent starlight in the skies.

"Soot and ashes," I whisper, for I've never seen anything like this in my life. High above, the two moons glow, and their reflections dance on the rippling waters of the marsh, but I can barely notice them through this wonderland of lights, swirling around us like twinkling snow.

"The marsh is something at night," Griffin says, his voice velvet beside me. The lights shine on his face in a dance of gleaming stars, sparkling off the beads laced on his arm and the lustrous shells strung around his neck. "But it's still treacherous to walk, I'm afraid. Stay close."

He opens his hand, palm outstretched. The motion reminds me suddenly of Jonash offering his arm to me in the firefly-lit outlands, when I had no choice but to accept. Now I have every choice, and I want to take his hand, but the guilt of the parallel memory floods me with shame. I have to tell Griffin that my path isn't mine to choose. I have to tell him before it's too late.

But I can't find the words, not in this land of luminous stars. Instead I thread my fingers through his, and we walk forward carefully, the mud sticking to our boots, the murky water lit with glowing minnows. I want to walk through this dreamscape with him. I want my life to fade away into the shadows so I can have this moment forever.

We walk for another half hour, until my feet ache from the day of wading through mud like gooey honey. I don't feel like I can go on, and from the way Griffin is stumbling, he must feel the same.

"We can stop and rest if you like," he says, but we may as well be in the middle of an ocean. The paths of reeds have become so thin they're nearly engulfed by the thick curls of water. There's nowhere to sit, and if we're going to stand around like scarecrows in a field, I'd rather keep walking. I tell him so and he laughs, his voice strained and exhausted.

"All right," he says. "How about one hundred more steps, and then I'll ask you again."

A smile curves its way onto my lips. "I could do two hundred," I tease.

"Three hundred, then," he teases back, the iridescent fireflies strung through his hair like a fairy crown.

He turns, and counts. "One. Two. Three."

I laugh, following carefully where he walks.

"Four," he says. We step again.

"Five."

And then with a horrible splash he's gone, and there's nothing there but the ripple of dark water slicking over his head.

SIXTEEN

"GRIFFIN!" I SHOUT, staring into the murky water. Panic seizes in my throat and my blood runs cold. I wait for him to surface, sputtering, but he doesn't.

Fireflies circle the ripples lazily. He doesn't come back up.

"Where are you? Answer me!"

The dread overtakes me, the wet and the mud and the dark between the showy lights. Can't he swim? Is he tangled in some reeds at the bottom?

He's running out of time. He can't hold his breath for this long, can he?

I jump in, thinking only how desperately I need to save him. The water rushes over me like a wintry blast, the ripples sealing over my head like a dank tomb. The water is pitch-black down here, cloudy and freezing and incredibly deep. I turn my head slowly, searching for Griffin, but I can't even see the bottom. Here and there the schools of minnow glow, their ghostly radiance shining like search beacons through the muddy water.

I hear the struggle before I see it. Griffin's limbs tear through the water with bubbling fury as I swim toward him. The heavy water pulls my waterlogged dress toward the bottom, and I fight against it to get to Griffin. If I'd been thinking straight, I would've taken it off before leaping in, but all I could think—all I can think—is to save him.

A group of minnows flash like lightning in the sky, and they illuminate the thick curve of something massive in the water. It's coiled around the seabed like a snake, each loop of its body the width of a giant cedar trunk. The scales glitter a cool blue in the minnows' glow, and there are spots of dim blue glowing up the back of the coils. Each light pulses at the end of a long spike, and the spikes are knit together down the monster's spine by stretched, leathery webs of skin.

The water goes dark again, except for the dim blue lights down the monster's back. My body chills with a frost icier than this frigid water. It's a sea serpent, almost as huge as the massive dragon that snatched the cat for its dinner.

We can't fight something like this. It's enormous—how could we even make a scratch?

The schools of fish flash again like lightning, illuminating the endless coils of the serpent. I can see two pairs of wing-like fins near its head, all spikes and ripped, webbed skin and scales. And then I see Griffin, floating directly in front of the serpent's gaping maw. Griffin's hands are shoved against the monster's top lip, pressing its cavernous mouth open, while his feet are wedged between the fangs on its lower jaw that try to snap closed. He struggles against the monster's attempt to chomp him in two. The serpent shakes its open mouth, showers of bubbles and dark water rippling toward me. Its forked tongue darts out, black and leathery. The minnows flash their lights, illuminating the struggle—and then the lights go out, nothing but darkness.

There's no time to let the fear seize me. I'm nearly out of breath, and Griffin's been down here even longer. If I don't act, he'll drown before the monster can take a bite out of him.

I pull my dagger from its sheath, fighting against my heavy skirts as I swim underneath the sea serpent's massive jaw. I shove the dagger into its skin with all the might I can muster. The serpent lets out a shrill sound that echoes through the water at an ear-piercing frequency. It shakes its head back and forth as black blood curls into the water like smoke. It tosses its head above the surface with Griffin still in its mouth before the head comes crashing into the water again. The waves toss me backward, head over feet. I hope the time above water was long enough for Griffin to get in a good breath. I swim to the surface myself and gasp in the muggy marsh air.

Ducking below the water again, I struggle to see the sea serpent in the flashes of light. The monster is writhing around in the water, and Griffin's managed to stab its eye with one of his daggers. Bile and blood stream out of the monster as it screeches, its fin-wings furling and unfurling, its claws slashing the water. I swim toward it again and stab my dagger into its chest, but the scales clink like chain mail, metal on metal; the hit is harmless. The sea serpent turns its head toward me, and while it's distracted Griffin goes for its other eye. It lets out a screech that sets off a tidal wave, and we're both thrown swirling through the water, the bubbles rising around us like a curtain. The minnows flash again, light and dark, and I see the serpent writhing, and then nothing, and then in another position, like a slow flip of illustrations. The glowing minnows dart in and out of its jaws quickly as it chomps and froths the water, looking for its escaped prey.

Griffin grabs my hand and tugs as he swims upward. My skirts slow us down, but we fight the pull with energy we didn't know we had. My heart is pumping and my pulse is throbbing in my ears as our heads break above the water. I gasp in a breath as Griffin presses my hand to a tangle of reeds. He pushes my back to help me climb onto the floating island. My dress is so waterlogged that it feels like an anvil pulling me back into the water. I wonder if I could've climbed the reeds without his help. As soon as I'm up, I turn around to help him onto the island. He sputters a spray of water with every breath, coughing as he kneels on the reeds, the island sinking into the water from our weight.

The sea serpent's head crashes above the surface, his long sleek body uncoiling as he towers above us like a mountain. I hesitate, transfixed with fear.

Griffin nocks an arrow dipped in chimera venom before I even know what's happened. I feel the slight breeze as it zings past my ear. The serpent cries out as the arrow lodges in the soft skin just below its throat. Griffin sends another one airborne, but this one clanks against the thick scales on its chest and tumbles into the water below, where it floats, useless.

He readies a third arrow, pulling back and loosing it so quickly the string sings. This one lodges beside the first in its throat, and the serpent twists its head and shrieks. We put our hands over our ears as the wail forces us to our knees on the reeds.

The serpent crashes below the surface again, the water frothing with foam as it closes over the monster's massive head.

"Come on," Griffin says, and jumps across to another platform of reeds. It's too dark to hurry, but I follow him. With every step I wait for the reeds to give way, for the icy water to envelop my body. But we never dip deeper than our knees as we struggle forward, our path lit by the eerie marsh lights.

The serpent's head lifts up again, but not as high as before, and now it's behind us. I wonder if the chimera venom is taking hold, if it's slowing him down. Black-tinted water streams out of its eye sockets as if it's crying black tears. But it can't see us, and its screeches can't bounce off the air like they can in the water to find us.

We stumble forward through the mud and the knee-deep water. And then the serpent dips below the surface, and it doesn't rise again.

I keep waiting for it to reappear, to shake the reeds below us as its sharp fangs bite into us. But the bite doesn't come, and soon the marsh is quiet and calm, a complete betrayal to what's lurking beneath the surface.

"You all right?" Griffin pants, and I nod. It's too much effort to respond. My hair is a cold, muddy tangle against my neck. My skirts drag with water and muck, the soaked karu fur tugging at the strings around my neck that choke me. My muscles ache and protest every step, and every breath comes out as a sputtering cough. How much water did I swallow? I wonder.

After a few more minutes, I manage to wheeze, "What... what was that?"

"Dark Leviathan," he answers. "They're stronger and bigger than the Leviathans in the rivers and lakes. I thought Dark Leviathans only lived in the oceans, but...I guess I was wrong."

So there are more of them on the earth, no matter what their size or strength. I shudder.

Thunder rolls in the distance, and before we know it, a cool rain is plummeting down on the marshlands. I can't get much more soaked than I am, but I shake in the bitter cold.

We're not counting steps anymore, and I can't see the mountains in the glittering lights around us. I have no idea how long or how far we've walked. It feels like the night's gone on for days. Griffin finally stops in front of me and points to a group of shadows looming on the left.

There are eight or nine thick tree trunks, so large that if we each hugged one side our hands wouldn't even touch. Four of them have rope ladders tossing in the wind and rain, and a fifth has a frayed rope that perhaps was once a ladder, as well. It's hard to see in the strobe of lights, but every ladder leads up to a structure like the one at the beginning of the marsh, each in a different state of disrepair. Some sort of small village had its life here, a group of small tree-dwellers eking out an existence in the marshes.

Griffin leads me to the tree that has the best surviving structure attached. He pulls on the rope ladder to test its strength and then tells me to wait while he checks it out. I nod, unable to answer because my teeth are chattering so badly.

He lifts his foot into the third rung and pulls himself upward, his movements numb and rigid like a doll's. When his right foot goes by, I see the dark ooze of blood that's plastered all over the back of his leg. "Griffin, you're hurt," I say, but either he can't hear me over the pouring rain or I'm shivering too much for the words to come out coherently. Some of it could be the Dark Leviathan's blood, but there's a slice down the back of his leg that leaches with every step. How has he walked this far on it without me knowing?

He's at the top of the ladder now, and he pulls himself into the structure on his stomach. I wait for a minute, and then his head appears and he shouts at me. I assume he's telling me to climb, so I lift my weary legs and pull myself up with a last effort of strength that I didn't know I had. The rope ladder sways and twists as I try to climb, and the top seems so far away. At last Griffin is grabbing my arms and pulling me through the collapsed doorway of the tiny house, into the tangled branches of this ancient, gnarled tree.

The rain drums against the crumpled roof and leaks through a giant hole in the ceiling, but it's a relief to be able to sit down anywhere, especially in a place that is mostly sheltered from the wind and rain. The back wall is leaning forward, but in one piece, and the other three walls have gaping holes where there were once windows, doors or pieces of wall that were crushed by the caving roof. In the far corner, coated with rainwater, are smashed and cobwebbed basins and jugs of clay, and the splintered pieces of what may have been a chair.

We sit and catch our breath, our karu furs dripping onto the paneled wooden floor. I lean out the doorway and wring my skirts over the edge, and then I collapse backward, staring up at the crooked, unstable roof. I've never felt exhaustion like this. My legs and ribs burn like fire. Neither of us can speak, basking in the refuge of the tiny tree house.

I'm shivering in the cold, and I wrap my arms around myself, but it does little good.

"Here," Griffin rasps, and his fingers go to the cloak string around my neck. His hands are shaking as he fumbles with the knot. The fur falls from my back like a brick I hadn't realized I was carrying. He unties his own cloak, and smooths it out on the floor to dry. "I'm not sure I can make a fire."

"The only kindling we have is soaked," I say, pointing to the wreckage of the wooden chair. We could maybe rip up some floorboards and burn those, but we might set the whole place on fire, or have it collapse in on us.

"It's not long until morning," he says. "Try and get some rest, and the sun will warm us. The storms here are thunderous, but they're always over quickly."

I remember the rain on my first night on earth, alone. It did come and go abruptly, and I hope this will be the same.

"Your leg," I say, remembering.

"I could've lost it, without your help," he says. He laughs, but it comes out as a sputter. "You must be thinking, 'some monster hunter he is.'"

I'm not, not at all. That we survived a beast that giant is miraculous, a bounty from the Phoenix herself. I know she fueled the courage in me to swim toward Griffin in the water. I know she gave me the strength to walk all this distance. But then I remember that I can't be sure the Phoenix is watching over us at all, so all I say is, "Without you, I would've been eaten by the chimera."

"I'm grateful to you, as well," Griffin says. "You swam

right at that Dark Leviathan with your dagger. I've never known such bravery from a fallen. You saved my life."

His eyes are deep and lovely, even in the darkness surrounded only by the gleaming marshland outside. The hazel of them draws me in like the Phoenix's flame, healing the aching in my ribs and the pain in my legs. I don't feel quite as cold when I look into them. "Can I do anything for your leg?"

He shakes his head. "I think the main thing is to stay off it for a bit," he says. "It doesn't look that deep, and if I made it this far, then it can't be too serious, right? I'll have a better look in the morning. Rest now."

I nod and roll on my side on the wooden floor. I shiver, wishing I had the warm, plush blankets in my bedroom back in the citadel. I miss the crackle of the flames in the fireplace, the comforting sound of my father's voice in the corridor. The iridescent lights of the plants and fireflies make gleaming spots on my eyelids even when they're closed. I tremble and pray for morning, pray for the rain to stop.

"Kali," Griffin's voice says, and it's so close to me that I turn to look. He's lying on the floor beside me, his lips nearly blue as he shakes from the cold. He's pulled his wet cloak over himself, and as he lifts his arm, the fur raises up like a wing.

I sidle against the paneled floor until I'm nearer to him, and he drapes the wet fur over both of us. It's heavy with marsh water, even though he's wrung it out, but it's the best we can do to keep in what little heat we have. He lies beside me, his shell necklace clinking against the floor as he adjusts the fur over us. There is little heat radiating from him, but it's more than I had alone. After a few minutes

I stop shaking, breathing in the small warmth from our bodies side by side.

I feel safe next to him, enjoying this closeness that I know is only meant for survival, but feels like so much more. Slowly, I press the backs of my hands against his bare chest. Our skin feels like fire and steam against the sopping wet cold. Griffin doesn't move from my touch. Instead he drapes a weary arm over me, pulling me closer into the little warmth we have.

My eyes close with exhaustion. Griffin is already breathing heavily, lost to dreams and sleep. Everything feels like ice and fire, heat and cold. *I want to tell him everything*, I think as I drift to sleep. *I will tell him everything, and then I will be free.*

SEVENTEEN

WHEN THE BIRDS begin to chirp, my groggy, water-logged brain realizes it's morning. I open an eye; sunlight streams in from the holes in the roof and the walls. Griffin is still asleep, his expression peaceful like a child's. I watch as his body rises and falls with each breath. His face is smeared with blood and mud, the yellow and purple paint under his eyes smudged by the Leviathan struggle and the endless rains of the night. There are no more iridescent stars floating around the marshlands, only sunshine in the pale morning sky.

I shift under the karu fur and find it's less heavy than it was several hours ago. Most of the fur is sleek and dry, though my dress is still damp beneath it. My leg seizes up, and I stretch it to stop the cramping. The night's walking, the fight with the Dark Leviathan—they all seem like dreams as I stare up at the clouds drifting above the shattered roof.

I get up as quietly as I can, but the motion stirs Griffin from sleep. He groans, rubbing at his eyes with the back of his hand. "Don't tell me the sun's risen already," he says, and in spite of everything, I almost laugh.

"It's nighttime still. Go back to sleep."

"Liar."

I look out the doorway of the hut and across the marshlands. The surface is calm and misty, covered in the swirling labyrinth of reed paths and water channels. The land looks more solid to the south, the reeds clumping together and the grass turning greener. The mountain range is so close I don't even see it at first, expecting it in the distance. I look straight up, the peaks high above. We're nearly at the base, and the sight of it raises my spirits.

"Griffin," I say. "We're at the mountains. We've made it!"

"Great," he mumbles, flipping over under the fur. "Now all we have to do is walk straight upward."

My stomach grumbles, and I sit down near the doorway, opening my pouch for some of the hazu jerky Sayra packed for us. Griffin sits up finally, stretching his lean arms behind his head. His weapons lie in a pile on the floor beside him, and he begins to strap the leather lacings on. I try to look away, remembering how closely we slept together last night. It felt so nice to be together, a warmth rushing through my veins when I think of it—when I think of him. I never felt that with Jonash. I tried, and I couldn't. With Griffin, I try not to, and I can't help it. And I don't even want to help it.

I shake my head, taking another bite of the jerky. Aliyah saw it from a mile away, and now I have to tell Griffin the truth, no matter how he reacts. My life isn't my own.

I'm used to it, and yet I feel that familiar panic rising up in my throat, the kind that makes me want to run to my outcrop on Ashra and be alone with the thistles and fire-weed and greedy pikas.

We eat and drink in silence as the sun rises outside the tree house. The room is thick with unspoken words. The night made me brave, but the sunlight makes me afraid, frightened that I'll lose everything I never knew I wanted.

Griffin gives voice to it a moment later. "If we're fast enough, this could be our last couple days together," he says.

I need to go home...don't I? This is what I wanted. This is what I must do. So why do I feel so unsure?

Come with me, I want to ask again. Instead I say, "Do you think the airship will see me?"

"You'll need to signal them somehow. How often do they fly over the mountains?"

I chew the last bite of a jerky strip thoughtfully. I've lost track of time, but the crowds from the Rending would've returned maybe five or six days ago. I can't be sure. "I know airships travel between Burumu and Ashra at least once a week," I say. "Sometimes twice. I'm not sure if they'll still be looking for me. And if they are, they won't think to look on the mountains." It's so far from the edge where I fell. Ashra looks so much smaller from here, like an ink-blot floating in the sky.

"I'll wait with you until they come," Griffin says. "As long as it takes."

We climb down the rickety ladder, our arms and legs aching and sore. Griffin washes the back of his leg in the marsh water until only the long jagged slice from the Dark Leviathan's fang is left. He says he might need to stitch it up if it bursts open, but otherwise no harm done. I can't imagine him taking his bone needle and sinew, stitching up the wound himself without a medic. But he says it wouldn't be the first time.

We walk across the last of the reed islands and onto the greener grass, where our footprints don't flood with murky water as soon as we've stepped onward.

An hour's walk and there's nothing but mountain straight ahead, a winding pathway making its way up the nearest peak. The sun is high in the sky because of our late start, and the hot breeze swirls around us, drying our cloaks and our clothes as we start up the mountain pass. After another hour or two, the path forks.

"Straight ahead is the pass," Griffin tells me. "We need this route, which goes up to the summit."

"What's on the other side of the mountains?"

Griffin smiles. "The ocean. It's where my father's village used to be."

The ocean? My eyes widen. So close to the vision I've always wanted to see. I'm tempted to forget Ashra and her lands. They can survive another week without me, or a month, or maybe my whole life. I could take Griffin's hand and race along the pass, and in a few days we'd be waist-deep in the cool salt water, surrounded by fish and dolphins and seashells.

It's a lovely dream, but that's all it is. Griffin looks at me, waiting. I know he'd take me if I asked. But without a word, I turn up the winding path to the summit, and neither of us talks about it at all. I'm the wick and the wax. My life isn't my own.

I wonder what kind of monsters the mountains hold, but Griffin says there aren't many. "Slim pickings for lunch up here," he says. "No humans, so there aren't any monsters bigger than basilisks, and they're only the size of deer."

The mountain path is hard sand stomped flat, and it reminds me of the paths from the citadel to Lake Agur and the outlands. The fields around the path are crammed with wildflowers in vibrant yellows and pinks, flaming oranges like Phoenix wings and blues like the storm dragon's scales. The red bees swarm the blossoms, gathering nectar to make scarlet honey, while the flicker wasps flap their wings lazily in the heat. We wind around the mountain over and over, like a carousel from the annals, always spinning higher to the top.

By dinnertime, the breeze around us has grown colder. It reminds me of the wind on Ashra. It reminds me that I'll never feel warmth in the wind again. We've stopped for the day, since there's no airship in sight, and we could step right off the mountainside in the dark. There's a thin waterfall running down a jagged outcrop of rock, and a small hollow underneath its ledge where we'll sleep for the night. Around us, the trees are full of mournful birds, chirping as they anticipate sunset.

As we sit chewing the dried berries from our pouches, there's a sound like hissing and slithering. Griffin jumps up, his bow and arrow in hand. A basilisk rounds the corner, looking as startled to see us as we are to see him. He fans out webbed skin like a mane around his face, shaking his tail with a rattling warning. The sun beams off his scales in a rainbow of iridescent colors. The monster's forked purple tongue darts in and out of its mouth as it hisses at Griffin, unsure whether to lunge or retreat.

Griffin holds his arrow ready, nocked on the string, but doesn't let it fly. Suddenly the basilisk lunges forward, and the arrow looses straight into its neck. The basilisk hisses and chomps his toothless maw at Griffin, who leaps out of the way and holds the monster behind the frill of its mane. The basilisk tries to charge at me, snapping and rattling his tail, but Griffin holds him back. The two tangle about until the chimera venom takes hold, and then the basilisk's eyes roll upward and his head hits the ground.

I help Griffin slowly carve away at the rainbow scales that I remember now he's promised to Sayra. Each is the size of my hand but barely weighs a thing. I wonder if she'll make necklaces out of them, but Griffin shakes his head. "They're pretty, but they're also impossible to cut through. They'll make good armor, if Sayra has time. If not, we can sell them when we make our next trip to the weapon smith in the lava lands. They disintegrate, though, so the armor's only good for a couple months."

"What's it like in the lava lands?" I ask, prying another rainbow scale off the basilisk. "Is it hot there? With...what are they called...volcanos?"

Griffin laughs. "Not where we lived," he says. "Much farther northwest there are a few active ones. The soil is rich and black from the lava flows, but there are hard ridges of stone rippling across the land. Not so great for farming on those, so you have to pick your field carefully. Plus behemoth packs like to hide in the ridges. But there's lots of iron in the rock, so it's a good place to be a weapon smith. The lava lands start just north of where I found you, around the other side of Ashra's shadow."

"I wish I could see it," I say, clinking another scale onto the pile. "The land where you grew up."

Griffin smiles and rubs the sweat off his forehead with the back of his hand. He gathers the scales into his pouch, then starts to carve some meat for us to roast. "I wish I could see your home, too," he says. "In Ashra. Do you and your father have a farm?"

The truth is filtering in again, no matter how much I want to block it out. "Not really," I say. "But my friend Elisha lives on one. She owns pygmy goats and chickens, and bakes the most delicious bread."

"Bread," Griffin says, his eyes gleaming. "Like my mother's, hot from the oven."

"You'd burn your fingers over Elisha's bread, too," I say. "There's nothing like the first loaves of the Ulan harvest."

I gather branches to make a campfire while Griffin prepares the basilisk meat. The sun is low in the sky, the colors of sunset spilled across the heavens like upturned paint cans. The view from the mountain is breathtaking. It isn't as high up as Ashra, where the earth looks like a flattened, dead painting. From here, everything is vibrant and moving. I can see the hazus and dragons circling over the plains in the fading light, the water of the marshlands reflecting the falling sunlight like a shattered mirror. I can see the river looping toward the forest where Aliyah and Sayra must be. And past that, the floating shadow of Ashra, looming silently in the sky.

Who could guess that a world overridden with monsters wouldn't itself be monstrous?

Griffin's voice is quiet beside my ear. "You can still change your mind."

I turn to face him. His hazel eyes are gleaming, his floppy brown hair falling into his eyes. I've never been given a choice before, not really. But he's ready to support any path I choose. We're standing so close to each other that the world seems to fall away. I could move toward him now, and I think he would let me. I could wrap my arms around his neck and see what he would do—to see what I would do. There's nothing in the world but us, and it's all in my hands.

And then Griffin erupts into a string of curse words I've never heard before and dashes back to the campfire where the basilisk meat has lit on fire. I hurry over and we blow out the flames on the meat, laughing until tears spring to the corners of our eyes. We peel off the charred outsides and eat the steaming meat inside, and then douse our burning fingertips in the waterfall. The water mists over our faces with its cool droplets, and suddenly the sky has turned a pale purple, and the sun is gone, and the day is over.

It's warmer by the fire, but Griffin insists we sleep in the cavern under the waterfall ledge. "Basilisks have bad eyesight at night," he says. "I've seen them walk straight off the mountain's edge before. But they won't miss us in the open next to a fire." The mountain breeze is cool, but the tiny cavern has trapped the warmth of the day's sunlight and keeps the wind away. Griffin spreads out his karu fur on the ground, and I spread mine out beside his. The cloak has dried from the long trek in the sunlight and the fur is soft and warm. We watch the stars alight in the sky around the sides of the waterfall's veil.

"It's probably a full day's walk tomorrow," he says. "From there we'll wait until the airship comes by. Do they travel at night?"

I shake my head. I've only ever seen them travel by daylight. "They're not the most stable machines. Our technology is pretty limited."

"Ours, too," Griffin says. "Scholars always get picked off first. No fighting skills. That's why monster hunters are trying to make a safe space, so we can get civilization running again."

"You said there might be a whole village left on the Frost Sea."

"There are a couple villages rumored to be left. But the Frost Sea is so far, and I haven't dealt with many ice-type monsters. If there is a village there, they must have good monster hunters of their own."

"When I... When I get on the airship," I say slowly, "what will you do next?"

Griffin stretches his legs out, resting his arms on his knees. "I'll head back to Aliyah and Sayra and see if they're still in the haven," he says. "If not, I might head to the lava lands to drop these basilisk scales off at the weapon smith. And then? I'll keep roaming, fighting monsters that are threatening survivors and keeping my eyes on the sky for more fallen, like you." He takes a drink from his water flask and corks the lid back in. "And you?"

"I..." I've been so desperate to get back, to escape the earth. And for what? The rebellion worries me, yes, but I know my father will deal with it swiftly. And then life will go back to those quiet times in the library, reading the annals and dreaming of the world below. I'll sneak out to Lake Agur and to my outcrop, dodging responsibilities with Elisha at my side. Then, next year, I'll marry the Sargon's son, whom I don't love. I'll take on all the responsibility that awaits me in a life I dread. I want to be with my father again, yes...but I know more now. I've seen more. There's a whole world down here that I want to explore.

"Kali."

I look at Griffin, his face earnest and concerned. "You've got that look again."

I lift a hand to my cheek. "What look?"

"Like the world is on your shoulders. Whenever you think about going home, you get this faraway look. I know it well. It's something monster hunters do, too." He rests his hand on the karu fur and nudges himself closer to me. "Give up our lives for others. But you don't look like it's a choice you made. It was made for you."

I don't say anything. He's right again.

He shakes his head. "I wish you'd tell me," he says. "It's important to give of ourselves for others, yes. But you look so unhappy when you talk about going home. You have to give yourself a choice, too, Kali." His face is so close to mine now that his breath gently ruffles the wisps of hair that coil near my ears. "What do you choose?"

What do I choose? I've asked myself so many times, but the choice I've made has always been with others in mind—my father and his respect, my people. I've never been forced, but guided toward a path. And I chose it because I felt like I didn't *have* any other choice, because I didn't want to let anyone down.

But looking into Griffin's gleaming eyes, I know that I can choose for myself, without worrying yet about the consequences.

I choose this moment, I think. *I choose this chance.*

My voice comes out as a whisper. "I...I choose..."

Griffin's hand rests on my cheek, his palm calloused and warm. His eyes are endless hazel like the fields at harvest-time, like comforting bread, warm from the oven.

I lean in toward his soft lips, only inches away. I don't want to think anymore. I don't want to care.

I choose Griffin.

His eyes close, and he leans in toward me.

And then I realize with horror that I've betrayed him. The only person who ever truly asked me what I wanted. I can't let him get hurt like this.

I turn my head to the side and look down. His lips stop near my cheek, and his eyes flutter open, confused. "I'm sorry," I whisper. "I'm...I'm engaged."

Griffin exhales, the breath warm against my cheek. He leans back on his karu fur, staring at his hands.

"It's not by choice," I say quickly. "I don't love him. I don't even like him. But I'm bound." There's so much I've been keeping to myself that it floods out in a horrible gush that I can't stop. "I'm the daughter of the Monarch, the heir to Ashra and her lands. That's why my life isn't my own, Griffin. I'm supposed to take over ruling the floating continents. I'm supposed to be the wick and the wax, the Phoenix's heir. I'm supposed to burn so the people have light."

He doesn't say anything at first. Then he says quietly, "When candles burn, Kali, the wick gets charred and thrown away. The wax crumbles into nothing. And then the light goes out."

"I didn't mean to keep it from you. I wanted to tell you. But after Aliyah told us about Operation Phoenix, and all the horrible things our people did... And before I fell, I found out about a rebel force moving in Burumu. I have to warn my father, and I have to stop it. I'm so sorry, Griffin. I didn't want you to think the humans up there haven't changed. I didn't want you to think I chose someone else. I only wanted to go back and fix everything."

Griffin is silent, and I know I've hurt him. "Of course you wouldn't want to tell me all that," he says quietly, and he's so giving and forgiving that my heart aches and my conscience wails at me. He looks at the waterfall, at the ripples that form on the surface of the little pool that laps against the rock. "What's his name?"

I don't want to give it voice, to make it real. But he deserves the truth. "Jonash. He's the son of the Sargon, who governs the continent of Burumu."

Griffin lies on his side with his back to me. I want to reach out to him, but I don't know how. The scars carve down his back in their crescent shapes, and I can only think how I've scarred him now, too.

"Griffin, I want to fix it," I say. "I'll go back, and I'll break off the engagement. I'll tell my father I'm alive, and I'll get everything sorted out. And then I'll come back."

"You can't," Griffin says, turning to look at me. "They can't know humans have survived down here. We know about the past, like the fallen they've tossed over the edge. The rebellion has found its way to us through them. They'd think we were part of it, and they'd hunt us down."

I shake my head. "They won't. My father isn't like that. He'll listen, I know it."

"But you promised Aliyah," he says, and the weight of the promise in his eyes burdens my own heart. "You promised you'd keep our secret."

The last of the sunlight has faded, the world around us growing dark. I listen to the rush of the waterfall. This moment is slipping from me like the water, rushing through my fingers no matter how hard I try to hold on.

"It's my father," I say quietly, lying on my fur beside Griffin. He rolls onto his side to face me, even though we can't see each other well in the dark. "He thinks I'm dead. I need to see him again, to let him know I'm all right. I... I have to go."

Griffin reaches for my hand in the darkness, lacing his fingers through mine. "I know," he whispers.

There's nothing else to say. The current has pulled the bubbling moment away from me. Whatever this was, whatever it could have been…it's past now, shining like an ancient star floating in the sky.

EIGHTEEN

THE NEXT MORNING we climb in silence. We climb
before the sun rises through the plumes of fiery orange and
red that saturate the sky. We climb through the hot mid-
day sun and the cool of early evening. We wrap around
and around the mountain, and I keep trying to think of
ways that I can be with Griffin and go home, but I keep
coming back to the same fork in the road.

I haven't known him that long, I understand that. But
there's a spark that spreads through me when I look at him.
I want to know more. I want to tell him more. I want the
fire I feel to kindle and blaze beyond stopping. I want to
see what's left when it's all ashes, whether it will rise anew
like the Phoenix, whether it will burn through to the real
core of me.

I feel like it might.

Instead, we trudge up the mountainside without even
a basilisk to distract us. We stop near a plum tree and pick

from the laden branches. The fruit is sweet and juicy, a luxurious treat after the dried jerky and berries and gamey basilisk meat. Griffin scales the tree to the very top and picks the finest plum he can find to toss down to me. It makes my heart ache.

I tell him more about the strange scene I saw between Elder Aban and the lieutenant. He doesn't patronize me the way Jonash did. He asks questions, ponders the meaning, validates my worries. "Something's not right," he says, and I see the concern for me in his face. "Shouldn't the Sargon be more capable than that?"

"He should," I say. "My father is well loved in Ulan. I can't imagine a reason for rebellion to rise, unless the Sargon isn't ruling fairly. I'll launch an inquest when I get home."

"But the rebels," he says.

"The Elders and Elite Guard would never let anything happen to me," I reassure him, but when I think of the lieutenant's face when he burned that paper... I'm not sure anything's under their control at all.

By the time the sun is setting, the air around us has grown so cold we wrap the karu cloaks tight about our shoulders. Frost dusts the ground with a glittering crystal sheen. The sun is setting, and before the world turns dark, I search the skies for airships. But there are none, and we sleep in a small crevice of rock near the summit.

The next day we reach the very top and look out over the world. Everything is miniature from here, but not as small as from Ashra. I can still make out the dragons and hazus on the plains. One of the dragons' screeches carries on the wind, the frequency of it carving through my skull like a migraine. The power is awe-inspiring.

"Try this view," Griffin says with a smile, and I turn away from the plains to look at the landscape from the other side of the mountain.

I can't breathe for a moment. In the distance, in the sky, I can make out the floating continent of Burumu. But on the ground—no trees, no plains, no marshlands. Just glimmering azure blue, as far as the eye can see.

The ocean. It's the ocean. I can see tiny white caps of foam like snow spread over top. The water is turquoise near the shore, where a thin strip of white sand snakes between waves and land. There are a couple small huts on the coast, though they're probably long since abandoned like the other dwellings we've passed through. Gulls spread out their wings and float above the sea, hovering on the salty air.

Just then the sun blazes from behind a cloud and lights the whole ocean on fire. It gleams and sparkles like the wings of the Phoenix. I've never seen anything more beautiful in my life. The illustrations in the annals could never have captured what it's truly like.

Griffin passes me a plum and we sit watching the ocean from our mountaintop. We're too high up to hear the gulls or the water. I wonder if it babbles like the stream, or rushes like a waterfall. We watch the ocean until the light fades, and even then I can still see it in my mind. I dream of standing on the shore with Griffin, searching for seashells and driftwood and slippery silver minnows.

In the morning, Griffin shakes me awake. I rub my eyes while he points upward. "Is that it?"

There's an oval shape up in the sky, heading toward us over the plains. I can't see its color, only the black shadow of its underbelly, but the way it tilts and sways, there's no doubt. It's an airship.

Adrenaline courses through my veins. The moment has come. The airship is puttering on its path to Burumu, and I have to make sure it can see me. But I frown as I watch it approach. "It's still too high up," I say. "They'll never see me."

"On it," Griffin says, and he's gathering armloads of branches and tufts of dry grass. I gather even more as he strikes his flint and blows gently on the cluster of tinder in his hand. It smokes, the thin trail curling in the cool air.

When the fire has caught on the kindling and is spreading to the branches, Griffin opens his pouch and places the basilisk scales around the fire. He finds rocks to tilt them upward, so they reflect the firelight into the sky. "We'll make a beacon they won't miss," he says. "Hope I don't blind the pilot."

The flames are soon roaring into the sky, the basilisk scales glowing brightly with the firelight. It must look as though the mountain is on fire, I think. There's no way they can miss it. Griffin stands me beside it; it's not long before they'll fly directly overhead.

"I have to get out of sight," he says, and that's when his words bring me out of the frenzy of building the beacon. This is it. Our final moment together. I'm not ready, but I don't think I ever could be.

"I'm sorry," I say. "And I'm grateful."

Griffin reaches around his neck and unties the cord of seashells. He wraps them around my neck, and I breathe in the warmth of him as his floppy brown hair tickles my cheek. He ties the necklace gently, his hands resting on my shoulders for a moment. Then his hands drop, and his eyes gleam like the garnet gem on my dagger.

My dagger. I move to unlace the sheath, but he shakes his head. "Tell them you found it," he says. "Tell them you found the karu fur and the dagger on the remains of a fallen monster hunter from a hundred years ago."

I want to give him something, too, but I have nothing. In desperation, I reach into my pocket and find I still have the piece of flint I'd attached to my flimsy wooden spear. It's all I have to give, and I place it in the palm of his hand, folding his fingers over it.

"What's this?" he says.

"A spark," I say, and he smiles. I want to kiss him more than I've wanted anything before, to rest my lips on his and hear my heart break. But it wouldn't be fair of me to do that to him, and I wonder if he's thinking the same, because he doesn't lean in. Instead he puts the flint in his pouch and takes my right hand in his. His lips press against the back of my hand, and I think how soft and smooth they are when the rest of him is calloused and strong.

"Goodbye," he says, his eyes meeting mine. "May happiness follow you."

I blink back my tears. I'm the wick and the wax, I think. I'll burn for you, so you don't have to. This memory will keep me alive when I'm crumbling to nothing. I don't want him to burn with me. I want this to hurt as little as possible. "And you."

The airship putters and snorts, and Griffin slips into hiding in a fracture under the rock ledge where we sat and watched the ocean.

I have to wait several minutes until the airship is close enough. I throw more logs on the fire and wave my arms wildly. The mountain summit is bare and pale brown, with a dusting of crystal-white frost. The deep scarlet fabric of my dress will surely stand out as much as the flames on the fire.

I wave until my arms ache, until my eyes blur with tears and I can barely see the airship in the sky. I jump up and down and shout, and I race around the fire in a circle, not knowing if any of it will make a difference.

But then I see the airship getting larger and turning toward me. It's descending. They've seen me. They're coming.

I cry and laugh as I wave wildly at the oncoming ship. I'm heartbroken and elated, lost and found. I will see my father again. They'll know I'm alive. Elisha will be waiting on the landing pitch with Elder Aban and Father, and there'll be feasting and celebrations and the music of the goat-string harps and the whittled wooden flutes. I'll warn my father of the rebellion and stop it in its tracks.

The airship moves slowly, and still I keep waving and jumping. I let the fire start to die down, because it's served its purpose. Griffin will collect the basilisk scales when I'm gone.

I should've kissed him. I should've had the courage. Why did I give up the chance? But it's too late to think about that now. I have to move forward, as painful as it is.

Two panels open along the sides of the airship, almost the length of its belly. Metal pipes slide out and into place with a sound like a hundred gears catching against each other. I wonder if it's landing gear. I'm not sure quite how they'll land on the summit with the fire roaring away. I guess I'd assumed they'd put down a rope ladder.

The pipes wail and spin, clicking and whirring as they zoom in on the mountain top.

When I went on the Rending Anniversary tour with my father, we rode on an airship, but I don't remember it ever using landing gear quite like that. Why on the sides, and not on the bottom?

And then I hear Griffin's frantic voice. "Kali! Kali! Get away!"

Get away? I don't dare look at him and give away his hiding place, but something's not right.

The airship's nearly stopped in the air, swaying like a balloon as the pipes whir and home in on me. They're hollow inside.

"Kali!" he shouts again, slipping out from under the rock. He's on the summit, racing toward me.

Panic catches in my throat. They'll see him.

"Griffin, no!" His karu fur is swinging around his neck as he bolts toward me. We collide and he shoves me to the ground.

The metal pipes on the airship fire rounds of ammunition at the place where I stood. One of the bullets ricochets into the fire, and the branches snap and collapse, exploding with flame.

I look over Griffin's shoulders at the bullet-ridden ground, then at the airship. It hovers there, its metal pipes slowly turning toward our new location.

"Come on," Griffin says, pulling us to our feet.

The airship is low enough now that I can see into the row of windows that runs along the perimeter. I can see the wide eyes of soldiers from the Elite Guard as they stare at us. Shouldn't they have returned to Burumu weeks ago?

And there at the helm, a familiar face looks back at me,

his blue eyes wild and panicked as he hunches next to the pilot.

Jonash?

"Jonash!" I call out, waving my arms. He has to recognize me now. But Griffin grabs my arm and pulls me away as another round of bullets drum against the summit, landing a step behind us as we run.

I follow Griffin, my thoughts reeling. None of this makes sense. Jonash saw it was me—I could tell from his expression. If he was close enough for me to see him, then he would definitely recognize me. Maybe he's afraid of Griffin, but that wouldn't be any reason to fire on us.

The airship putters around the mountain, following us like a wobbling bubble that we can't escape. We're trapped on the mountaintop; every time we wind down, the airship lowers to our height and fires. If we wait, it putters around to the other side where there's no shelter. If we can get to the cave with the waterfall, perhaps we can hide behind it, but it's a full day's walk down the mountain, hours and hours below.

We spiral as quickly as we can, every breath burning in my chest. We stumble across a surprised basilisk, which startles and dashes into a fissure in the rock face. I'm scanning the landscape for a place to hide, but I can't find one.

Then the airship is in front of us, and a second pair of metal pipes clank into place behind the first two. We dash out of the way, but the ammunition explodes behind us. I hear Griffin cry out as I go flying through the air. It feels like I've fallen off Ashra again, like I'm tumbling toward the earth. The cliff of the mountain races away below me, and there's nothing but underbrush and green and the earth far below.

I hear Griffin shout, "Kali!"

And I feel the impact as my body collides with the jagged bushes that cling to the side of the mountain.

And then my eyes close, and the world goes black.

NINETEEN

THE WORLD IS too bright when I try to open my eyes. There's a sound like rushing wind, but I don't feel cold. It takes a while for things to come into focus—the sunshine is bright in the room, the walls whitewashed and clean. I turn my head and hear the whistling of fabric against my hair. I'm in a bed, covered with patchwork blankets. White bandages are looped around my right arm up to my elbow and around my head. I'm not in my red dress now, but a simple white linen shift.

My head throbs as I try to remember what happened. Then it floods back, hitting me with the force of a tome dropping on my skull. The airship—Jonash staring at me with wide, panicked eyes. The ship firing on me. *Firing.* Tumbling over the mountainside into the prickly branches, and darkness after that.

I try to speak, but it comes out as an incoherent moan.

I hear a chair push back and someone stumbles in the

corner of the room. Warm, calloused fingers slip through mine. "Kali," Griffin says. "I'm here."

"Where are we?" I blink a few more times, the room coming into clearer focus. There's an arched doorway and a window; the breeze is pleasant and salty and warm.

"The ocean," he says.

The ocean? "What's that sound?" The rushing rises and falls, but the wind is steady, so it can't be the same.

"It's the waves," he says. "The waves on the shore. Remember when we saw the huts on the shore from the mountain? We're safe for now. Don't worry."

"I can't remember what happened," I say. "After I fell into the bushes."

"They thought you were dead and just came after me," Griffin says. "So I led them away from you and managed to fool them into thinking I was dead, too. When the airship was gone, I managed to reach you and bring you down the mountain."

He's saved me again. He probably came here remembering the huts, thinking I was in no condition to cross the marshlands back to the haven.

"Ashes," I say. "My head feels like a stone wall collapsed on top of me."

Griffin laughs gently and reaches to smooth my hair behind my ear. "You'll be okay."

"She's awake," says a voice I don't know, and there's a new person there, blocking the light streaming in from the doorway.

He's tall and slender, dressed in cropped brown furs and leather. There's a medium-sized dagger hanging at his hip and a shorter one beside it, but the double sheath is made of braided palm branches instead of leather. His hair is black and cut short on his head. He wears one of the brown furs as a cape, the way Griffin and I wear the karu cloaks—his is sealskin, Griffin later tells me, a brown creature from the ocean. And the man's ear is pierced with wire, attached to a dangling spiral of iridescent shell.

He reaches his hand out to me, and I take it. His fingers are much thinner than Griffin's, but also calloused. His arms are less muscled and tanned, but there's a strength to him that I can feel in his hands. He's worked hard to stay alive—it shows in his chestnut eyes.

"Welcome, Kallima," he says. "My name is Tashiltu, but you can call me Tash. And I'm glad to see you feeling better."

"Thank you," I say, but I'm thinking what a strange name he has. It sounds a bit like the names we have on Ashra, inspired by the words associated with the Phoenix. But I've never heard a name quite like it.

"Kali," Griffin says. "Tash is the one who dressed your wounds. He's one of five survivors here. Five! Living in one place!" His eyes are gleaming. It's small, but this is one of the rumored villages that he'd hoped existed. This is a place of survival.

Tash nods. "We're not as brave as this monster hunter here. We've survived by hiding, mostly. We fish, and we hide from the airships. There aren't many monsters in this area except Leviathans, and they don't often come this close to the shore."

"You do get behemoths, though?" Griffin asks.

Tash nods. "It's hard to find a landscape that doesn't. But the barren shoreline makes them easy to spot."

Something he's said sluggishly makes its way through my

aching brain. "You...hide from the airships?" I say. "Are you fallen? From Burumu?"

"Ah," Tash says, exchanging glances with Griffin. "We can talk about it when you're feeling better."

I sit up, and immediately wish I hadn't. The room spins, and I have to lie back down. Griffin reaches for my arm with concern. "No," I say. "Tell me everything. Please."

Griffin nods at Tash, who takes a deep breath.

"I'm not fallen," he says. "I'm Benu."

My thoughts swim. Benu. Where have I heard that before? Then I remember—Aliyah's story of Operation Phoenix. "The Benu were the original people on the floating continents," I say. "But they were all killed three hundred years ago."

Tash shakes his head. "Most were," he says. "We've survived in secret, just handfuls of us."

"What? But..."

"Show her, Tash," Griffin says.

Tash nods, and turns around. He slips his seal fur to the side, and my aching head can barely understand what I'm seeing.

Wings. Wings that burn with red-and-orange flame that somehow don't ignite anything they touch. The plumes are folded in tightly from shoulder to hip, with broad spikes of bone at the tops, like a cross between dragon and bird. They look like...like the wings on the Phoenix statue.

The seal fur swings in front of them again, and Tash turns around.

"I don't understand," I say.

"They say we are half monster, descendants of the Phoenix over thousands of years. And since Operation Phoenix, the Elite Guard of the floating lands have hunted us down," Tash says. "That's why we hide from the airships. There are Benu surviving everywhere, even on the floating continents."

"That's impossible," I blurt, trying to sit up again. Griffin reaches out a worried hand to support my back. The room spins a little, but only for a moment. "I would've seen people with fiery wings."

Tash shakes his head. "The Elite Guard catch them when they're born," he says. "If they have wings, they rip them out. And if the parents can't keep the secret, then the children are taken."

"Taken?" It gets more ludicrous by the minute. And yet, there's a horror to it that sinks into my skin. Is it true? Could it be? "Tash, with all respect, I'm the daughter of the Monarch. We'd notice if babies started disappearing, or were born with flaming wings."

"Kali, listen to him," Griffin urges gently. I look into his hazel eyes as they plead with me. He trusts Tash. There must be truth to it, but I can't understand.

Tash sits at the foot of the bed. "Let me explain," he says. "The population on the floating continents is small, yes? And when a baby's born, a representative of the Elders always comes to present a gift."

I nod. They bring a customary red feather as a sign of the Phoenix's blessing. Mine was the good-luck charm I told Griffin about, the plume that swirled over the edge of the outcrop long ago.

"But what they're really doing is checking the baby for Benu heritage. If one of the parents is already tagged and on file, they know what's coming. But sometimes even the mother or father doesn't know the origin of the scars on their back from the ripped-out wings. Their parents never told them, and so they're alarmed when their baby has them."

The midwives are Initiates of the Elders. And it's true that sometimes, very rarely, a member of the Elite Guard will follow up on an Elder's visit to a newborn.

"There are only a handful of Benu on the continents, mostly in Burumu. And if the family refuses to cut out the wings...well, sad to say, no one bats an eye if one baby doesn't survive its infancy. And if the parents can't deal with the truth, then they are silenced, too."

I swallow, a hard lump in my throat. "The fallen," I say, and Tash nods.

"Only, the truth is starting to get around, and we've had many fallen over the last year. Things are getting worse in the outer continents."

"Tash and I have been talking," Griffin says. "We think it's related to the rebellion you told me about."

"We have contacts in Burumu," Tash says. "The unrest under the Sargon is reaching a critical mass. There isn't enough food or housing. And instead of managing things, he's riling up the population by blaming the Monarch. Some of the rebels even believe he's secretly aiding them, that he's the one who printed the papers to pass around about the true origins of the continents."

The paper the lieutenant burned. I can hardly speak. "But why? Why would he do this?"

"Using the timing to his advantage," Griffin suggests. "To take control of Ashra. It's what a monster would do. Take a moment of weakness to use for his own gain."

"The Sargon isn't a *monster*," I say. "He's the Eye of the Phoenix that watches over us. It's always been that way. And I'm marrying his son, for ash's sake. He's already secured the Eternal Flame through our betrothal." Griffin's face blazes red.

"But he didn't know for sure until your engagement was announced," Tash says. "And now that you've fallen, he's back to his original plan, I imagine. This has been building for years, Kallima. It's just coming to a boil after all this time."

Then Jonash and I have been nothing but pawns in a dangerous game of politics. How dare the Sargon use us like this to his own gain? But Jonash...he fired on me. A chill swirls around me as I start to wonder. Could he be in on it, too? Was he not ignorant when I asked him, but merely pretending to be?

And my heart breaks for the children and the parents thrown over the edge of the continent, without my father's knowledge, or mine. Betrayed because their child was born with wings and they refused to rip them out.

Outside, the waves wash against the shore in their soothing rhythm. It's warm inside the hut, and Griffin's karu cloak hangs over the back of the chair in the corner. He turns to look at Tash, and I see the crescent scars on his back, still as deep as ever, while the hazu bite has paled to almost nothing.

And then I put my hand to my mouth as the realization hits me.

The warm bread his mother used to bake. The toddler found crying in the fields below Ashra. The scars on his back.

"Griffin," I breathe. "It was you. You were the child in Ulan who fell off the edge fourteen years ago." The one whose mother jumped to her death with grief—or, perhaps, was pushed when she threatened the truth.

"Yes," Tash nods, as Griffin's eyes gleam with the weight of the realization. He and Tash have already figured this out while I was resting. "The scars on his back are those of the wings ripped out in infancy. He's a fallen, and he's Benu, from the royal lineage of the Phoenix herself."

"But the barrier—your mother. She must be alive somewhere!"

"It's possible," Griffin says, but his eyes show he doesn't believe it. "It was fourteen years ago. Even if she survived a while, she would've lacked the skills to fight monsters. She's likely long gone by now."

Did Griffin tumble from Ashra's edge? Was he thrown? I can't be sure anymore, but I do know this—Griffin is from the floating continents. He's from Ulan. He was born to my world, and he is Benu, descendant of the Phoenix.

And he's one of the rightful heirs to the floating lands.

"Is that why the Elite Guard fired on us?" I ask.

"Their lieutenant is probably worried you've found out the truth," Tash says, tapping his finger thoughtfully against his cheek. The motion makes his earring spiral and sway. "And when they saw Griffin with you, wing scars or not, they'd know you've seen the survivors."

My head throbs with confusion. "But they don't know humans are alive down here."

"They know the fallen are here," he says, "and they know somehow they're getting allies into Burumu and Nartu. They're frightened, because the humans and Benu are forming an alliance to confront the Monarch, and somehow dropping them off the continents isn't stopping the rebellion or the word from getting around. The rebels are planning to overtake the Monarch to stop the atrocities against the Benu and our allies."

"That can't be right," I say. "If my father knew, he'd stop it immediately. He wouldn't tolerate treason from the Sargon, and he'd certainly never stand for children being victimized like this. If he knew of survivors struggling down here, he'd welcome them to the floating continents."

"Your father is the one who ordered the rebels thrown off Burumu," Tash says. "And one of his duties is to oversee the register of Benu children."

"My father would never do that," I whisper, but I'm not sure what to believe anymore. I fall back to the bed, my head spinning.

"It's too much," Tash says. "I'll see if Lilia can bring something for her."

"I'll stay here," Griffin says, wrapping his warm hands around mine.

Tash smiles. "You always do," he says, and then he's gone, the sunlight streaming in from the doorway where he stood.

"Griffin, it's not true," I tell him. "My father wouldn't do that."

Griffin holds my hand tightly. "I believe you."

It's horrible that there was a massacre. It's horrible that those who are finding out the truth are being thrown over the sides of the continent like unwanted garbage. But I can't understand exactly why this is all causing such unrest. Should we be ashamed of a massacre from three hundred years ago? Yes. But we aren't the same generation who made that decision. Surely we can acknowledge it and try to do better. Why would the Elite Guard rip out wings and throw people over the edge and incite anger?

I switch gears in my mind, access my regal tutelage to decipher the politics of it. Conditions on Burumu must be terrible. Food and housing shortages, long work hours in the mines and industries. And the Sargon, fearing for his own family and seeing an opportunity to advance, pins the blame on the Monarch. The rest—the Benu, the concealed shame of our origins on the island, the truth—is oil spilled on a flame, igniting in a blaze that will destroy thousands.

It makes sense, unfortunately. How could we have not seen it coming? We must stop it before it's too late. But how?

"I have to get back," I tell Griffin. "I have to talk to my father."

He nods. "Then we'll get you back. Whatever it takes. I promise."

Lilia brings fish soup a while later, her curly red hair framing her shy face. She curtsies as she come in and helps me drink the pale broth as she talks about her childhood in Burumu. When she turns to put the bowl down, I see the scars on her back, the same as Griffin's.

"My parents managed to keep the origin of my scars a secret, even from me," she tells me. "They were too afraid to share the truth and put the watchful eye of the Elite Guard on me. But I met another girl with the same scars, and her parents had told her the truth. We heard there were others with more knowledge about who we really were, about the Benu and their history. I wanted to know more about where I'd come from. But there was a raid by the Elite Guard that night, and we were caught and thrown over the edge."

"I'm so sorry," I say. "If my father had known, he never would have allowed it. We would've come for you."

She smiles, but I can't tell if she believes me.

"And the other girl lives here, too?" I ask.

She shakes her head. "A Leviathan attacked her fishing boat a year ago," she says, her eyes misting with tears.

I don't know what to say, so I apologize over and over, and she tells me it's all right.

When she leaves, Griffin helps me stand and we walk slowly along the shore of the ocean together. It isn't the way I'd imagined seeing it, surrounded by sadness and confusion and the embers of rebellion. But I'm here, and Griffin's here, and I never dreamed I'd see it in any way except the faded red–brown ink of the annals.

The sand is almost white, and it sinks beneath my feet like warm, soft moss. The grains stick to my soles, and they're sharp, but pleasantly so. It's not like the sand around Lake Agur, which is dark and packed and fine. I kneel and scoop a handful of it; some of the grains are tiny fragments of shells or colored glass. They're like collected shards of memory, millions of forgotten stories laid out against the turquoise of the lapping water.

Griffin and I dip our toes in the cool foam of the waves as they rush up to the shore and soak into the sand before they retreat. Tangles of seaweed are tugged back and forth by the waves, and tiny mussels lie scattered in their dark brown shells. I pick one up and toss it as far into the ocean as I can. It disappears into the water with a slurp.

Above us the gulls call to one another, dipping and diving on the warm salty wind. One of them dives down to catch a fish, but a small Leviathan arches into the air and catches it, disappearing under the surface of the water with a splash of white foam. I shudder, thinking of the Dark Leviathan who almost ate us.

Beauty and danger go hand in hand on this earth. And

yet there's freedom here, a peacefulness in my soul. I'm still with Griffin, and he's with me.

I slide my fingers into his palm and lean my shoulder against his.

"I'm going to make everything right," I say. "And when it's done, I want to come back here with you and see the ocean again, with only gladness in my heart."

Griffin says nothing, but his fingers squeeze mine more tightly, the beads and lacing on his forearm pressing against my skin.

TWENTY

WE SPEND A few more days recovering in the tiny fishing village of winged and de-winged Benu. It's getting less unnerving to see the flaming feathers peeking out from under their seal-fur cloaks. Tashiltu and I have been talking about how to get back to the floating continents, although he's not as supportive of my plan to get home.

"Things are tense there," he says. "If the Elite Guard fired on you, you can be sure your return won't be welcomed with open arms."

"I just need to get to my father," I insist. "It has to be a misunderstanding. The Elite Guard has always protected my family."

"We're going to find a way, no matter what," Griffin says. "So it'll save us a lot of time if you could just help us."

Tash sighs, rubbing his forehead. Then he nods. "Pax and I can fly you two up to the airship near the coast of

Burumu, and from there you must make your way to our allies. But it will be up to you to get to Ashra safely."

"Thank you," I say, knowing how much they're risking to take us.

"There have been too many airships lately," he warns. "Our allies have reported that new recruits are flooding in to the Elite Guard to deal with the rebellion. They're growing their numbers for what I only hope isn't a full-scale civil war."

"Whatever it is, I'll stop it in its tracks," I promise.

We must fly up to Burumu during the day, because at night the Benu's wings glow and spark with endless flame. I have to leave my red dress behind because it's too easy to recognize. Lilia has given me a plain olive jerkin and the cream-colored leggings she was wearing when she was thrown from the continent. I have to leave my laced leather boots behind, too—they'd raise suspicion—so I wear a pair of flat sandals that Tash has woven from dried palm branches. I tie Griffin's shell necklace around my neck, and Lilia cuts my hair short with my dagger. Griffin, too, is given clothes from Burumu—a plain leather jerkin, black leggings and boots. He's allowed to keep his bow and arrows—hunting is common on the floating islands—and a row of daggers fastened under the hem of his jerkin. We must go unnoticed through the crowds, not only to prevent mass panic, but also to avoid any extremists who might use the opportunity to hold me hostage.

A few weeks ago I never would've dreamed the people of the floating lands were capable of these things. The whole world has changed around me, or perhaps I am the one who sees it with new eyes.

Pax and Tash wait indoors with the rest of us until another Benu waiting on the mountaintop spots an airship puttering toward Ashra. Once it's near the mountain range, we walk onto the shore. Burumu floats high above, casting its shadow on the ocean.

Tash and Pax have tied a rope in an X across their chests, and now they wrap the cords around our waists, as well. They don't think their arms will fail, but if they falter mid-air, the ropes will stop us from falling to our deaths.

I wrap my arms around Tash's neck, and Griffin wraps his around Pax's. Lilia stands at the edge of the tiny village, her eyes bright and worried. She knows their village could be in jeopardy if we're caught, but she also knows I've promised to save them from the threat of the Elite Guard.

Tash loosens his seal cloak to the shore, his wings spreading out behind him like a wildfire. He flaps, and the salty ocean air wafts into my lungs. One flutter, and another, and slowly my feet lift from the ground. I hang on to him with all my strength.

It's like falling upside down—now the floating islands are the earth I once feared. Burumu is so far above that I can't imagine how long it will take us to get there, or if Tash's wings will hold out. He tries not to speak; it's taking all his energy to fly us upward. I watch our shadows as they drift over the ocean, as the village huts and Benu living there become as small as red bees buzzing around clusters of flowers. There's a dark, curling shape threading through the ocean waves below—the giant loops of a Dark Leviathan prowling the waters.

Tash's forehead is dripping with sweat. I reach for the flask around his neck and tip the water into his mouth, the rope keeping us tightly linked. We've passed the summit of the mountain range now, and I can see across to the plains and marshlands on the other side. The shadow of Burumu still seems so far up, but the airship is nearly above us.

There's nowhere to hide in the sky, but the layer of clouds is thick, and the hope is that no one will see us out the narrow airship windows. Pax and Tash both turn so only their wings face the airship, and we hover far below its path, trying to imitate hazu and dragons and other sky beasts that might be overlooked.

When the airship is directly above, the Benu beat their wings furiously. We rise up with a speed and urgency that our lives depend on. The plum balloon of the airship draws nearer and nearer, and finally we're hovering just below the belly of the wobbling vessel. Tash flaps carefully as I take another length of rope and thread it through the wooden braces on the bottom of the airship. I tie the knot with trembling fingers, then tie the other end around myself. Tash unties the rope that attaches us together, and with his help I carefully slide onto the wooden railing, the soft fabric of the airship fluttering in the wind above us. The railing is like a bench in the sky as I cling to it, the ocean sparkling far below me. I can't even make out the shadows of the trolling Leviathans from here.

Beside us, Griffin and Pax have done the same at the other railing. The plan is to wait for the landing gear to descend, which the pilot lowers as he reaches the continent's edge. Then we'll have to drop down from our ropes and hope for a safe landing opportunity before the ship reaches the centralized city of Burumu. Usually the airship flies over a lake, which is our best bet, but sometimes they circle across the fields, and that will be a bumpier landing.

Tash pulls a bag over his shoulder and passes it to me. He flies beside me for a minute, his face full of concern. "Be safe, Kallima," he says. "Remember that the barrier will catch you if you fall from Burumu. We'll keep watch for the lights above the water. Jump if you need to save your life."

"Thank you for everything, Tash. But I'm afraid you won't see me again until I've stopped this war from happening."

He smiles, and then he folds his wings behind himself, dropping so rapidly through the sky that my stomach knots just watching him. A moment later his wings spread out and he glides across the skies above the ocean, looking every bit like another circling monster. A moment later Pax is by his side, and then it's just Griffin and me on our tiny trapeze in the sky, waiting for the airship to float us to Burumu.

It's another hour of lifting upward and bumping forward until the edge of Burumu comes into view. A tiny azure eye glitters among the emerald grass, and I realize we're coming up over the lake. I look at Griffin, who nods, holding tightly to the rope as we wait for our chance.

Slowly we putter over the lake. The landing gear whirs and clicks into place, our tiny benches lowering toward the water. It's smaller than Lake Agur, but it's a softer landing than the fields. Griffin holds up three fingers, then two, then one. I fight every instinct flaring in my body and climb down from the wooden brace, swaying from the rope I've tied around it. We lower ourselves in unison, unsure if our body weight will tip the unstable airship and alert the crew on board. We move carefully, but we're nearly past the small lake, and we'll miss our chance if we don't descend a little faster.

I reach the end of the rope and wish immediately we'd brought a longer one. It's still quite a drop from here, my legs dangling over the crystal waters teeming with tiny fish. Griffin looks at me, but I can't hear him over the choppy wind.

Be strong, I think to myself. *You've survived chimeras, Dream Catchers and hazus. You've bested karus, Leviathans and basilisks. You've fallen from the edge of the world to another, and it was full of brilliance. What's one more fall?*

I look at Griffin, my jaw set, my chin high.

I let go of the rope.

The wind rushes in my ears, and it snaps back the memory of falling from Ashra. But this fall only lasts fifteen seconds, and then a foam of bubbles blasts into my ears and nose and the world turns liquid blue. A moment later Griffin shoots into the water across from me, surrounded by bubbling foam. We spread our arms and kick our way to the glittering surface.

I gasp in the cool air as Griffin surfaces beside me, and we swim toward the rocky shore. The stones slip as my sandaled feet crunch against them, and I collapse on the shore, completely drenched. The air is cold as it whips through my wet hair. The tiny hairs on my arms stand on edge.

Griffin is still panting from the effort, which surprises me. I've seen him run and tackle monsters and not even break a sweat. "Are you all right?"

He puts a hand on his forehead. "I feel dizzy," he says. "Like I can't get enough air."

The cool sky breeze presses against us, and I realize the problem. "It's the altitude," I say. "You're not used to it."

"I'll be okay," he huffs. "Just...just a minute." He sways a little as he walks toward the edge of the forest by the lake.

I look down at the bag Tash gave me and pull open the flap. Inside are directions to the allies' house and a patched lavender cloak. I unfold the wrinkled fabric and fit it around my shoulders, tying the strings in a bow. The hems are puckered and ripped, smooth sealskin sewn over the moth-eaten holes and tears.

I hear Griffin retching into the bushes, and I whirl around, the cloak twirling in a circle around me. "Hey." I touch his back gently until he's finished. "Do you need to sit down?"

He tries feebly to laugh it off. "Nah," he pants. "Never felt better. Although…let's get to the allies. The sooner I can lie down, the better."

But he takes another step and falters, and I convince him to rest for a moment before we go on.

I pull my knees up to my chin and study the directions Tash has given us, and then I slip them into the bag and stare across the water's surface. It glitters in the sunlight, but it's nothing like the sight of the ocean spread out as far as I could see. It was as if the whole horizon had drowned in the rich, deep waters, like they had no end.

After a few minutes, Griffin forces himself up. "We don't have time," he says, his voice faint. "Let's get going."

"Are you sure?" But a little color has returned to his face, and he looks determined. It reminds me of all the times I was stubborn on the earth, when he knew I wasn't capable, but he let me do things anyway. I nod, and we start down the path toward the city.

Burumu is the second largest of the floating continents. Nartu and the Floating Isles aren't even half the size, and the fragments are far too small or inhospitable for anyone to live on. But even as the second largest island, Burumu was only a piece torn from Ashra's side long ago. And so the population is forced into a very dense city surrounded by the small lake and forest. There are a handful of farms, whose harvest is supplemented by Ashra's crops, the iron mills, and the caves and mines. They have to be careful not to mine too deeply, or they'll go right through the bottom of the continent. So far we still have resources, but we know they're limited. So we try to use renewable ones as much as possible, which is why I'm stunned that the airships have been equipped with metal pipes and ammunition. How can we afford the use of iron as weapons? How far has the Sargon let things get out of hand?

The pathway is short, and we soon arrive at Burumu's towering city. It gleams in the low afternoon sun. The buildings are pressed together and several stories high, each housing several families. To compensate for the claustrophobic feel of the city, most of the buildings are painted in vibrant reds and oranges, like the wings of the Phoenix. Others are blue like the lake, and most are made of wood siding, a resource we can regrow, but one that's dangerous kindling waiting to spark. The city also has something Ulan does not—lampposts, set at intervals down the street. Most of them are painted crimson poles, with a lantern at the top and candles made of beeswax and goat's milk. The lanterns have swirling patterns of plumes and stars cut into them that remind me of Elisha's lantern, but the cutouts are much larger to keep the streets well lit at night.

I lift the cloak's hood over my face and keep my eyes downcast as much as possible as Griffin and I navigate the narrow, busy streets. There's so much noise here in Burumu. Everything feels cramped and uneasy. People are shouting in alleyways while merchants shove the first of the summer plums and peaches in our faces. A vendor calls about his honeyed ale as we turn the corner to a quieter street, heading for the neighborhood Tash has instructed us to find.

When we arrive, the house looks like all the others. It's four stories tall and painted a vibrant orange, with tiny red plumes running in a border along the base of the wall. I look at Griffin, and he nods. I reach a nervous hand out and rap against the planks of the door.

The voices inside go quiet. I wait a moment, then knock again.

The door creaks open and I look down, frightened to be identified if we have the wrong address. A slender man steps out, his hands on his hips and a golden necklace sparkling against his dark skin.

His voice is gruff. "Can I help you?"

"We're looking for friends of Tashiltu," Griffin says quietly.

The man says nothing, but looks up and down the street before stepping away from the door. "Welcome," he says then, and we step into the tiny room as he closes the door behind us.

The curtains are drawn over the windows, and slowly our eyes adjust to the light. And that's when I see the black-haired, olive-skinned girl at the table, a map laid out in front of her.

Her eyes meet mine, and despite my cloak and cropped hair, there's no mistake that she knows me, or that I know her.

"Elisha," I breathe, and her eyes fill with tears as she stumbles over the bench and into my arms.

TWENTY-ONE

I HOLD MY best friend tightly as the tears blur in both of our eyes.

"I thought you were dead," she whispers.

"I thought I'd never see you again," I answer, and for a moment everything else is forgotten. I can't believe she's here, and we're together again.

She leans back to look at me, her arms still grasping mine. Her eyes are wide and confused, like she's looking at a ghost. She speaks, her voice barely above a whisper. "How? How did you come back?"

Where to start? "There's a barrier," I explain. "To save those who fall off the edge. It broke my fall."

"They've told me about the barrier," she says, looking at the man who opened the door for us.

"I'm Aksel," the man tells us, while the others put water and food on the table. Griffin sits down shakily, his head in his hands.

"This is Griffin," I say. "He's the one who saved me on the surface."

"A fallen?" Elisha asks. How does she know about the fallen? And why is she here?

"He's the one from Ulan, Elisha. He's the child that fell when we were kids."

Her eyes turn round and wide, staring at him with disbelief. "But…"

"Now he's a monster hunter on earth. And he…he saved me." I wonder if Elisha hears the tenderness in my voice. Self-conscious, suddenly, I feel the heat rise to my cheeks as I turn to Aksel. "Can you help him? He's having some kind of reaction to being on Burumu."

"Altitude sickness," Aksel says. "Come with me. You can lie down in the back." He leads him away, and from the other room I hear him add, "We owe you a great debt for saving the heir."

They know, then. Even with my hair cut and the cloak over my face, they recognized me. I knew from the way he looked at me outside the door.

"I don't understand," I say to Elisha. "Why are you here in Burumu?"

"To find you," she says, and she pulls me over to the table where I gulp down a glass of water. "At least, I held out hope. So much has happened since you've been gone."

"Then…you thought it was possible I survived?"

"With the monsters, I…I didn't think…"

I grab her hands with urgency. "My father. Does he think I'm dead? Is he looking for me?"

"I don't think he could come to terms with it," she said. "He's in denial."

"Please, Elisha. Tell me everything."

She nods. "That night, when you fell off the edge, Jonash just about lost his mind. He was shouting about how you'd tried to throw him over the side, but that you'd fallen instead, and how he couldn't save you. He was weeping and ranting, and I could barely understand him."

"What? I never tried to throw him over the side. He was walking too close to the edge. I ran to save him."

"I knew you didn't like him much, but as if you would do something horrible like that. It was ridiculous. I tried to calm him down. He said how you accused him of some kind of conspiracy with Elder Aban and the lieutenant. I was confused, because you had been talking about it, but not about him being involved."

Is that why he had fired on me from the airship? Did he really believe I was a threat? That seemed too far-fetched to be true.

"Your father didn't believe it, either," Elisha said. "He accused Jonash of conspiring against you, but when Jonash started sobbing in the audience hall I think the Monarch didn't know what to believe. He sent out airships to search, but no one believed you could have survived the fall. It was... It was a mission to recover your body. But it was no use, because the airships can't fly that low."

I shiver to think of my father ordering a search for my body. I long to tell him I'm alive, and that will be the first thing I'll do.

"Jonash headed the search, but after a week, the efforts were given up. There was so little they could see from up here. Jonash came back to Burumu, and then the Sargon accused the Monarch of sabotaging the engagement by attempted assassination of his son."

I can't keep my voice down. "What? That's absurd!"

Elisha nods. "The Sargon used the news to stir up more unrest in Burumu. It was propaganda against the Monarch, that he had found a way to break the engagement and keep control of Ashra and her lands by assassinating Jonash. That you fell was a tragic mistake. The lieutenant, who had failed to protect you, resigned, and then he disappeared. Jonash became the leader of the Elite Guard. None of it sounded right to me. I started to look into what you'd been talking about that night, about the meeting with Aban and the lieutenant. And my search led me here to Burumu. I've been staying with my uncle and trying to piece together the truth. And then I found Aksel and the rebels."

I've returned to a complete political mess, and the prospect of war is closer than we'd thought. Aksel returns from the back room without Griffin and sits at the table with us.

"I imagine your friend has been filling you in," he says. "What I believe happened to you is that you uncovered a truth the Elite Guard didn't want you to know, and that is why Jonash pushed you."

"Pushed me?" I shake my head, remembering that night. "No. He was walking too close to the edge. He'd only just learned to see the crystal edge of the rock bed, and he was dangerously close. But my weight threw us off balance, and then…"

"Kallima," Aksel says, putting his hands on the table as he leans in. "Jonash is the son of the Sargon. And Burumu was fractured from the side of Ashra three hundred years ago. Do you not think we have the same glittering crystal edge around our continent that our prince can easily recognize?"

My face crumples in confusion. "I don't understand."

"You were set up. Jonash meant for you to fall."

My heart races. I think of how pathetic his attempts were to save me that night, threading my hands through the useless tufts of grass. I remember him falling belly-down to save himself at my expense. And I remember Jonash's face as he ordered the airship to fire. Did he... Did he really intend to throw me off the continent? Did he intend for me to die?

Elisha's gentle hand presses against my back. "The Elite Guard have strict orders to get rid of anyone who finds out the truth about Operation Phoenix or the Benu. We think Jonash panicked. He had his orders, but he didn't know if they applied to his fiancée. I think that's why he was try-ing to persuade you not to talk about what you'd seen. And when you were adamant..."

"But he doesn't know about the barrier," Aksel says. "He's brainless, that boy. He only acts to please his father, the Sargon. And the Sargon wants to control the lands of Ashra, if not by his son's marriage, then by an uprising and civil war." Tash and Griffin were right, then. That's ex-actly what's happening.

I can't believe it. I was pushed. I was meant to die. And by the same man that I tried to respect and love, that Griffin and I held back for because we felt such guilt and remorse.

"These secrets only have power in the dark," Elisha says. "If everyone knows about the Benu and the genocide that occurred, then we don't have to fear anymore. The Phoenix has listened to our prayers for three hundred years. Even if the Benu are half monster, why should we fear them?"

"The Sargon is the real enemy here," Aksel says. "He's using the rebels and the Monarch against each other. The rebels are a decoy to keep the Monarch distracted and to provoke him to war. Between new recruits and reinstated

members, the Elite Guard has doubled in size this past
month. Grief has pushed the Monarch past reasonable reaction."

"I have to get to my father, then, and warn him not to
bite," I say. "The Elite Guard's loyalty should be to him,
not to the Sargon. If they see I'm alive..."

Aksel nods. "This was our hope," he says, "but we had
no way to be sure we'd find you, or that you'd survived.
But now you're here, we can stop all this."

Another rebel puts a plate of honeyed chicken in front
of us as I nod my gratitude.

"There's an airship for Ashra in the morning," Elisha
says. "I'll take you back with me."

"Won't I be recognized?"

"We'll do our best," she says. "Just wear that cloak and
look down."

"Everyone thinks you're dead," Aksel says, "and people
see what they want to see." It's true, I think. So many were
witness to the massacre three hundred years ago, but they
chose to look away. Taking over the continent saved the
human race. They were willing to forget the dark price it
cost, the blemish staining our history.

"Remember," Aksel continues, "the Sargon is using the
rebellion against the Monarch. We can't be sure what you'll
find on Ashra, but you can be certain that your father is
in danger."

"Thank you for your help," I tell him. "I will get there,
and I will stop all of this."

Aksel nods. "I'll look into acquiring tickets for the airship," he says, and excuses himself to talk to the others.
I watch him leave, and then I catch Elisha staring at me.

"What?" I say, meeting her amused eyes.

"You're different," she says, resting her head on her hand, her elbow propped on the table. "You used to have this look in your eyes, like you were far away. Like you were dreaming. But now...you look like you've woken up."

"I missed you," I say, and I hug my dearest friend close.

After we eat I check on Griffin, but he's fast asleep, his face pale. Elisha stands in the doorway with me, her eyes curious, but she doesn't ask me. I tangle my fingers in the shell necklace, toying with the string as the circles clink against each other. She can tell from the way I look at him, I think. Nothing needs to be said—only that he saved me, from the earth's surface and from myself.

Elisha slips back into the front room, and I go to lie down beside Griffin. Outside, a lady is setting a ladder against the lamppost and climbing up to light the wick. The sun is setting, and the world is fading behind the closed curtains of the house.

I tuck my head into the curve of Griffin's neck and lace my fingers with his. He wakes slowly, and I lean back to look into his confused hazel eyes as he remembers where we are.

"Are you feeling better?" I ask quietly. He breathes slowly, his hand reaching to my cheek. His calloused fingertips are warm against my skin.

"I got you to the floating mountains," he murmurs. "I kept my promise."

"You did," I smile, and then I press my lips against his, taking back the moment stolen from us. It is everything I had hoped it would be—softness and tenderness and honeyed sweetness. It is flames curling on my skin and electricity sparking through my blood like the crystals of a storm dragonling.

I close my eyes, and we are in the house in the tree in the marshlands. We are in the cave on the summit of the mountains. We are deep beneath the earth in the dugout haven.

We are in each other's arms, and promises have been kept.

Griffin has brought me home.

The crowds are thick to board the airship as I stare down at the sea of leggings and sandals and cloak hems. I pull my cloak tighter around me, praying to the Phoenix I won't get caught. I know now she's a myth, but I've believed in her my whole life, and so it feels natural to look to her for protection.

Elisha's handed the guard our tickets and he's looking them over. Immigration to Ashra is tight, and citizens of Burumu are often trying to smuggle people in. "Who did you say this was again?" he asks, thumbing toward Griffin.

"My cousin," she says. "My uncle's son. We need some extra help for the coming harvest. You can see I've already bought his return ticket."

He flips through the documents, checking the details. "And her?"

I stare at the ground, saying nothing.

"My sister. She came with me to Burumu to fetch our cousin."

"What's your name?" he says to me. I continue to look down, the blood racing through me like flame.

"She's can't speak, sir. She's mute."

"Hmm."

"Will you hurry up the line?" a man shouts several people back. I recognize Aksel's voice, and I know he's trying to pressure the guard. "We've been waiting all morning!" he adds, and others in the line being to mutter, as well.

The guard flips through the documents, but you can tell he's nervous about the long line and the delay it might cause to the departure of the airship. He glances at his superior, who is dozing off in a chair nearby. "These seem to be in order," he finishes weakly and hands Elisha the papers.

We step on board the airship, taking seats near the back.

Griffin brushes his hand against my cloak, just for a moment, but the gesture gives me courage. He still looked a little pale this morning, but managed to eat the eggs and honeyed peaches on his breakfast plate.

The airship fills up, and before I know it, we are wobbling and puttering our way toward Ashra. Many of the passengers are members of the Elite Guard, easily recognized in their white uniforms and red-and-gold plume pins. I long to look out the window and see the mountain range as we float over it, but I don't dare lift my head. There's plenty of time to think on the journey, and I try to sort out everything that's happened. The marriage to Jonash, which my father thought would strengthen the bond of the continents, was a ploy of the Sargon's to take control of our lands. The whole rebellion has been cultivated by his lust for power. And the discussion between Aban and the lieutenant led Jonash to push me off the side of Ashra on purpose. He panicked, and then probably realized how stupid his decision had been. Maybe you could make an unknown in Burumu disappear without a trace, but a public figure? That wouldn't go unnoticed. The Sargon, with no claim to the throne by marriage, built an army in the Elite Guard and would take our lands by force. Only my father stands in his way, and he thinks the real problem is the rebels.

It's a complicated tangle, but I know how to unravel it. I'll go to my father immediately and cut the knot through the middle, the rope pieces shriveling like Dream Catchers pierced by the truth. And the truth will shine like a basilisk scale, like the fiery surface of the ocean, reflecting everything in undeniable veracity.

The airship touches down on the landing pitch near the citadel, and my heart pounds with anticipation. We wait for the others to disembark while I stare out the back window at the familiar forests that border the citadel. I'm home, and it floods me with joy. I reach for Griffin's hand and squeeze it as he stares out at the forests for the first time in fourteen years. This is his home, too. We've both returned.

Elisha pats my arm, and now it's time for the three of us to descend the plank to the landing pitch. The shining blue crystal of the citadel refracts the afternoon sun into dancing patterns on the ground. We walk through them, the blue striping across our toes and ankles. The Phoenix's colors are red and orange, and I always wondered why the citadel's crowning crystal was blue. I asked my father once. He told me the hottest fire, the deepest part of the blaze, is not orange or red, but blue. It looks cool and calm, but it carries in it the strength of the strongest spark.

I walk toward the citadel with this memory in my heart.

I will not be the wick and the wax any longer. I will be the flame, and I will light a new world for us all.

TWENTY-TWO

AS WE ROUND the landing pitch, we stumble upon a strange gathering in the courtyard of the citadel. It's like I've gone back in time to the Rending Ceremony. Some of the banners and garlands are still strung across the courtyard, although the flowers on them are wilted and collapsed. It's like a forgotten birthday party, the decorations collecting dust, the cake gathering mold. "It's because you fell," Elisha whispers to me as we duck under the faded bunting. "All the efforts went into finding you, and then the threats and blame started." She looks at the faces of the crowds as we push our way through.

"They look possessed," Griffin murmurs beside me. "Like they're in a Dream Catcher's vision."

"Dream Catcher?" Elisha asks. It brings the memory flooding back of the dream the monster put in my own head. The Rending Ceremony, with red petals falling like blood. With the dying garlands and the crowds, the shriveled petals strewn across the ground, it's almost like a prophecy now, like the monster knew what would happen. I'll have to ask Griffin later if it's possible. I don't know enough about any of the monsters on the earth yet. I want to know everything he does.

I'm trying not to look anyone in the face. It's hard to know who my allies are and who my enemies. I feel like I'm on the plains in my karu fur, hiding from hazu birds, trying to blend in as something I'm not. My karu cloak, back in the village, is the color of the pack leader. I'm not a youth hiding in the forest anymore, but the one leading the hunt.

On the plains, I was a scared human hiding in a monster's fur. Now I'm a force of reckoning hiding in a peasant's cloak, trying to look feeble. I will not let the Sargon and his son manipulate our futures.

We push through the crowd toward the sound of a voice. The gathering is thick with villagers from Ulan, and at the front a circle of Elite Guard soldiers keeps them back from the courtyard. Griffin gently bumps into me as I look over the shoulders of the guards. It's a familiar sight, only now I'm on the outside.

Elder Aban is standing in his white-and-red robes, his hands clasped and his face grim. He's droning on with some sort of invocation of the Phoenix, one of the many I've heard thousands of times before. Everyone stands solemnly, and I think about how none of them know what really happened, how we've all blindly accepted what we think our history is.

Then the crowds erupt around me as the doors to the citadel creak inward. The trumpets blare and my heart stumbles over itself. He's there—my father, the Monarch.

He's wearing his circlet of golden plumes that clinks and jingles as he walks. His golden cloak adorns his hunched shoulders, the red-plumed hem sweeping against the steps. His face looks weathered and older than it was a few weeks ago, and I unconsciously press against the guards in front of me as I strain forward. They push me back just as Griffin and Elisha each take my arms.

"I know how you must feel," Elisha says quietly. "But we have no idea how this crowd will react to the news that you've survived."

"They could riot or panic," Griffin says. "Better to approach your father quietly after."

I hate that they're right, and the chance of a riot seems so small. But I listen, if only because I'm in shock at being back here in the courtyard of the citadel, with my father, Elisha and Griffin.

And then another figure steps out of the doorway to the citadel and down the long stone steps. He's dressed in the white uniform of the Elite Guard, the golden plume of leadership pinned to his lapel. Around his head he wears a circlet of etched golden feathers, the mark of the Phoenix's royal favor.

My blood runs cold. It's Jonash.

He stands beside my father. The one who pushed me off the edge, if I believe Aksel. And as I stare at my once fiancé, I do believe him. I believe with all my heart that he knew about the crystal edge of the outlands, and that he walked along it to stage the accident.

The crowds fall silent as my father stretches out his hands, but it is Jonash who speaks. "To our family in Ashra, visitors of Burumu, and kin of Nartu and the Floating Isles," he says. "Thank you for gathering this day. Many of you have heard rumors and have troubled hearts. We are here to put those rumors to rest, so that you can all know the truth of what is happening."

The truth that you pushed me? I think. *The truth that you and your father have stirred up fear of the rebellion and the genocide to your advantage?* But I feel Griffin's fingers on my elbow, and I take strength in him, waiting for the right moment to act.

"The truth is," Jonash says, "that all our hearts are broken at the passing of my fiancée, our beloved Monarch's only child. She was the Eternal Flame of Hope, the heir of the floating continents, adored by us all. She would've been our queen. My queen. And my heart breaks that her life was taken from us by the lies of the rebels that seduced her."

"That dirty cinder," Elisha says beside me. I can think of stronger words, ones I learned from Griffin on the mountain when the basilisk meat burned. Those words bounce off the walls of my mind as I force myself to stay quiet.

"Many of you have heard that she fell from the outlands while trying to throw me off of Ashra." He pauses, scanning the crowd. "This is true. But I do not blame her. The rebels twisted her understanding with their lies. And now they hope to twist the rest of you to their side, as well."

It's ridiculous, yet the people hang on his every word. My father merely hunches like an old man. Why is he letting Jonash go on and on like this? He must know it's utter nonsense. He must think more of me than this.

Jonash makes a fist. "But my father and I are loyal to the Monarch, and united, we can stand against this rebellion!"

Some of the crowd cheers, but most still look confused. Elder Aban steps forward, raising his hands for the crowds to silence. "It is true, my dear ones," he says, "that there is an abomination in our midst. And we have been protecting you all as part of our duty to the Monarch for the last three hundred years. There were those perverse souls who joined with the monsters and longed for humanity's destruction. They were called the Benu. And the Elite Guard and our brothers and sisters, the Elders, have both protected society for as long as we could in our own ways. But now we have joined together, for the abomination has grown, and like weeds, must be cut down for the health of the crop."

I can't stand to hear any more. I lurch forward, but Elisha and Griffin pull me back. "Let me go," I say, and press forward again, but they pull me back and I lose my balance. I bump against one of the guards, and he turns to see who's causing trouble.

"Quiet there," he says, and turns back to the speeches. *We have to get out of the crowds,* I think. *We have to get to the side entrance of the citadel.* I jostle through the throng to leave, and my friends follow.

Jonash is speaking again as we weave through the gathering. "Rebels and Benu are to be executed on sight," he says. "Benu can be recognized by two crescent-like gashes on their back from shoulder to hip. Rebels do not have this marking, but can be recognized by a disdain for our Monarch or the Sargon. They will speak of the Benu with reverence instead of disgust. If anyone has information about a suspected rebel or Benu and does not come forward, they, too, will be charged with treason."

Why won't my father speak up? They're inciting madness. We round the base of the Phoenix statue as I approach the side doors. The crowd is thinner here, and I stop for a moment as I consider breaking through the guard. Surely this charade has gone on long enough. I look at Griffin. I wonder if he can see the flame burning in my heart. He nods, and I know he trusts me to do what I need to do. I only need to trust myself.

I take the edges of my hood in my trembling fingers and step toward the guards. "Let me pass," I say, my throat dry and the words barely coming through.

The guards look at me, eyebrows raised, hands on the hilts of their swords.

I grasp the slippery fabric tighter and press the hood backward. It slides from the short curls of my cut hair as I lock my fierce gaze with the guards. "Let me pass," I command.

Their eyes widen like they've seen a ghost, and they hesitate, stepping aside just enough that I can push through. Griffin and Elisha follow me toward Aban, Jonash and my father. My beloved father, who is looking at me in disbelief.

"Father," I say, willing my voice not to shake too much. The crowd is watching in stunned silence. Jonash's face is pale and frightened. "My friends and kin," I say to the crowd. "You have been misinformed." I glare at Jonash. "I am very much alive."

"Kallima," my father stammers. He holds his arms out and I long to run into them, but one thing I've learned from Griffin is caution around monsters, and there's one standing beside my father now. I focus on Jonash as I stride nearer.

"What Jonash has told you are lies," I say. "He is the one who pushed me. I stumbled upon a conversation between the lieutenant of the Elite Guard and Elder Aban about the rebellion and the truth of the floating islands. And Jonash threw me down to the earth's surface to cover it up."

Jonash says nothing, his face pallid and swirling with panic and embarrassment. The words are caught in his throat.

"I have been, and always will be, loyal to Ashra and her lands," I say. "But the Benu are nothing to fear. They are our brothers and sisters, and have lived among us peacefully for three hundred years. They are the ones who fear us. We need not fear them."

I have reached my father, his face bewildered. I hold him tightly in my arms, and feel the warmth of his hug as he embraces me. "Kallima," he whispers. "My daughter."

"I'm home, Father," I tell him, and I blink back the tears, because there is still work to be done. I tilt my chin up and glare at Jonash. "I hereby arrest you for treason, son of the Sargon. You threw me from the edge of the outlands, and when there was a chance to rescue me by airship, you fired on me—your very own fiancée and future Monarch. Treason!"

"Lies!" Jonash shouts, and the sound of it almost jolts me backward. "The lies of a traitor. She has survived the fall and come back to lead the rebels. She's not to be believed."

"Oh, stuff it, you bag of hot air," Griffin says. "If you truly loved her, you never would have pushed her, not for any reason."

"And who is this *gentleman*?" Jonash asks, the patronizing disdain clear in his voice. He glares at Griffin as he stands beside me.

"My name, that you will know, is Bazh," Griffin says, and it startles me. "And I lived among you once, in Ulan. Before I fell to the earth fourteen years ago."

Bazh. The name he held before he was Griffin. One of the only memories he has of Ashra—an ancient name and chubby fingers burned by a crust of fluffy bread, hands kissed better by a mother whose fate is uncertain.

The crowds mutter, for they remember the toddler and his mother who fell. How could they not? And one of them says, "It's in his eyes. Look! He has her eyes." And another says, "He's the spitting image of his mother, no mistake."

"I'm here to tell you that you've been deceived," Griffin says. For an inexperienced speaker who hunts monsters alone, he has a surprising amount of charisma with the crowds. I swell with pride at his voice. "There's a barrier surrounding the continents that protects those who fall. It was put in place by the rightful heirs to the floating mountains—the Benu." The crowds mumble among themselves; he's almost lost them. He shouts over them, "They aren't monsters! They were and are our allies. If you'll allow me to explain—"

"There's nothing to explain," Jonash says. "It's clear you are the one who has confused my fiancée. Kallima, we're grateful you have returned, but I have been nothing but faithful to you and your father in your absence. This ruffian has filled your head with lies."

"You're wrong!" Elisha says. Aban stares, unsure what to make of it all as the crowds become uneasy. Jonash's eyes are shifting through the crowd as if he's looking for someone, but perhaps he's only looking for support. None of this has gone the way he intended it.

"Daughter," my father says quietly. "Is this true?" He looks at Griffin thoughtfully. "Are you the one who saved her?"

And then everything happens at once. Jonash shouts, "Your Majesty! Look out!" I turn to stare at the crowds, and there are two men dressed in dark cloaks and golden winged masks, like an ominous masquerade ball. And one has in his hand a crossbow, and it's lifted toward my father's chest.

TWENTY-THREE

I SCREAM AS the string of the bow snaps loose. I know the bolt's in the air, and I can't react fast enough. But Griffin is standing at my father's right side, and he shoves him away in the quickest of movements. My father stumbles backward on the stone steps with Griffin over top of him, the bolt buried in the lean muscle of Griffin's bare shoulder.

Elisha screams, but Griffin is already up and running toward the crowd, the two men in dark stumbling through the stunned masses. Blood streams down his arm from the lodged bolt, but adrenaline has taken over, and he's hunting the men like a karu charging across the plains.

Elisha kneels down to tend to my father, but I can see he's all right—Griffin took the shot that was meant for him. I spring forward before I can think, the cloak slipping from my shoulders to the courtyard stones. Why aren't the Elite Guard chasing them? They seem more worried about crowd control.

I leap onto the platform of the Phoenix statue, the rough stone scraping against my knees and the palms of my hands. It's the quickest way to cut through the crowd and reach the fleeing men.

Griffin's already grabbed the first one, yanking his arm back and throwing him off balance. He's struggling to reach the crossbow while the man elbows him in the chest. The other one is sprinting away, his black cloak billowing behind him.

I leap down from the statue as the crowd parts before me. He's racing down the dirt path toward Lake Agur, past the landing pitch. He really hasn't planned this getaway very well. There are only so many places to hide on Ashra, and I know all of them. I wonder if maybe he's from Burumu, but why not plan an escape? It makes no sense.

The palm branch sandals Tash gave me pound against the ground as I chase him. I could never have run this far, this fast, without my past few weeks on the monster-ridden earth. My ribs have healed, and my breath doesn't sting or burn. I'm near the edge of the man's cloak and I pounce, grabbing fistfuls of the material to choke him backward. He stops running, pulling at the strings around his throat to untie them. The cloak falls from his shoulders, but it's slowed him down enough that we're side by side, and I wrap my arms around his legs to stop him from advancing.

Suddenly Griffin is beside me, tackling the man to the ground. The man grunts as he hits it hard, and struggles like a writhing worm, but we've got him.

"Where's the other one?" I pant.

Griffin nods back toward the courtyard. "The Elite Guard are holding him."

Good. They finally shaped up. We yank the man upward and back to the courtyard while more members of the Elite Guard dash forward to help us.

"Highness," one of them says as they take the culprit from our hands. I know I hardly look like the heir of Ashra now, panting and sweating, hair cut at odd angles by an old dagger.

They march both of the masked men into the courtyard before my father. Elisha is standing with him, her hands grasped lovingly around his. He looks flustered and confused, a shell of his former self. I look to Jonash, and he's standing there nervously, his face as white as the down of a hazu bird. He looks even more shaken than he was before I appeared, and it's making suspicions drift around in my head. Was he so worried about my father being shot? Why does he look more worried now that the moment has passed?

"Your Majesty," says the soldier holding the culprit. "The traitors." He clears his throat and averts his eyes, as if he's apologetic. Something's not right.

"I am grateful to your friend, Kallima," my father says, his eyes shining at Griffin. "He's shown more loyalty and usefulness than my own guards."

I look at Griffin, who's carefully pulling the crossbow bolt out of his arm. His face is one of concentration and control as he tugs the barbed tip out of his skin. The arrow clatters to the floor and blood seeps from the hole like crimson tears. I reach into my pocket for a handkerchief, and I press it to the wound for him. He looks up at me, his hazel eyes gleaming. He lives for this, I think. He's a monster hunter first, whether the prey is on four legs or six or two. He lives to save others.

"Kali," he says quietly, nodding at Jonash. "He motioned them, in the crowd. It's a setup."

I know it's the truth the moment I hear it. The assassination attempt is part of the ruse to spark a war against the rebels. That's why the Elite Guard were so slow to react.

I nod as he presses his hand over mine on the handkerchief. My fingers slip out from under his, and I step toward my father, who stands with Elisha and Jonash on the steps, Elder Aban a foot away from them.

"Well?" I say. "Unmask them."

The Elite Guard look nervously at Jonash, who nods. They must be in on it, too, at least partially. After all, he's their lieutenant now.

The golden plumed masks clatter to the stone courtyard, and two young men stare back with wild eyes. I don't recognize either. Likely they are from Burumu, because I know everyone in Ashra quite well, as least whether they're a familiar face or not.

"Rebels, I'm sure," says Jonash quickly. He's trying to cover, I think, trying to improvise on his feet. Aksel was right. He really is brainless. "I warned you all of the danger they posed."

He's not the only one who can think on his feet. I've been raised my whole life for leadership under pressure. The flame inside me flickers. "So you said," I say, stepping toward him. "And here they are, trying to assassinate our dear Monarch."

Jonash looks relieved, the color returning to his pallid face. "Then…you can see what I've said is true."

"The rebels are a threat, as you said," I repeat, and Jonash smiles. But here's where I drive the sword through his treacherous heart. "And so they must be executed."

His face is aghast. "Wh...what?"

"You said yourself," I say, sweeping my hand to the crowd. "All rebels must be executed." The two culprits look terrified, watching Jonash with big eyes. "Or are you not loyal to the Monarch and your own words?"

There is a long silence, as if the whole courtyard is holding its breath.

And then Jonash lowers his head. "Execute them," he orders to the Elite Guard.

The man who held the crossbow jolts forward in the guards' arms. "My lord!" he says, struggling. "You promised! You promised us safety!"

My father's brow crinkles, his face filling with life. "What's this now?" he snaps.

I look at Griffin, and we both grin. Monsters snared in their own traps. The best way to bring down a monster, he told me, is to use its own weaknesses against it. And Jonash has tangled himself in a knot of a web.

"Please, Monarch," the other culprit pleads as he falls to his knees. "He told us to do it. He promised our families a lifetime of protection and compensation from the Sargon. My family is starving in Burumu. I had no choice."

"As I thought," I say. "The Benu and the rebels are not our enemies. It is the Sargon and his son who have tried to assassinate my father. Spare the boys." I raise my hand and point at my once future fiancé. "And arrest him for treason."

"Jonash, why?" My father's face creases with sadness. "I treated you as a son, did I not? I offered my daughter's hand to you, and encouraged her to see good in you that was not there. Kallima, forgive me. I'm a foolish old man, and I'm ashamed."

But before I can say anything, it's Griffin who speaks. "There's no shame in seeking good in someone's heart, Monarch," he says. "Even when there's none to be found."

"Take him," I say to the Elite Guard, but they hesitate. None of this is going the way they'd expected. My father was supposed to be dead, bleeding on the steps, while Jonash and the Sargon mourned and reigned on his behalf with the support of the Elite Guard. I don't know how much the soldiers have been kept in the dark or brainwashed, or how much the Elders under Aban know, but I do know that the crowds are divided and confused in loyalty to their lieutenant and to me, their heir.

They step toward Jonash, and he's looking nervously around, trying to figure out what to do. Snivel for mercy? Bolt from the courtyard? Sweet-talk his way out? He hesitates, like a monster cornered.

I turn to Griffin to smile again, but his face is grim. And that's when I remember that he's warned me before. There's nothing more dangerous than a beast that's been cornered, a monster with nothing to lose.

Jonash starts to laugh, a cold and horrible sound that makes the guards approaching him halt. He looks up at me, his blue eyes shining. "Well," he says. "This isn't turning out the way I'd planned at all." There's an edge to his voice, and it's unsettling. "You're back from the dead and here to curse me, is that it?"

"Jonash," I say. "It's over."

He shakes his head. "It's only just beginning." The guards step toward him, and he throws out a hand. They stop. Griffin stands at my side, still holding the handkerchief to his shoulder. "You," Jonash says, pointing at him. "So you're the one they threw over the side, are you? The bastard from Ulan whose mother wouldn't shut up about him." He sneers, looking him up and down. "I see they've dressed you in clothes from Burumu, but that doesn't make you a gentleman. I bet you roll around in the mud with the monsters, hmm?"

Griffin doesn't flinch. He's beyond petty words. But he can't help taking the bait. "What do you know about my mother?"

"Oh, so now you want to make friends, do you?" Jonash laughs, full of spite. "Sorry, I'm not interested in anything but getting rid of all of you. You're wasting my time."

"How dare you speak to the royal family in this way," Elder Aban snaps, stepping forward. "Surely the Sargon himself would take offense to your tone."

A coolness flickers in Jonash's eyes. "The Sargon is dead."

The crowds gasp; Aban steps back as if he's been hit. "What...what have you done?"

Jonash's face is pure darkness. "Long live his successor."

He's gone mad. "You think the people will bow down to a murderer?"

"They can bow or they can die," he says. "I care not. Those who will not follow will be thrown off the continents to their deaths. Live and obey, or fall to the talons of the monsters below."

"At least monsters know when they're defeated," Griffin says. "You're a flicker wasp crushed beneath our feet, and you're still trying to sting. Give it up."

Jonash turns his head sharply. "What do you know of stinging? It's impressive that you've survived all this time, I'll give you that. But you're the one who was unwanted here. Did you ever think about why you and your mother fell? When so many other Benu could keep their mouths shut and survive? Your mother was the wasp, crushed under the Monarch's foot. She wouldn't shut up about the truth of the Rending."

My eyes widen. Griffin's mother had found out the truth? Had she been the spark that ignited the rebellion? I imagine the ember, the truth smoking from its burial in ashes, the flame growing over the years. And, overcome with grief, she must have approached my father. Was she thrown away to hide what she'd discovered?

"Enough of this!" my father shouts, life flowing through him again. "Seize him now!" The guards march toward Jonash on the steps, swords drawn.

And then there's a brilliant flash of light and the sound of fabric ripping. And Jonash isn't on the steps anymore but in the air, suspended by a pair of fiery wings. The flames ripple up them as they flap, holding him aloft above the shocked noises of the crowds.

He's a Benu. The Sargon and his son were both Benu, the same ones they threw off the continent. Have they been holding to the grudge against humans all this time, or is this just a personal struggle for power? There's no time to wonder because Jonash is swooping away from the court-yard and soaring over the forests toward Lake Agur. The crowds are screaming and shouting while the Elite Guard try to maintain control. Aban's face has gone as pale as his robe, and he whispers prayers under his breath, while my father's face looks sunken and defeated.

"It's happening," he says.

"What, Father?"

"This is why we've been throwing the Benu off the con-tinents for the last three hundred years," he says, and the words sting like ice. "To prevent them from using their power against us. And now it's happening again."

Tash was right. My father knew. He knew people were being rounded up and wings cut off, thrown down to the earth to die. And he'd let it happen. "Father...no."

"I am the wick and the wax," he says. "I must crumble, or the people will. Forgive me, Kallima." The betrayal cuts; it stings to think he knew of the genocide. That he continued it. He condoned it, for the people. I shake my head. I can't accept it. I can't believe that's the father I knew.

Griffin's gentle grip is on my arm, giving me strength. "Come on," he urges. "We can't let him get away."

I'm numb, but with Griffin's help I turn toward the forest and the lake beyond. I don't know what's happening, what power the Benu have that we need to fear. But I know that storm clouds are gathering in the sky, slate gray and laden with rain. I know thunder is rolling in the distance, and I know there was darkness flashing in Jonash's ice-blue eyes. The air buzzes with electricity, and I know something terrible is about to happen.

And I know that Griffin and I must stop it.

TWENTY-FOUR

"KALI, WAIT!" ELISHA calls after me, tripping over her sandals as she hurries forward. She takes my hands in hers, her eyes wide. "Don't follow him," she says. "I lost you once, and I can't bear it if I lose you again."

"Elisha, I have to do this. If I don't stop him, no one will."

Griffin rests a hand on Elisha's shoulder, and she looks up at his gentle eyes. "You won't lose her," he says. "You didn't the first time, and you won't now. Look at the fire in your friend's eyes, Elisha. It's tempering her into something stronger than steel. She won't fail."

Elisha looks at me, and I gaze at her with all the courage I have. She steps back, and Griffin and I run side by side to the path that leads to Lake Agur.

"I don't understand," I shout as we run. "If he's a Benu, why was he calling for the execution of other Benu? Shouldn't he want to save them?"

"Perhaps there's a power the Benu can wield that he's keeping from the others," Griffin shouts back. "Even the scavengers squabble among each other for the prime kill."

He's right, I know. My father feared some terrible fate from the Benu, but what? What is it that Jonash knows?

The citadel and the shouts of the crowd slip away behind us as we weave through the forest. It's at least an hour's run to Lake Agur, and I don't know why, but I know we need to hurry. I feel lighter on my feet as I race alongside Griffin, thinking about what he's said and what he thinks of me. He thinks I'm strong; he has faith in me. And all this time I'd been struggling alongside him as we fought monster after monster, knowing that he had a lifetime of hunting behind him and that I was useless. But he never saw it that way, not from the beginning. He believes in me. And that stokes the flames that are already lit, and together we're going to stop Jonash once and for all.

The path curves on and on, but high above us I can see Jonash soaring on the wind. I can't believe this secret has been kept for so long, that Jonash and his father are Benu. I wonder how many descendants of the Benu have been thrown over the edge in the past three hundred years to "protect" Ashra and her lands, to keep the Sargon's line the only permissible survivors from the original populace of the floating continents. They taught others to fear the Benu, when they themselves were descended from the same. It's sickening.

The lush green of the forest finally breaks away, and we're at the edge of Lake Agur, my ears filling with the rushing of the waterfall at its northern edge. The packed dirt beach gives way as we near the water, the quiet azure lapping gently against the shore.

Jonash is high above the middle of the lake and I'm not sure how to get to him. He holds his sword in his hand. The members of the Elite Guard each receive a standard-issue blade, although they're really more symbolic than for actual use—at least, that's what I'd been led to believe. Now I'm not sure what's true, but I do know that Jonash's sword is more elaborate than those of the Elite Guard. The blade is curved like a scimitar, the steel tinted a deep blue like the night sky. And dotted all over the blade are spots of shining silver that haven't been dyed, that look like stars gleaming. The hilt is made of elaborate swirls of silver that loop around his hand and catch what's left of the sunlight between the storm clouds.

"Come down and fight if you aren't a coward," I shout. Griffin has nocked an arrow with the chimera's venom, and he points it at Jonash while his wide wings flap silently.

"It's not cowardly to use my lineage as an advantage," Jonash shouts back. "If your Neanderthal friend here still had his, he'd be up here, too, no doubt."

Griffin tightens his grip on the bowstring and adjusts his aim. "I can face you without them. I've brought down larger beasts than you." He looses the arrow and it flies toward him, but Jonash wraps his wings around himself and plummets below the shot. The arrow splashes into the water's surface and floats there, bobbing as it's pulled by the current of the waterfall.

Jonash laughs. "Is any of this necessary? Don't waste your time and arrows on me. Go back to your barren earth and leave us in peace."

"You tried to kill my father," I say. "You threw me over the edge of Ashra and fired on me from the airship. You and your father tried to raise a rebellion against us. I'd say this is pretty necessary, yes." I draw my dagger, the sun glinting on the orange garnet set in the hilt.

Jonash shrugs. "As you wish," he says, and then he flaps his wings with a blast of air. He tumbles suddenly toward us and we brace for the impact. I lunge at his approaching shape with my dagger, but he's a blur, and his wing slaps into my face and knocks me down to a mouthful of sand. Griffin grabs a handful of feathers out of his other wing and punches him in the jaw before he can lift up again. Jonash collapses backward, the flames of his wings rippling against the ground. The water laps against one feather and it singes, sending a tiny spiral of gray smoke up toward the sky.

I quickly roll onto my knees and press on Jonash's shoulder with all my might to keep him down. He's beating his giant fiery wings and they're wafting uncomfortable heat everywhere, but they don't burn where they graze my arms. Jonash swings his sword and it clangs against my dagger with a spray of sparks that drops like shooting stars. His leather boot collides with Griffin's chest and he falls backward, gasping. Jonash grabs my hand on his shoulder and rolls sideways, pulling my wrist backward. I cry out and let go, and he's up in the air again, flapping higher. I grab his boot to stop him, but the rush of his wings beats against my face and I can't hold on much longer.

Griffin's there, grabbing at Jonash's wing. He has one of his daggers out and he's cutting into the quills in a crescent down Jonash's back. The prince cries out as the feathers drift like glinting embers to the sand, snuffing out as the water touches them. Jonash shrieks in agony and flaps wildly to escape Griffin, but he can't, and the whole scene is horrific, because this isn't a monster we're fighting but a person. Despite everything he's done, I feel pity for him as he wails like that. I think of Griffin screaming as a baby as they carved his wings off, too.

But it was my father who ordered it done. And the Sargon, too. If I let Griffin do it, am I not the same?

There's no time to know what's right, only to act on instinct. And so I grab Griffin's hands and try to pull them away from the quills. Only a half-broken wing remains as Jonash slips free into the sky. Griffin looks at me, questioning, but he's not angry, only confused.

"I'm sorry," I say. "I don't... I don't know why I did that."

I do know. Because I want to save Ashra and her lands. But I don't want to be a monster, too.

"I get it," Griffin says, looking at my confused expression. Somehow he knows what I'm thinking even as I'm just sorting it out myself. "We'll bring him down, but I won't kill him."

"Such grandiose ideals of mercy and justice!" Jonash shouts from above. He flies lopsided now, lurching and panting as the one good wing beats and the other flaps, frail and fragmented. "My thanks to you, dear fiancée, but I'm afraid your heart will get you into more trouble than it's worth. If you hadn't cared so much, I never would have had to throw you from the edge."

"Bah," Griffin says, though his cheeks flush at the use of fiancée. "Save us all some time and come down now. Then maybe the Monarch won't have you executed."

"I don't fear the Monarch," Jonash spits back. "Or you, wingless abomination and disgrace to the Benu. No, I'm here to fulfill a prophecy made long ago, to ensure the rule of Ashra belongs to me and mine for aeons to come."

What's he even talking about? What prophecy?

Jonash laughs, his one wing holding him crooked and aloft above the lake. "You look confused, Kallima. Have you forgotten the prayer to our divine ancestor?" His lip curls in a threatening smile, his blue eyes gleaming as the thunder claps in the sky. "May she rise anew."

The Phoenix. He's talking about the Phoenix.

"Joke's on you," I shout back. "There never was a Phoenix. It was only a military code."

The thunder is louder now, rolling in around us. The ashen clouds have blotted out the sun, and the world is dark and ominous. "Oh, there was a Phoenix," he says in a dark voice. "She was the ancestor of the Benu. And it's time for her to rise again and purge all who will not follow her prince."

Jonash begins speaking another language, its intonation ancient and strange. His tongue curls off the syllables, and I remember vaguely hearing something like it once before. Then I remember—when Elder Aban read from that secret first volume of the annals. That archaic tongue must have belonged to the Benu. Was it passed down the Sargon's line all this time?

The thunder rolls, the lightning claps. The cold wind whirls around and nearly knocks us over. The surface of Lake Agur is pockmarked and murky, the roar of the waterfall overcome by the fury of the storm.

Griffin nocks an arrow, but in this wind there's no way for it to hit its target. He lets the bowstring snap and the arrow flies astray, spinning head over tail before it splashes into the lake far to Jonash's right.

There's a strange mist lifting off the waters. It's floating upward in spirals of white around the arrow's shaft. It's curling in clouds of fog near the waterfall, and then it's rising from the entire surface of the lake. The wind is whipping the mist away as quickly as it forms, while Jonash's voice drones above it all, echoing with a strange vibration that makes the ground shudder.

I crawl toward the edge of the water and put my hand over the curling white wisps. The water condenses on my palm like drops of thick, hot rain. I pull my hand back and look at Griffin.

It's steam. The white mist is steam.

And now the surface of the water is rippling more than before, and it isn't the wind stirring it up. The white mist is frothing and roiling. Fish are going belly-up, and frogs are hopping onto the shore by the dozens.

Lake Agur is boiling. It's bubbling like a stew pot over a fire.

And then there's a flash of yellow light so blinding that even with my eyes closed I can see searing starbursts on the insides of my eyelids. The water surges everywhere with the roaring crash of a tidal wave. It floods over Griffin and me so that suddenly we are drowning, pulled backward by the immense current. The wave slams against the shore and far into the forest before it retreats back to the lake. I sputter and rub my eyes, searching the ground for my dagger. It's buried in the sand tossed around by the wave, a tiny fish flopping around on the hilt. I grab the weapon in my hand, the freezing wind whipping against my soaking wet skin. I look into the sky, and there's a light as bright as the sun, so bright that I have to squint to see its shape.

The Phoenix. She has risen anew.

Every feather smolders with flame, the very sky around her rippling with waves of intense heat. Her wingspan is as wide as the lake that tosses against itself as it resettles. Her beak gleams with golden fire, her talons a darker gold, and a bronze ridge of bony plates runs down the back of her spine. Her eyes glint black like hot oil, and flames roll off her like a blazing fire in the sky. Her tail trails behind her in a feathery fan, three extra-long plumes hanging from the end of it like the strings of a kite blowing in the wind.

She was sleeping in the lake all this time. Three hundred years, since the Rending? Or three thousand since the Benu created the floating isles? I don't know when, but she was here the whole time on Ashra, and she is magnificent.

Jonash flies beside her, his eyes glistening. He's as stunned as I am, just watching her. She's real. She's huge and benevolent and incredible. And for a moment I forget everything else. I've looked to her my whole life to protect me, and she was here in the wilderness of Ashra, in one of the places I've always been drawn to.

She opens her beak and lets out a shriek like a hazu bird, a great screech that seems to shake the very sky. The thunder claps in response, which startles me. She's so brilliant that I'd forgotten the dark storm clouds around us.

Griffin's hand clasps mine, and I look over to him, speechless. But he's not stunned like Jonash and me. He's not taken in by her beauty. "A monster's a monster," he says quietly.

But not the Phoenix. She's the only monster who ever looked after us. That's what we've been taught.

Jonash knows, too, as he hovers beside her in the sky, as she flaps her great wings gently and tilts her head to look at him.

"Sacred Phoenix," he shouts at her. "I am Jonash, your devoted descendant. I have called you forth once more to purify the lands of Ashra with your intense flame. Restore this land to its rightful heir!"

His words don't frighten me. I've served the Phoenix my entire life. She will not betray me now.

The Phoenix opens her beak widely, her feathers flapping in rippling waves as she soars through the sky toward Jonash. He spreads his arms, a smile on his face. He reaches a hand out to catch hold of the flaming plumes on the back of her neck, but he never gets that far.

She snaps him in her beak as he shrieks. She shakes him back and forth, lifting her sharp talons up to his struggling form.

The world is devoured in panic and flame.

I scream. Griffin grabs me and holds me to his chest, turning me away from the nightmarish scene. Jonash screams again and then is silent, and I manage to pull away from Griffin in time to see the starry blue scimitar splash into the lake below.

The tears flood my eyes as the Phoenix circles over the lake, screeching as her giant wings flap gales of hot wind against us.

And then the Phoenix stops circling and sets her wings flat and tilted forward. Lightning streaks in the sky behind her, and she is closer now, diving toward us, her beak open and her eyes wild.

And I only have a moment to realize that Griffin is right before we turn to run.

This is not the Phoenix I've prayed to, the one romanticized over hundreds of years of tradition and storytelling.

This is an ancient sky beast, one so powerful that she was said to have rent the floating continents from the very earth, leaving craters of shadow and death behind in her wake.

She is a monster on an epic scale, larger than one ever faced before.

A monster is a monster. And she will do what monsters do.

She will kill us.

TWENTY-FIVE

THE WORLD BUBBLES with heat as we run, the air wavy and streaked like a mirage. We dive for the tree line as the Phoenix swoops over us and into the sky again. The air is heavy with the smell of burning wood as we look up. The trees above us are lit with flames, all burning down around us. Birds and pikas are scattering with a flurry of squawks and chatters as the Phoenix makes a wide loop around the edge of the continent.

This can't be happening. The Phoenix was the defender of the floating lands, but she's lighting them on fire like she doesn't care.

And I remember then, looking at Griffin's grim face as we hurry back to the lake—she doesn't care. She's a monster, and we're prey, and that's it.

We have to stop her, and I can't let my upbringing hinder me. I can't revere her, I can't hesitate, or all of Ashra will go up in flames.

"What do we do?" I shout to Griffin. The only monster I've ever seen that nearly rivaled the Phoenix's size was the dragon that carried off the striped cat.

"Same as any other monster," Griffin yells back over the thunder and winds. "Find its weakness and bring it down."

The Phoenix is on fire as she flaps her wings, rounding the distant cloud of mist at the northern waterfall. "Water, right?" Water puts out a fire. But the Phoenix was sleeping inside Lake Agur, and she only made the water bubble and boil. It's not enough to extinguish her flames.

There's no time for Griffin to answer, because she's swooping again. Griffin has one of his venom-tipped arrows nocked, and he looses it at the Phoenix's chest. It lodges in the feathers and promptly burns up like a stick of kindling. I don't know how long the chimera venom stays potent, but I doubt it's strong enough for a tiny dose like that to affect such a huge sky beast.

The Phoenix opens her beak and lets out a deafening screech. I clasp my hands over my ears, unsure which way to run. The forest is burning, and large branches snap off with ancient groans, blocking the way back to the citadel. We could run into the eastern forest, but we won't make the edge before she reaches us.

"Come on!" Griffin shouts, and he wades into the water toward the flaming monster. The water feels thick as honey around my calves as I force myself to run faster toward the center. Just as the Phoenix swoops over us, we plunge under the cover of the lake's surface. It's barely deep enough, and as she passes, the water splatters like scalding tea across my back. I cry out, my shout nothing but bubbles in the warm water. I splash upright and Griffin's already there, another arrow flying toward the Phoenix. There are only a handful of them left in his quiver, and I'm not sure what else to do.

"Can we drown her somehow?" I ask. "Put out the flames?" Then the rains finally break loose from the slate clouds and pound the lake's surface around us. They rise like steam off the Phoenix's back, and her feathers tinge with blue, the color of an even hotter flame. She's compensating for the rain, I think, so it won't put out her fire.

"Maybe her wings are like the Benu's," Griffin says. "Maybe they won't burn us." He has a dagger in his hand now, his eye on the monster as she curves gracefully through the sky.

"They're not," I shout back, my own dagger held upright for whatever good it will do. "They boiled the lake and singed my back. They're hot."

"But that part," he says, pointing at the Phoenix's back. There's that long line of ridges down her spine, chinked together like scalloped plates of armor. They end near a tuft of yellow feathers on the top of her head, and they're the only part of her that doesn't seem to be on fire. They look like they're made of shining bronze, and I doubt we could stick a dagger in. Even if we could, it would be like a pinprick to a beast like that.

"I'm going to jump on," Griffin says.

I can't have heard him right. "What?"

"Next time she swoops by," he says. "We're no use down here on the ground. Use a monster's abilities against it, right?"

"But you'll get burned!"

"We'll see," he says, and the mass of light is coming toward us again as the rain pounds and steams off her back.

I brace myself. He's right—there's nowhere to go but up.

She opens her beak and screeches, diving toward us with her claws and wings outstretched. Every nerve in my body pulses with a panicked scream to run, but I fight it and brace myself.

I'm the heir of the Phoenix. I will break her.

Griffin and I wait until she's so close that she can't alter her course. Then we spread apart just enough to avoid her oncoming claws. We both reach for the tufts of fiery yellow plumes that cover the skin where her wings meet her body. I grab tight with both hands. The weight of her knocks me off my feet, but I hang on with all my might as I lift with her into the sky. The skin on my fingers is burning and peeling, the Phoenix tilting her black oily eye to stare at me. Griffin is on the other wing and has already pulled himself up onto the ridge just behind her head. He braces his legs and reaches for me, but his hand is too far away. My brain shrieks at me as my fingers blister and scald under the feathers, like I'm grasping a blazing hot pan handle. I can't hold on—I let go and fall through the air, tumbling down toward the lake below. I plunge down in a flurry of foam, bubbles fizzing in my ears as I swim toward the surface. The lake water is still warm, but it soothes my burned hand as the skin peels away before my eyes. I come gasping to the surface, my dagger still in my other hand. High above the Phoenix is soaring with Griffin on its back. He's like an insect on her spine, but he's hanging on to the ridges tightly as he crouches behind the tall back of one of the plates. They're not scalding, then, or he would've jumped down by now. I hear a cry from the Phoenix. Has he stabbed her? I can't see anything over the thick curtain of rain.

The current of the water is strong and pulling, but at

least I'm not weighted down by the dress I wore in the marshlands. I kick toward the shore, the rain pelting down around me. But I'm not getting closer to the shore. In fact, the edge of the lake is getting farther away.

I clamp down on the dagger with my teeth so both hands are free, and I swim with all my might toward the edge. I don't understand. I've crossed this lake hundreds of times before. Am I too exhausted from fighting the Phoenix? My heart is thrashing against my ribs and my blood pulses like it's on fire, but it only makes me feel more alive, more desperate.

Then I hear the rush of water, and I realize the problem. I've dropped into the lake too close to the waterfall. When she arose, the tidal wave must have broken away the crust of earth and turned it into a roaring flood of water. The current is pulling me to the edge of the continent. I'm going to go over, to fall back down to the earth.

I thrash my legs through the water, my arms crashing through the surf. But the shore keeps shrinking away from me. Mouthfuls of water splash in with every heaving breath, and I cough and sputter, lungs burning. I know now about the barrier surrounding Ashra. I know if I fall I will likely survive. But if I fall without Griffin, if I break a leg or an arm or pass out, I will be easy pickings for any monsters prowling below. If I fall now, unless Griffin can take out the Phoenix, Ashra will burn and the people will die. Ashra will burn to ashes, its namesake, like the Phoenix burned before it.

The current batters my shoulder against a sharp rock and I cry out, spinning helplessly through the water. I feel blood oozing down my back, sticky and cold as it spills into the frothing waves. Thick brambles of entangled vines stretch out over the rocks, and I grab at them with blistered fingers. Their thorns stick into my skin, but they hold as the current grasps at my tired legs. I'm safe for a moment, and I hold on with every fiber in my being.

And then the thought strikes me. The words of the annals that Elder Aban reads from every year at the Rending Ceremony. The Phoenix burned herself up in her effort to rend Ashra from the earth and throw it into the sky. Water will not douse her flames, but if she overexerts herself as she did then, wouldn't she turn to ash and soot? Already her flames are heating up, her plumage no longer the first brilliant yellow we saw but flaming in reds and oranges, her back tinting blue where the rain is hitting her.

We can't douse her flame, but we can burn her out.

I have to tell Griffin. I have to let him know how we can defeat her. He knew all the weaknesses of the monsters on the earth, but I'm the one who knows the Phoenix's weakness. This time I'm the one who knows what to do.

My muscles burn as I grip the vines stretched over the rocks. I'm not sure I have the strength to pull myself out of the water, or whether the vines will hold my weight. I kick against the current and pull myself up to see over the boulder. Flames lick the far ends of the vines—the whole shore is on fire. The rain beats down on the smoldering foliage, producing a thick layer of smoke that spreads over the rocks like gray mist. Climbing up isn't an option. I hang on to the vines as the water pelts my skin, not sure what to do next or where to go.

"Kali!" Griffin's voice shouts over the storm in a faraway cry. "Kali!"

I see the Phoenix high above, Griffin crouched on its back. She's in the eastern sky above the lake, and Griffin is holding tightly to the bronze plate with one hand and waving with the other. "Wait!" I think he shouts, but I can't be sure.

Wait? It's not like I can do anything else.

But I see him reach into his dagger belt and take out a blade. He sticks it deep between the ridged plates and the Phoenix lets out a screech, turning her head to snap at him with her golden beak. The feathers at the tips of her wings flare blue as she lowers in the sky. Griffin drives in another dagger with his foot, and the Phoenix turns her head to the other side, shrieking at him. They dip below the edge of the continent and out of sight.

A moment later I see her wings flapping, and they surface just to the northeastern edge of the waterfall. And I know what Griffin's doing.

If I can let go at the right time, he's going to try to catch me.

If I miss, I'll plummet back down to the earth, my future uncertain.

It's a huge risk. But my fingers ache and sting tangled in the briars. I can't hold on much longer, and I can't climb up to the burning shoreline. There's nothing to do but go over the edge of the waterfall.

I watch the Phoenix approaching. She tries to fly away from the edge of the continent, but Griffin uses the daggers he's driven into the ridge to steer her down and around. I can't believe he can command a monster that big. He must have struck nerves in her spine or something—either way, she looks irritated and unhappy, completely distracted.

I look at the misty edge of the falls, bordered by outcrops of sharp rock. I have to time it carefully. There's only one chance.

They're close now. Griffin shouts at me before they duck out of sight, but I can barely hear him over the roar of the storm and the waterfall. Did he say five? Or dive? Or maybe something else? Five seconds sounds about right to time the fall.

There's no time to think. My grip won't hold out for them to make another loop around me. I squeeze my eyes shut and count down the last three seconds. Then I open my eyes and let go.

The vines thread through my open fingers as the current pulls me to the edge. I hold my dagger in front as a feeble attempt to ward off sharp rocks. The spray from the waterfall is so thick I can barely see, the water roaring in my ears.

And then I'm swept over the side and I'm falling, the earth dark and far below the storm clouds. But there's a gleaming light down there, too. The Phoenix with Griffin on its back, and he's looking up.

My mouth fills with frothy water, the spray all around me. But the light is hurtling toward me, and I have to get this right or it's all over.

I land against something hard and uncomfortably warm. It's a bronze ridge near the Phoenix's tail. I grab with all my might as the waterfall tries to sweep me off. My dagger clanks against the side of the armored plate and tumbles toward the earth. Another flap of the monster's wings and the waterfall is gone, but the rain is still pounding away, and my hands are throbbing and aching. I scramble to get my legs up the side, but the heat of its feathers scalds my soles through the thin palm branch sandals.

Then two strong arms grab mine, and Griffin's face is above me. He's shouting something, but I'm so tired and panicked that I can't make it out. He heaves me up onto the bronze ridge as the Phoenix flaps up and down, the motion jerking us both around like a kite in a storm. Far below I see a flash of brilliant light—my dagger hitting the barrier and setting off a pulse.

Griffin's strong grip holds me steady as I pull one leg over the ridge. I'm on my stomach, both hands on the plate like the front of a saddle from those long-ago horses. Griffin slumps back, and we can both finally breathe.

The Phoenix screeches and flies lower, the edge of the continent dangerously near. The bottom of the island, tangled in roots and dirt, comes into view. "She's going to try and scrape us off," I shout.

"Come on," Griffin says, and with his help I rise. We walk carefully along the bony bronze, hunched low so we can grab the ridges as we climb toward her head. The feathers on her wingtips are a pale blue now, almost lavender, and the color is spreading toward her body.

"Griffin," I say as we climb. "I know how to use her weakness against her. Water won't work, but exhaustion will."

He turns, his hand grasping the next armored plate. "Come again?"

"When the Phoenix has used up all her strength," I pant, lifting my leg carefully over the next tall ridge, "she'll burn up to ashes and soot."

"Then we better be over the continent when it happens," Griffin says. "Or we'll go down with her."

The earth is laid out like a painting below us, speeding away at a dizzying pace. We wouldn't pass through the barrier if we fell from here. There'd be nothing to slow us in the air.

The Phoenix hovers directly below Ashra as she flaps

her wings. The bottom peak of the continent touches the bronze ridges by her tail in a flurry of sparks. A whole chunk of rock shears off and tumbles toward the shadow-lands below. The Phoenix readies herself to ram against Ashra a second time, but we're up near her head now. We brace for the impact, holding on with blistered fingers.

The collision tosses us to the side, but we don't fall. The Phoenix stumbles in midair and flaps her great wings, the blue flame spreading along the sides of her body.

"Come on, girl," Griffin says, patting the monster on the ridge. "You can fight harder than that!"

She screeches and bumps against the continent again. It wavers in the sky like an upset top. I stare with wide eyes. Is she really capable of capsizing the continent? "Griffin," I shout, "we have to get her back up!"

"On it," he says, driving the daggers into a gap between the ridges with his feet. The Phoenix squawks and dives toward the earth and up again, circling around Ashra. The plumes that tuft around the top ridge ignite blue, and then we have a problem.

Griffin's dagger blades turn yellow-white and melt, the metal oozing into a silvery puddle against her plumes. The hilts tumble off the sides of her neck and down to the earth below. Griffin takes a fresh dagger and gently prods the tip into her skin and lifts it up. The end of the blade is warped and melted, gleaming with heat.

He looks at me and I stare back at him. Our steering mechanism is gone. We've lost control.

TWENTY-SIX

"HANG ON," GRIFFIN shouts, and we duck as the Phoenix approaches Ashra's rim. From here we can see the forest burning, the crowds shouting and staring and pointing from the village of Ulan. The shining blue crystal of the citadel gleams with reflected firelight as we pass over it. Elisha and my father are down there somewhere in the chaos.

The Phoenix flies over the outlands and past the outcrop of rock that stretches from the side of Ashra—my realm of one, the fireweed drowned out by the raging rains. The thunder and lightning have moved on, but the rains pelt down. The winds are blowing the clouds toward Burumu, and soon we won't have the storm to dampen the Phoenix's strength.

We need to bring her down now.

Griffin grabs the last of his arrows and shoves it firmly into the gap in the ridges. The Phoenix screeches and the arrow lights with instant flame, the arrowhead melting into her skin.

That's it. We're out of weapons.

"Is that all you can do, you roasting chicken?" Griffin shouts. "Come on! I thought you were a beast of legends. You're just someone's dinner caught on fire!"

He's grinning. Has he lost his mind? I doubt the monster understands what he's saying. But she squawks, and blue explodes down the trailing kite feathers of her tail. She might not understand the words, but she understands the tone.

Griffin jumps from side to side on the ridges. "You going to let your prey take you for a ride, are you? Let's hope the dragons and hazus aren't watching. For shame!"

"Stop jumping around!" I shout. "You're going to fall."

"We have to bring this bird down with us," he says, his eyes gleaming. And the Phoenix's whole tail and wings are rippling with blinding blue as her beak snaps at Griffin. It's working. I run down the ridges of her back and stomp on them, shouting at the monster with all my might.

"You liar!" I shout, and I'm surprised at the strength of my voice. "We believed in you as the protector. And you're nothing but another stupid sky beast!"

The Phoenix snaps at Griffin and he flips out of the way, steadying himself two ridges behind. The feathers around me are undulating like a lava flow as we jump and shout at the bird.

"I trusted you!" Tears blur in my eyes. I can't tell if they're from the smoldering heat or the frustration and heartbreak, but the world is distorted and hazy, the thick raindrops clinging to my hair and skin. "I was ready to let my life burn for you. But now I'll burn for myself." I stomp around a bit more, and the Phoenix is circling, distracted, over the gleaming blue crystal of the citadel.

And then there is a roll of repeated thunder, only it's not thunder at all. The airship is rising from the landing pitch into the sky, its metal pipes clanking into place and aimed at the Phoenix.

They fire.

The ammunition smashes into the Phoenix with the weight of iron cannonballs. They melt on impact, falling to the ground half-shaped, but the impact is enough to send the Phoenix spiraling through the sky. Griffin and I hold tight to the ridges as we spin upside down over and over. I can't tell which way is up and which is down, and somewhere in the light and dark and rain and sky there is another volley of fire, and the world ignites in pure, gleaming blue.

The Phoenix lets out a horrible screech that rings in my ears and through my head. She beats her wings furiously as we lurch through the sky. Griffin has been thrown back to the ridge beside me. The beast's plumage is pulsating with blue light, and her flames crackle with electricity. It's like the storm dragon's crystals lighting up. And I know what happened the moment after that.

I grab Griffin's hand and we look at each other, the only constant as the world around us spins and burns. We have to let go and hope there's land underneath. "Time to go," I say. And he trusts me. We drop from the monster's back.

The world is wind and pelting rain as we fall. But after a few seconds we land on my outcrop, the fireweed trampled underneath us as we roll across the grass. Griffin tumbles past me and over the edge, but our hands are tightly locked and I pull him back up. We lie there gasping while we hear a third volley of ammunition from the airship, whose puttering form is slowly chasing the lurching Phoenix. The beast lets out one last horrible shriek and crashes hard into the side of the continent.

The Phoenix bursts like a star exploding, in a blue-and-silver blast so blinding that the whole world seems to light on fire. Ashra shakes with the fury of an earthquake as it topples from side to side. The blue-and-white burst of light blazes across the visible sky, everything turning to sparks and radiance, like we're inside the shower of a blinding firework.

I can't see anything for a moment, my blistered hands threaded through Griffin's fingers and the soft, waterlogged fireweed. I have to blink five times before the light of the blast dies away. The sparks of the Phoenix are glittering and drifting like the silver stars on Jonash's blade. It's the most beautiful thing I've ever seen.

But Ashra is tipping and rumbling underneath us, the whole continent groaning as though it were alive. I look at Griffin to see if he hears it, too. Then I turn from the outcrop to look for the airship, but it's gone. Maybe the blast lit its wobbly linen balloon on fire. In the distance, the blue crystal of the citadel is gleaming with a bright light I've never seen. It isn't reflected sunlight, or the Phoenix's stars. It's lit from within, flashing like a beacon and humming as Ashra shakes.

Then it goes dim, and there's a horrible cracking sound. Ashra shudders and splits, the rocks rending into jagged edges that break apart. The pieces of my world crack and tumble toward the earth.

The continent is falling.

"Griffin!" I shout. We try to stand, but the world is rumbling and collapsing, and we keep stumbling as it shudders.

Griffin reaches for me and pulls me close to him, his warm arms around me.

If the world is ending, I'm glad I'm with him.

Ashra crumbles to fragments around us, some pieces falling slower than others. The tiny rock bridge I'd climbed to my outcrop so many times is one of the first to shatter, detaching us from the rest of the continent. We fall sideways onto the grass and manage to rise to our knees, still clasped in each other's arms. We're drenched and sweating, blistered and bruised, but I'll hold on until the very end here on my realm of one—no, my realm of two.

There's a sound like buzzing, a humming sound like millions of red bees or flicker wasps. It's slowing to a drumming, and then the world around us lights in rainbow colors. They dance off Griffin's shell necklace still around my neck. They weave across his face in light and shadow, flickering on his face like the stripes he sometimes paints there. The world is sticky like scarlet honey, and everything has slowed.

"The barrier," I say.

And then there's a sucking sound, and the world tumbles down into the crater below with an earth-shattering crash.

My world goes black.

"Kali." There's a girl's voice in the darkness, a voice I recognize that's calling me. "Kali." Someone shakes me gently. "Two shining moons, girl, now is no time to snooze."

I blink, the world slowly coming into view. The clouds above have drifted away, the sunlight streaming down. And there's a familiar face leaning over me, her golden earrings dangling against her long neck.

"Aliyah."

She smiles, her skin crinkling below her eyes. "You're all right," she says.

It all comes flooding back to me—the Phoenix. The continent. Griffin. "Where's—"

"Right here," Griffin says from my right, taking my hand in his. His face is smudged with soot and dried blood, ashes strewn through his tangled brown hair. His fingers are blistered, and there are burns up and down his arms, little diamonds of scalded red skin between the wrapped leather strings and beads.

He's beautiful. He's Griffin, and he's alive.

I sit up slowly, supported by Aliyah's and Griffin's caring hands on my back, and I look around.

The shadowlands below Ashra are gone, filled with shattered fragments and boulders of what was once our home in the sky. In the distance is a crushed silver machine, crumpled over like a giant broken lamppost.

"The Phoenix's last burst of fire overheated the generator," Griffin says. "Without the generator to keep it afloat, Ashra came down. Burumu, too. The blast was that strong."

My eyes widen. "Burumu, too?"

"Your soldiers saw it fall from their airship," Aliyah tells me. "Just before their ship went down."

The Elite Guard. So they're here, too.

"My father," I say. "Elisha. Is…is everyone okay?"

Aliyah's smile drops from her lips. I look to Griffin, but he won't meet my eyes.

"Stay optimistic," Aliyah says. "There are many survivors, and we haven't found everyone yet." She stands, lifting her behemoth fang staff from the ground and reaching her hand out to me. I rise slowly, Griffin hovering to catch me if I need help. "We did find this," Aliyah adds, and from her pouch she passes me the garnet-hilted dagger that fell to the earth with a flash.

I flip it over in my hands, the blade dusty with soot and ashes. I brush it off with my hand and return it to its sheath tied around my waist. Then Aliyah passes me a water flask and I drink, and I think how strange it is to be talking with her when I thought I'd never see her again.

The landscape is jagged and uneven, and we make our way slowly. Griffin limps as we walk, but doesn't utter a word of complaint.

"We were on our way to the lava lands after you and Griffin left," Aliyah tells me. "A storm dragon dug too deep into the roof of the haven, so we had to leave before it broke through. It would be a shame to lose another safe place."

"Where's Sayra?"

"Tending the wounded," Aliyah says. "And getting the able-bodied organized into a monster patrol on the perimeter. We don't want any more lost today."

The thought strikes me like an electric shock. The people of Ashra have been taught to fear the monster-ridden earth. There could be outright panic. And what's more, a gathering of humans will definitely attract monsters. It's only a matter of time before they come.

Ashra and Burumu, gone from the sky. Tash and Lilia will surely help the people of Burumu, though I'm not sure how many they can reach. The continent will fall into the monster-infested ocean, and I don't know if it will float like a raft or crumble, or if the Dark Leviathans will gather and consume it. And Nartu and the Floating Isles, those smaller fragment islands, are so far to the east that they're probably completely unaware of what's happened to us.

They'll still be hovering aloft in the sky with their barriers and generators intact.

We walk for nearly half an hour with no one else in sight, picking our way through the jagged boulders and upturned earth along the dirt path Elisha and I once hurried down for the Rending Ceremony. Dragons and hazus soar high above, circling where the continent used to hover among the clouds. It's strange, being on Ashra and on the earth at the same time. The two worlds are one again, colliding the way my world intertwined with Griffin's. And this time Ashra's fate was definitely shaped by the Phoenix, but not in a way anyone expected.

We near the blue crystal of the citadel, now shattered in jagged shards strewn across the ground. It looks like an ancient ruin, like the destroyed houses in the marshlands. The long stone steps are cracked and uneven, the ribs of the library's arched ceilings exposed and the annals strewn about in the rubble. I see a man in a white robe, his gray beard covered in soot. He's piling the dusty red tomes on top of each other with a blank look on his face. It's Elder Aban, and I shout out to him. He stares at me with the same vacant expression, and I realize he's in shock. I wonder if he thought the Phoenix wasn't real all this time, or if he believed in her and can't fathom that she attacked us, or that Ashra fell from the sky. It's not something I can comprehend myself, yet.

I stumble over the rubble toward him.

"Kallima," he says. "Thank the Phoenix you're safe."

No thanks to her, I think, but there's no point in aggravating things. "Aban, have you seen my father?"

He blinks slowly and says nothing, as if he's lost his mind. "Your...father," he says eventually, as if the words have no meaning, as if he's never spoken them before. He says nothing more, but after a moment reaches into the rubble again and scrapes the dust off another of the annals, placing it on top of the tall, wobbly pile he's made.

"Poor soul," Aliyah says as we turn to leave. "Somewhere between panic and disbelief he's lost himself."

"He'll be all right," Griffin says. "The fallen always struggle at first."

We step through the bones of my destroyed home. I'll never return to my room again, my fireplace crackling with comforting warmth, my blankets snug around me as my father's soft voice murmurs in the hallway. Those blankets are somewhere under the piles of stones, covered in dust and ashes. But the breeze on earth is so warm. It drifts over me with its own comfort.

There are villagers from Ulan wading through the wreckage. Some are on their knees, crying. Others have their hands held up, as if the Phoenix will return and reverse our fortune. They can't accept what's happened. Others call out for their children or their parents or their siblings, everyone searching, everyone disoriented. But among them I see helpers, soldiers of the Elite Guard in smudged uniforms, holding the hands of children as they help them search for their parents. I see Sayra in the distance, a bow and quiver looped over her arm as she searches the skies for danger. She holds a water flask in each hand, passing them to those in need who drink and smudge the soot off of their faces.

And there, in the courtyard, I see my father lying down, the Phoenix statue shattered beside him, a piece of the azure tower crystal pierced straight through his chest.

I let out a horrible cry and run toward him, tripping over

the stones and fragments of our old life. Elisha is beside him, blood trickling down her forehead where she's been struck by a stone that's fallen. She's covered him with the lavender cloak I shed before I chased Jonash to Lake Agur. The cloak is stained dark, and I don't want to know why.

"Father," I say, kneeling at his side. His face is pale, his eyes closed, but they flutter open at my voice.

"Kali," he says, his voice just above a whisper. "You're all right."

Elisha's face is streaked with dried tears and ash. "I've been doing everything I can," she says, her voice tired and strained.

"I know," I say, tears blurring in my eyes. She's bundled his golden cloak like a pillow under his head, and she sits so her back shades him from the gleaming sunlight. She's done everything, but his body is destroyed by shards of crystal and stone. Beside us the Phoenix statue's wings lie in sharp, fragmented pieces, scattered wide across the courtyard. The world of the Monarch is broken. My father is dying.

"I love you," he tells me, and I squeeze his hands tightly. It's horrible to know that he kept the truth of the Rending from me, that he ordered the Benu mutilated or thrown from the edge in what he thought was the best way to protect Ashra. But he is my loving father, who was always good to me and who always tried to do what was best for the people. I do not love what he did, but I love him, and now he's being taken from me.

"I love you, too, Father," I say, and the world is blurred by my tears as I shake with sobs.

Aliyah and Griffin kneel on either side, resting their hands on my shoulders. I want to beg them to do something. Aliyah must know some kind of herb or poultice that can soothe my father's pain. But I can see how stained the cloak is, all the puncture wounds from the crystal shards. I know there is no hope for him.

"I have burned to the wick's end," my father murmurs, closing his eyes. "I'm tired of lighting the way."

"Rest now, Your Majesty," Griffin says. "We will protect Kali in your stead."

My father clears his throat, turning his head to the side. "She is...just like her mother," he manages, his voice frail. "A free spirit that flies where it will. All she needs, young man, is the sky."

"Father," I whisper, pressing my forehead to his as I close my eyes.

And then he lets out a tiny breath, and I know that he is gone, that his own spirit is flying with Mother's in a field of thistles and fireweed and song.

TWENTY-SEVEN

THE REST OF the day is spent searching for survivors of Ashra's plummet from the skies. The village houses and barns in Ulan are mostly in ruin, but there are some that are good enough for a night's refuge while we try to hide everyone from the hungry eyes of the circling sky beasts. The change in altitude is dizzying for some, the air thick and warm down here. There are many broken bones and missing people, but the barrier has saved many of us. Most are in shock, barely able to accept the food and water that Sayra and the Initiates take from shelter to shelter. Chickens and pygmy goats wander the wreckage, pecking and braying at the strange landscape. The Elite Guard have formed a protective circle around Ulan, swords drawn and arms shaking. They've never seen monsters as close as the ones in the sky, never had to use their swords to fight anything but illusions of danger.

All our lives are at risk in the open like this. There is no fence to protect us, no door that can be latched against the fangs of the shadowlands and sky beasts.

As the sunlight fades and the sky streaks with orange and purple, as the stars begin to shine and the moons wax new, Griffin and I sit down on the side of the steep cliff where I once fell alone to a frightening world. The smoke from the campfires in the village spirals into the sky.

"They will look to you to guide them," Griffin tells me. "You're the heir."

"As are you," I tell him.

"Yes, but I'm illegitimate," he says, amused. "And I have no training, so I can slack off. It all falls to you." I know he's trying to cheer me up, but his words are dry in the early evening, tainted with more truth than either of us wants to admit.

I rest my chin in my hands as we watch the soldiers guarding. Elder Aban is still stacking books in the ruins of the library. He's got ten swaying towers of them now, as tall as he is, and an Elder Initiate, the one who hurried me into the citadel for the Rending Ceremony, is gently tugging at his arm to pull him to the shelters. He yanks his arm away, still shocked and lost somewhere in his own mind.

There are too many of them. The monsters will come, and they will come hungry. They don't stand a chance.

The only airship on Ashra, the one that fired on the Phoenix, has a massive rip from one edge of the balloon to the other. Nartu is at least a month's trek away, and with this many traveling, maybe more. I'm not sure how to transport this many people safely. And Nartu is too small to hold them all, even if we had the airships from Burumu to use. And there's no guarantee what's happening there, either, in the little village at the ocean's edge.

"I don't know how to save them," I say. The words are terrifying to hear aloud.

Griffin's hand finds mine, and he squeezes my fingers. I want to run away with him. I want to soar all the way back to the ocean, to stand on that shore how we did once when I promised to see it again with him. I don't want the responsibility and sadness that's been weighted onto my shoulders.

"When you fell from the sky, you were lost," he tells me. He nods at the ruined valley below us. "Now they're lost, too. They need someone to save them."

"Like you saved me."

Griffin laughs. "I only found you," he says. "You saved yourself first."

"Can we go to the ocean?" I ask. "Just you and me. And I'll collect shells and breathe in the salty air and let the waves lace my ankles with foamy surf."

Griffin laughs warmly. "I'll take Tash's fishing boat and spear Dark Leviathans until the waters are safe enough to swim in."

The mention of the sea serpents drains the ocean from my thoughts. I think of the Phoenix circling Ashra, of how she rose out of the lake that I swam in so often with Elisha. I look out at the campfires, at all the survivors waiting to see what will happen. Their Monarch is gone. The Sargon and his son are dead.

"What will you do?" Griffin says gently.

I want to run away. I want to help them. I want to do what's right and not lose myself.

"The lava lands," I say finally. "Let's take them there. Your village is still standing, right? Are there enough houses for them all?"

"Maybe," he says. "But they'll need some work. It's been many years since they were lived in."

"Are there other havens, like the one underground in the woods?"

"Some, yes. And there's the ocean with Tash and Lilia. They can surely support at least a few families there, depending on Burumu's survivors."

"And the village near the Frost Sea?"

An amused smile tugs at Griffin's lip. "It's a rumored village," he says. "But, yes, there are safe places about."

"Why are you smiling?"

"Because," he says, "you sound like a Monarch."

I find myself smiling, despite everything. "I think I'm growing my wings."

"One of us should have them," he teases.

The best way for the people to survive is to split up. In the morning, Griffin and Aliyah will help with basic monster training—the types to look for, the tactics they use. How to use their weaknesses against them in order to survive.

And then we'll tell them the choices—north, to the lava lands and Griffin's village, and farther on to the Frost Sea; south to the mountains and the ocean, through the dangerous marshlands and the hazu-infested plains. East toward the dugout havens in the woods, and farther still to Nartu's shadow and the Floating Isles. West toward a great desert and the unknown. Or to stay in the shadowlands and build a new Ulan, fortified and protected by walls built from the ruins of our old life aloft in the sky. The choice will be theirs to decide. There is no need for an heir anymore. Their lives are theirs, and they must choose how they will walk.

In the morning, Griffin and I will lead the willing to the lava lands, and I will see the fields and lava flows that shaped his early life. I will hunt the behemoths with Aliyah and Griffin, and Elisha will herd the pygmy goats and the chickens to the once-deserted barns.

The world has not ended with Ashra's descent. It has begun, and we will not let the monsters stand in our way. We will rend a new world from the old, one where we look to each other and not to the Phoenix for strength.

And when the world begins to thrive, when the villages are restored and a new generation of hunters have beaten the monsters back, then Griffin and I will return to the ocean, letting our footsteps sink into the sand and the foam of the surf. We will let the grains stick to our soles, and we will float on our backs without monsters lurking in the water, without shadows floating in the sky to blot out the warmth of sunlight enrobing our skin.

This is our world now, no longer a sheltered life aloft. We live on the ground, surrounded by beauty and danger, by risk and by possibility. This is humanity's new dawn, a fire lit from a single smoldering ember of the past.

May we rise anew.

★ ★ ★ ★ ★

ACKNOWLEDGMENTS

SINCE I WAS LITTLE, floating continents have been hovering in the corners of my thoughts. They drift about there with cities and waterfalls, mountains and plains. What would it be like to live on a floating world? What would it be like to survive on the earth below, looking up?

Thank you to my editor, T. S. Ferguson, for helping me answer these questions in the most elegant way possible. Without your help and your amazing edits, I could never have woven the stories of Kali and Griffin together in the way they needed to be. Thank you to the Harlequin TEEN team for all the work you put into this book, from the cover to the interiors, copyedits and promotion. It's all most appreciated.

Melissa Jeglinski, it's such a privilege to have you as my agent. You're always there for me, and you lift me up when I feel like something is beyond what I can write or accomplish. Thank you!

To my sister, Jen Conquergood, for her love, friendship

and massive support with my books and my life. You keep me going and you're always there for me. I'm the luckiest in the world to have you as my sister. Love you so much.

To my dear friends, for their support and inspiration—the MSFVers, the Lucky 13s, Tanya Gough and Lance Schonberg for your camaraderie with this writing thing we do.

Julie Czerneda, thank you. You're an inspiration to me, a friend and a mentor. Your encouragement pushes me to improve with each book, and it's thanks to your belief in me that I continue to grow.

And to my own family, Mum and Dad, who stand by me during the entire emotional arc of creating a book, and Kevin, Emily and Alice. Without your constant support, I couldn't raise floating continents into the air at all. From the long plot conversations, park visits and gaming matches while I write, to your support and encouragement for what I do. Emily and Alice, you're the reasons I paint worlds and adventures on the page for you to explore.

To readers, who climb floating islands and tumble off edges with me. Thank you. You keep me aloft.